D0464257

how it feels to fly

ALSO BY KATHRYN HOLMES

The Distance Between Lost and Found

how it feels to fly

KATHRYN HOLMES

HARPER TEEN

An Imprint of HarperCollinsPublishers

Library of Congress Control Number: 2015950991
ISBN 978-0-06-238734-9 (trade bdg.)

Typography by Carla Weise
16 17 18 19 20   PC/RRDH   10 9 8 7 6 5 4 3 2 1
❖
First Edition

FOR JUSTIN, WHO HELPS ME FLY

one

I FOCUS ON THE MOVEMENT. MY ARMS EXTENDING away from my shoulders. My back curving and arcing. My knees bending and straightening. My feet pressing into the floor.

I focus on all that, and for just a moment, I'm able to forget that I'm in a cozy meeting room, not a dance studio. That my ballet slippers are brushing across carpet. That I'm holding the back of a folding chair instead of a barre. That I'm seeing my reflection in a dark window instead of a mirror.

In that window, I'm not much more than a shadow. Ghostly. You can see right through me to the trees outside.

Even transparent, you're fat. Look at you. You're disgusting. You're—

I flinch, turning away from the window. I rearrange my face into its usual pleasant mask. I try to let the choreography distract me.

In front of me, Jenna's doing the same series of movements. I watch her extend her leg into a high développé and then lower it, with control, back to the floor. Her legs are lean, her muscles streamlined. Her thin arms move through the port de bras like clockwork. She's a blade slicing the air, petite and precise.

She's a figure skater, but she clearly has ballet training. *Proper* training. Russian, maybe. As we turn to do the other side, I tell her, "You're really good."

"Thanks," Jenna answers coolly, giving me a brisk nod as she settles into fifth position. She doesn't say anything else. Just waits for the music to cue up.

I take my own preparatory position, right hand on my folding chair-barre. Then I unfold my left leg into the air in front of me, pointing my toes as hard as I can. I try to keep my port de bras soft and airy, even as my quad quivers with effort. I carry my leg to the side, then to arabesque. I drop my face toward the floor in a deep penché, my toe pointing straight up to the ceiling.

My muscles feel strong and limber. My form feels perfect. But then I look past my own standing leg at Jenna, behind me.

She's judging you. Your bubble butt and your thunder thighs and your C cups and the way your stomach pooches out. That's why she didn't say anything back when you complimented her earlier. That's why——

My knee buckles a little as I pull myself upright. I move from arabesque to a back attitude, lifting onto demi-pointe. I bring my arms to fifth position overhead. I balance, and I breathe, and I smile.

Because that's what I do. I don't let anyone see what's happening inside my head. Not my friends, not my classmates, not my mom. It's a performance that never ends.

Jenna and I move on to battements. I kick my legs up and up and up, punctuating each downbeat in the music with my pointed toe. I try to bring my focus back to the movement. The movement is what matters.

But just as I'm getting into the zone, the door swings open, slams hard against the wall, and bounces back. Zoe, my roommate for the next three weeks, catches it in one hand. "What are you two losers doing?" She walks over to the stereo and switches it off, midcrescendo.

"We're exercising," Jenna says, sounding annoyed. "You might want to try it while you're here. Twenty-one days is a long time without a consistent training regimen."

I ask Zoe, "Do you want to join us?"

Zoe barks out a laugh. "Um, no. *This*"—she rises onto her tiptoes and flutters around, mocking us—"is not exercise. And who says I want to stay in shape while I'm here, anyway?"

"Suit yourself." Jenna slides into a split on the floor, forehead touching her knee.

I give it one more shot. "Seriously," I say, "you're more than welcome to—"

"Whoa, Ballerina Barbie. What part of 'no' do you not understand?" Zoe saunters over to the sofa on the other side of the room and grabs the TV remote. She flips channels, stopping when she comes to a horror film. There's a skinny blond girl in a torn T-shirt and underwear running from a guy with an axe. The camera cuts in close on the girl's tear-streaked face as she screams. Zoe turns the volume up. "This won't mess up your concentration, will it?" she asks, grinning.

I turn around, wanting backup, but Jenna is already standing to leave. "I'll stretch in my room," she says, picking up her folding chair and leaning it against the wall.

"Oh. Um, okay." I'm surprised that she's giving in so easily.

And now I'm torn. I don't want to tick Zoe off—she looks like she could break me in half and would enjoy doing it, never mind the whole we-have-to-share-a-bedroom thing. But I'd planned on getting in at least another hour of strength training and light cardio tonight. It's really important that I stay in shape while I'm here.

In shape. Ha! No such thing.

The panic swirls up. It's like there's a tornado brewing in my belly. But I don't let it show on my face.

I say, "Stay, Jenna, please."

Jenna looks at me over her shoulder. "Sam, no offense— you seem nice and all—but I'm not really here to make friends." She pauses. "If you want, we can do barre again tomorrow. Good night." She glides from the room, leaving me standing there.

"Burn," Zoe says from the couch. "And props to her

for pulling out *that* line. Welcome to America's Next Top Neurotic Teenager, the group therapy camp where we are absolutely not here to make friends." She laughs to herself as, on-screen, the axe murderer finally catches up with his victim.

I consider staying to work out alone, with screeching violins and screams as my soundtrack, but the magic is gone. I used to be able to completely lose myself in dance, no matter where I was or what was happening around me. Ballet was my safest space. Then my body changed. I got curvy, and I got self-conscious. I couldn't stop thinking about everyone looking at me—what they were seeing. When the comments started coming—both painfully kind and sweetly cruel—I heard them echo inside my head. Before long, my nasty inner voice had more to say about me, and worse, than anyone else ever could.

You're fat. You're weak. You're worthless.

You might as well—

I can do my conditioning exercises upstairs, in the thin strip of space between my bed and Zoe's. That'll have to work, despite the storm in my stomach. The only way to kill the panic is to dance through it.

Even that barely helps these days.

But I'm coping. I am.

And Perform at Your Peak, a summer camp/treatment facility for elite teen artists and athletes with anxiety issues, is supposed to give me even more coping mechanisms. That's what the website says. It's what Dr. Debra Lancaster, the director here, talked about earlier this evening, at orientation. When she was telling the six of us campers about all the different types of activities we'll be doing—one-on-one therapy sessions with her, group discussions, simulations of real-life situations we might face—she sounded so confident. She's sure we'll get something positive out of this experience.

I want to believe her. It's just so hard to ignore the voice in my head.

Everything about you is wrong. Nothing can make it better. Nothing except—

I look at Zoe, who's lounging on the sofa with her feet propped up on the wooden coffee table. She's drumming on her thigh with the remote, eyes narrowed at the screen. When a guy jumps out from behind a shed and tackles the axe murderer to the ground, only to get immediately axe murdered, she throws her arms in the air and cheers. "Way to die, idiot!"

"So, um, see you upstairs?" My voice comes out more like a squawk than I want it to.

Zoe doesn't even glance my way. "You're still here?"

The other thing Dr. Lancaster kept mentioning at orientation earlier was group cohesion. She wants us to bond with one another, so we feel comfortable discussing our feelings. She made us do all these getting-to-know-you exercises. We had to toss a beanbag around the circle, shouting a random fact about ourselves each time we caught it. And we played a version of Simon Says where we took turns giving instructions, going faster and faster. It might've all been okay—if we were anywhere else. And clearly, the bonding didn't take. Not with sarcastic Zoe, and not with frosty Jenna, and not with the other three campers—Katie, Dominic, and Omar—who vanished to their rooms the moment we were released.

Not that I blame them. The games felt so forced. Like a distraction from why we're really here, or a trick to get us to let down our guard. A bait and switch. That doesn't mean it wouldn't be nice to have someone to talk to for the next three weeks.

I walk out into the hallway. It's empty. I'm alone.

I let my face relax. My cheeks are sore from smiling. I massage them with my fingers. I dance more than twenty hours a week, but lately it's been the muscles in my face that hurt the most.

I pass the stairs to the second floor and head for the kitchen. I'm thirsty. I'll need to stay hydrated if I'm going to keep exercising. Plus, filling my stomach with water will distract me from the hunger that's creeping in. I don't eat after eight p.m., as a rule, so water will have to do until morning.

When I enter the kitchen, the fridge door is open. I can see a guy's legs sticking out underneath. At the sound of my footsteps on the tile, the door moves. A head pokes around it. It's the guy counselor—I mean "peer adviser." Andrew. He and our other peer adviser, Yasmin, are former campers at Perform at Your Peak. Success stories, according to Dr. Lancaster, who looked like a proud mom when she introduced them earlier.

"Hey there," Andrew says.

Suck that gut in. Now!

"Hi," I say, my smile snapping into place as I adjust my posture.

"You hungry?" Andrew steps away from the fridge, letting the door swing closed. He's holding a loaf of bread, a pack of cold cuts, a hunk of cheese, a tomato, a jar of pickles, and mustard and mayo. All crooked in one arm.

"No, thanks. I just wanted a glass of water." At the sight of all that food, my stomach rumbles. I can't look at it, not for too long, so I look at him instead. He's cute, in a wholesome way. Like he should be on a farm milking cows or something. He has warm brown eyes. A nice smile.

He dumps his bounty on the counter, grabbing the pickle jar before it rolls off the edge. "Well, the first thing you need to know about me is I'm always hungry. I think it's a football-player thing."

"I think it's a guy thing," I say, moving past him to get a glass from the cabinet. "My boyf—my ex," I correct myself quickly. "He basically never stopped eating." I keep my voice light. Like thinking about Marcus, what he said to me a few days ago, doesn't hurt a bit.

Andrew laughs. "As a guy *and* a former football player, I eat twice as much as anyone else I know."

I barely register that he said *former* football player—if that's true, how can he be a Perform at Your Peak success

8

story?—before my nasty inner voice kicks in:

Imagine if you ate twice as much as anyone you know.

You look bad enough as it is——

I fill my glass with tap water and sit on one of the stools at the kitchen island.

"So, Sam-short-for-Samantha," Andrew says, quoting my stammered-out intro from orientation. He takes two slices of bread and waves them at me. "Prepare yourself. You're about to see something pretty special."

I raise my eyebrows and lean forward, resting my elbows on the gray marble countertop. "Oh yeah?" I make eye contact, smile, and then look down. Which is when I see how slouching like this is making my stomach stick out.

Ugh. You're disgusting——

Slowly, casually, I lean back and cross my arms in front of my midsection.

Better. I don't think he saw.

Andrew assembles his sandwich, stacking ingredients like he's building a Jenga tower. Pull out the wrong pickle and the whole thing falls down. When the sandwich is done, it looks too big to possibly bite. But he lifts it up, grins at me, opens his mouth wide, and shoves what looks like a third of it inside.

"Mmm." He chews and swallows. "It's good. Sure you don't want one?" He makes the cold cuts and bread do a little shimmy dance on the countertop.

"I'm okay. But thanks."

"How are you settling in?" he asks, before taking another

giant bite. Chew, swallow. "Orientation is always kind of awkward. Icebreakers are the worst." He gives me a knowing smile. "But do you feel like you'll get along with everyone?"

I don't know whether I should tell him about "I'm not here to make friends" Jenna or "what are you losers doing" Zoe. As a peer adviser, he's basically a camp counselor—not a trained therapist, but not one of the campers, either. I don't know whose side he's on. "Dr. Lancaster seems nice," I finally say. It seems like a safe statement.

"Dr. Lancaster's great. She really helped me when I was a camper here." Andrew finishes his sandwich and brushes the crumbs from his hands. "I think you're going to get a lot out of this program."

Yeah, right, my inner voice cuts in. *Like anything will make a difference for you at this point. Unless Perform at Your Peak is a front for Dr. Frankenstein's lab and you're about to get a total body transplant, you're out of luck.*

"I hope so," I answer, raising my voice so it drowns out the noise in my head. "I have a ballet intensive to go to when this is done. I'm really looking forward to it."

As long as they don't see how much weight you've put on since the audition and send you packing.

"That's great," Andrew says. "When does it start?"

"It actually overlaps with this place by a week. But my mom—she used to be a ballerina, before I was born—she and my teacher got permission for me to start the intensive a week late."

It's the only reason I agreed to come here. My best

friend, Bianca, got into four ballet intensives this summer, including her top choice. I was accepted to one program. I only have one shot.

"Since I can't do the whole program, they bumped me to the wait list, but my mom's not worried. Spots always open up. People pick other schools, or get injured. I'm definitely going." And I'm definitely babbling. Andrew's been looking at me long enough that it's making me uncomfortable. I don't really like it when people look at me. Not while I'm dancing, not while I'm sitting still—not ever.

"Well, I'm glad they could make the schedule work for you." He turns to put his plate in the sink, and I'm able to exhale.

"I guess. But I'd rather be dancing than . . ."

He finishes my sentence when I can't. "Going to therapy camp? I'm not surprised. But if you can't become a professional dancer—"

I'm on edge again immediately. "What do you mean, if I can't?"

"What you learn here should help you in any career—"

"I don't *want* any career. I want to dance. That's all I want." The panic is back. Rising from my swirling stomach, wrapping itself around my lungs, making it hard to breathe. I try to steady my voice. "This place is supposed to help me do that, right?"

My mask is slipping. Any second now, Andrew is going to see *me*. The real me. Messed up and broken and flailing. I can't let him.

Andrew runs a hand through his hair, frowning. "It's just that there are six of you here, and you probably won't all become professionals in your field. But you can learn how to take good mental care of yourself, whatever you decide to do—"

"So you think I can't be a ballet dancer. It's because of how I look, isn't it?" I clap my hand over my mouth and scramble down from the stool. "I didn't mean—never mind. I'm going upstairs. Forget we had this conversation." I practically run for the door.

Andrew calls after me: "Sam, wait!"

I stop, not wanting to look back. But because I'm a glutton for punishment, I do. I wrap my arms around my body, squeezing myself thinner, wishing I could make myself disappear entirely. And I stare at him.

"I'm sorry," he says. "None of that came out right. I didn't mean to suggest you won't be a professional dancer."

Sure he did. He said exactly what he meant.

And he's right.

"I was trying to say that this camp is about making you a happier, healthier *person*—beyond dance. Does that make sense?"

He's looking at me intently. I want him to stop looking.

"I'm sorry," he repeats. "Really, I am. Forgive me?"

"Sure," I mutter, trying to smile like it's no big deal. "Forgiven."

There are tears pricking at my eyes. I blink them away and start walking. Around the corner. Up the stairs, my feet silent on the plush beige carpet and my hand gliding along the dark wood of the banister. I feel Andrew's eyes following me. They burn into me, the way eyes always do these days.

I ignore them. If the past few months have taught me anything, it's how to ignore the eyes. How to pretend they don't hurt.

two

MY BODY DIDN'T BETRAY ME ALL AT ONCE. THE change was gradual. Stealthy. Like I was papier-mâché and the artist was adding one thin layer at a time, wrapping around and around until the new Sam started to take shape.

November to May. A picture-perfect, music-box ballerina to . . . something else. Someone else.

First my balance was thrown off. I couldn't find my center of gravity. My pirouettes were shaky, when I used to be able to spin like a top.

I figured I was having some bad dance days. I'd train harder. Get it all back.

Then I noticed soft curves where there used to be straight lines. Roundness and fullness. A hint of an hourglass.

So I cut calories. A little, then a lot.

But cutting calories didn't help. Exercising more didn't help.

The layers kept coming.

I hid my new body beneath loose warm-ups in class and rehearsal. I wore sports bras under my leotards. I learned how to suck it in, tuck it under—to camouflage.

None of that kept people from noticing. From commenting. From offering advice. From whispering behind my back.

It's amazing how much damage fourteen pounds can do.

Those fourteen pounds are all I can think about as I dig through my suitcase, then my dance bag, then my suitcase again. I'm searching for something that makes me feel confident. In control. Thin.

Nothing could make you look thin. Absolutely nothing.

"I know," I say aloud, to the empty room. But I keep digging.

Today I'm probably going to have to talk about how I've been feeling—how I ended up at this place. That's part of the therapeutic process, according to Dr. Lancaster. The problem is, I've trained myself *not* to talk about it. I've gotten good at nodding, and changing the subject, and pretending I don't hear things. And smiling, always smiling.

If it weren't for that one panic attack—not my first, but the first one other people saw—I wouldn't even be here. If I could have made it to the privacy of the bathroom in time, no one would have found out. And having everyone's eyes on me made it worse. I couldn't pull myself together, not with all of them gawking.

Miss Elise got to me before I had my walls back up. She

convinced me to confide in her—and then she told my mom what I'd said. Next thing I knew, I was here.

So much for following in your mom's footsteps.

Ballet never gave her *a nervous breakdown.*

After throwing outfit after outfit in a pile on the floor, I put on skinny jeans and a blousy tank. I glance in the mirror when I'm dressed and immediately wish I hadn't.

My muffin top. My mom was actually the first one to point it out. "Those jeans don't fit you quite as well as they used to"—that's how she put it. Then we had another chat about my diet. Her catchphrase lately has been "Make good choices." She and I have been "making good choices" together since my weight gain became obvious. Like it was my choice what happened to my body in the first place. Not a combination of bad luck and bad timing and bad genes.

I think she's disappointed in me. I think she thinks I'm not fighting my changing body hard enough. In reality, fighting's all I'm doing. It's just that it's hard to win when you're fighting yourself.

I pull my hair into a ponytail and sit on the bed. I should go downstairs. I'm already late. But I couldn't shower until the bathroom was empty, and I couldn't get dressed until Zoe went down for breakfast. Which, judging by the time, I've now missed. No matter—I haven't been great at eating in front of people lately. It's not that I don't eat. I totally do. But having people watch me eat makes the panic swirl up.

Missing a meal or two won't kill you. You're better off hungry.

The door slams open. Zoe scowls at me. "Dr. Lancaster

sent me to get you. What are you even doing up here?"

"Oh, hi! Sorry, I lost track of time. I'm almost ready!" I smile, but it doesn't matter. She's already walking back down the hall.

I stand, straighten my tank top, breathe in deep, and follow.

WE'LL BE HAVING our morning group sessions in the Dogwood Room—the room Jenna and I were dancing in last night. It's an open space with large windows looking out over a wide green lawn. There's a TV and a pair of couches in one corner. The carpet is a dusty rose, and pink and white dogwood flowers climb the wallpaper.

When Zoe and I walk in, everyone else is seated in a folding-chair circle.

I feel their eyes rake over me.

Dr. Lancaster smiles warmly. "Good morning, Sam. Welcome."

I sit in the only open chair, trying to look like I haven't just broken out in a cold sweat.

This is happening. I'm in therapy, disguised as a summer camp.

I don't need therapy. I was doing fine on my own.

But I can't face my mom if I don't at least try to get something out of this place. She's been working two jobs to cover the cost of sending me here *and* to my ballet intensive. In the car yesterday, she mentioned how exhausting it is to spend eight hours at the law office where she's an executive assistant, only to then head straight to my ballet studio, where she's been doing extra admin work for Miss Elise since April. I don't think she was trying to make me feel guilty, but . . . I feel guilty.

So I have to learn how to not have panic attacks. For myself, and for her.

"Morning, Sam," Andrew says from the seat next to me. "Sleep well?"

I glance at him, wary, but I keep my voice polite. "I slept fine, thanks. You?"

"Yeah, I slept like a rock."

I force myself to maintain eye contact despite how much I want to turn away. I can't believe I melted down in front of him last night. And now he's acting like nothing happened. Well, I can pretend too. "How do rocks sleep?" I ask him.

"Hard, I guess," he answers, grinning.

"Ha, ha." I roll my eyes, and he laughs. That's good—he can't tell how uncomfortable I am.

And then Dr. Lancaster begins. "Welcome to your first official day at Perform at Your Peak! Whether you're a dancer or a gymnast or a football player or an actor or a tennis player or a figure skater"—she looks at me, Katie, Dominic, Omar, Zoe, and Jenna as she says each of our specialties—"you can become more effective competitors and performers. You're all facing something that is keeping you from reaching your full potential." She spreads her arms wide, like the potential in the room is about to bowl her over. The movement turns the flowy, oatmeal-colored cardigan she's wearing into wings. "Over the next three weeks, we'll confront your anxiety issues and come up with strategies to combat them."

Strategies. I'm okay with strategies. Talking—not so much.

"Perform at Your Peak is about helping you achieve athletic or artistic excellence," she goes on. "But more than that: it's about learning to manage your anxiety so that you can enjoy mental and emotional well-being all the time—not just when you're on the field or onstage. And that's why I want to start today's session by having Andrew and Yasmin tell you more about themselves and how their lives have changed since their time here. Yasmin?"

Yasmin waves at us. "Hi, guys. When I was here two years ago, I'd just started writing my own songs. I'd taught myself keyboard and guitar, and I could sing and record in my bedroom, but I was terrified to perform in front of anyone, live. So when my best friend signed me up for an open mic night at a local college, and basically shoved me onstage, I totally bombed. I was *awful*. But it was like . . ." She pauses, looking thoughtful. "That experience made me realize that if I wanted music to be a part of my future, I had to get over my stage fright. So I came to Perform at Your Peak. In our one-on-one sessions, Dr. Lancaster and I talked about why singing in front of people freaked me out. What I was afraid of. We came up with ways to get rid of those fears. And now I'm a sophomore at Belmont

University in Nashville, majoring in commercial music and performing at open mic nights whenever I can! I'm hoping to record a demo soon."

Dr. Lancaster beams. "And Andrew?"

"Yeah, so, uh, my story's a little different," he says. "I came here because my dad and my coach wanted to make sure my head was in the game senior year, when we were looking at colleges. It can be a lot of pressure, dealing with recruiters and figuring out where you want to go. It's a huge decision. You have to play better than you've ever played before to get noticed. I was really nervous, and Dr. Lancaster helped me learn to stay calm and focused. I ended up getting recruited to play at the University of Georgia, but, um"—he clears his throat—"I quit the team after my freshman season. It was totally the right choice for me, and I couldn't have done it without everything I learned from Dr. Lancaster."

"That doesn't make sense," Jenna cuts in. "You're supposed to be able to advise us on being better competitors, but you got everything you wanted and just . . . quit?"

Dr. Lancaster holds up her hand. "As I said before, being here isn't only about competing or performing. It's also about learning to deal with anxiety."

"Dr. Lancaster and I talked a lot about my motivation. In college I realized I wasn't playing football for me," Andrew tells Jenna. "I was doing it for my dad and my coach. I didn't want to let them down. And I'd never thought about what else I might want to do with my life."

Jenna crosses her arms, letting out a huff of air. "But how—"

"Your dad made you play?" Zoe interrupts her, staring at Andrew. "You only did it because he forced you? For how long?"

"Zoe." Dr. Lancaster points at the poster on the wall by the door. Another thing she had us do during orientation: discuss what would make us feel safe in the group setting. We each got to write a rule on the poster, like, "Don't interrupt or talk over each other" and "Don't make fun of other people's experiences." My contribution: "It's okay to say 'pass' if you don't want to talk about something."

"Can you hold on to your questions for Andrew until Jenna has finished?" Dr. Lancaster asks Zoe.

"Whatever," Zoe mutters, slouching back in her chair.

"Jenna?"

"It's fine, I'm done," Jenna answers, voice tight.

"Okay. Zoe?"

"Pass," Zoe mutters.

Dr. Lancaster waits a beat, but no one else speaks. "Andrew and Yasmin were sitting where you are now, just a few years ago," she tells us. "They have a lot of insight into what you're going through. I encourage you to chat with them outside of the group setting, especially if you hear something from one of them that resonates with you."

I glance over at Andrew to see that he's looking at me. I look away fast, embarrassed.

"Now, I know it's not easy to open up to people you've

just met," Dr. Lancaster continues, "even with the icebreakers we've done so far. So I want to start this morning's conversation in a way that shouldn't be too intimidating. I want all of you to tell the group about a time you performed at your absolute best."

Crickets.

"Don't be shy. You're all highly skilled in your fields. Brag a little."

Go on. Brag, my inner voice snorts. *Like you have anything to brag about.*

I look around the circle, waiting for someone else to be the first to talk.

It's not that I haven't had great performances. I have. There are those amazing days when my body does exactly what it needs to. My spot is solid, so my pirouettes whirl effortlessly and stop on a dime. My jumps are buoyant and my leaps soar. It's like I'm moving in slow motion and fast-forward, all at once.

On those days, I almost forget what I look like.

The rest of the time, I'm chasing that high. I need to feel that joy, that power, that ease again. Those wonderful days remind me why I love ballet so much, in spite of everything that's clawing at me.

"I—I have something?" Katie speaks up from my left.

"Yes!" Dr. Lancaster looks thrilled. "Tell us."

"Um. I guess it was, like, a year and a half ago? At Regionals?" Her voice is high-pitched, and getting squeakier by the moment. She's turned a deep shade of pink. "I got a personal best on the uneven bars, and I came in fourth over-all. So I got to go to Nationals."

"Impressive!" Dr. Lancaster says. "What did you feel like that day?"

"Everything felt . . . easy?" Katie frowns and bites at her thumbnail. "Not easy, like *easy*. But I knew my body would do what it was supposed to. So I guess I felt ready. Oh, and my dad was there. He can't come to every meet, so I wanted him to see me do well."

"Wonderful, Katie. Thank you for sharing."

Katie smiles, relieved.

Dr. Lancaster looks around the circle. "Dominic. Tell us about your best game."

Dominic's been leaning back in his chair like he's too cool to be here. I can picture him in a classroom, in the back row, laughing with his buddies and throwing crumpled-up sheets of notebook paper at the nerds at the front. But when Dr. Lancaster calls on him, he startles. Then he puffs out his chest and sticks out his chin.

"My best game—you mean, like, all of 'em?"

"Pick one," Dr. Lancaster says dryly.

Dominic looks toward the ceiling, making an exag-gerated thinking-hard face. "Okay, so at last year's state semifinal, I threw six TD passes. No incompletes in four quarters. I was game MVP. Again."

"How did you feel?" Dr. Lancaster asks. "What were you thinking about?"

"I was pumped! And focused. I trusted my arm, and I

trusted my team. I knew we could beat those guys. And we did. Obviously."

"And did you have fun?"

Dominic snorts. "Course I did. Who doesn't love winning?"

"Thanks, Dominic," Dr. Lancaster says. "Anyone else?"

With a little nudging, Omar talks about playing George Gibbs in a regional theater company's production of *Our Town* last year. "It was my first dramatic role," he says. He moves as lot as he talks, shifting in his seat and pulling at the neck of his shirt. "Before that, I was just the scrawny, dorky kid who used to be in those cereal commercials. But after *Our Town*, I guess people knew what I could do onstage."

Then Jenna remembers the first time she landed her triple-loop, triple-toe-loop combination in competition. "I worked on it for months," she tells us, smoothing back a strand of black hair that's come loose from her slick ponytail. "It was exciting to stick it."

Zoe talks about playing tennis with her older brother when they were both kids. It's kind of sweet until she says, "And then my parents basically made tennis my job. Flashforward to me getting stuck here with you crazies. Which is *awesome*." She gives us a sarcastic thumbs-up.

I'm the only one left to speak. My mouth is dry. I can feel tension creeping up from my lower back, wrapping around my shoulder blades, gripping my neck. But I push all that aside. This isn't the time to use my "pass." Not yet. Not when we're talking about *good* memories. I say, "*Nutcracker* last December. I was alternating Dewdrop Fairy with one of the other girls. A senior."

"I'm sure you were exquisite," Dr. Lancaster says.

Exquisite—the last word anyone would use to describe you—

"Thanks."

"What made this performance so special?" Dr. Lancaster asks.

It wasn't special. You're nothing special.

"It was the best I've ever danced. Everyone said so. My mom was so proud. It was like I wasn't *playing* the Dewdrop Fairy, I *was* a fairy. Light and sparkling and—"

"Light and sparkling?" Zoe's eyes are rolled up so far into her head, they're about to fall out the back of her skull. "You can't be serious."

"Zoe." Dr. Lancaster points at the rules on the wall again but keeps her focus on me. I think that's supposed to be comforting, but it makes me want to become invisible. "What were you thinking about and feeling before that show?" she asks me.

"I—I was excited. I was thinking about how lucky I was to have the part. How much I wanted to dance it well. Do the choreography justice. And I felt . . ." I fade out. I've gone one step further than I wanted to go.

"You felt . . . ?" Dr. Lancaster prompts.

I spit it out all in one breath: "I felt really pretty in my costume."

25

Maybe you felt pretty. But you weren't. You aren't. You never will be.

"Thank you, Sam," Dr. Lancaster says. She turns away from me. I close my eyes and try to get my equilibrium back.

And then Andrew puts his hand on my shoulder. A jolt runs through me, like he's pinned me to my chair. I'm one of those butterflies in a frame. Caught and put on display. I don't look at him, but I feel him lean closer. "Thanks for sharing that, Sam," he says in a low voice. He leaves his hand there a second longer, and then drops it to his lap.

"So. When you did your best——" Dr. Lancaster starts ticking things off on her fingers. "You felt prepared to compete or perform. You were thinking about entertaining your audience or your fans. You had fun. You were in a no-pressure scenario. Or less pressure than usual. You felt grateful for the chance to be doing what you love. And your self-image was good. Right?"

Heads nod around the room.

"Over the next three weeks, we'll be working to help you get those feelings back. Whatever you're going through now, there's no reason you can't experience those happy moments again." Dr. Lancaster nods to Yasmin, who stands and leaves the room. "But before we dive in any further, we'll do another trust exercise. Here, you can say anything you feel. No matter how embarrassing. Or painful. Our job is to listen, not to judge you. And we're certainly not here to tattle on you to your parents or coaches. Confidentiality is important."

Yasmin comes back holding a bunch of bandannas and starts handing them out.

"Turn to the person next to you—it doesn't matter whether it's a camper or a peer adviser. You'll be doing this next trust exercise in pairs."

I look to Katie, but she's already talking to Dominic. Which means Andrew is my partner.

Dr. Lancaster goes on, "In order to trust one another with your emotions and your anxieties, it can help to trust each other with your physical safety."

"Seriously?" Zoe groans. "Trust falls? How cliché is this place?"

"We're not doing trust falls," Dr. Lancaster says. "You and your partner will take turns being blindfolded. Your partner will guide you in exploring the grounds. It's a gorgeous morning out there, and the property we're on is gorgeous as well. I want you to be each other's eyes. Share what you're seeing, to help the other person see it. Use your words, rather than just pulling the person along. Keep each other safe. And be back here in the Dogwood Room by ten thirty. Okay?"

"What if we just . . . don't do it?" Zoe asks loudly. Next to her, Jenna lets out an exasperated sigh.

"I suppose you could say that I'm choosing to trust that you want to learn something from this experience." Dr. Lancaster walks over and kneels right in front of Zoe, which makes Zoe squirm in her seat. "Just try it, okay?"

After a moment, Zoe nods. But her frown deepens.

"Ready?" Andrew's standing. Waiting for me. He holds out his hand.

three

WE GO OUT THE FRONT DOOR AND DOWN THE STEPS
from the porch. The gravel driveway stretches out ahead of
us, disappearing behind a grove of trees before it reaches the
main road. We're at the edge of a small college campus—
the school where Dr. Lancaster heads up the psychology
department. The house we're staying in has bedrooms,
meeting rooms, a kitchen, a front *and* a back porch—the
works—so the school rents it out for events and retreats.
And, apparently, summer camps for teenagers who are
stressing themselves into the loony bin.

"Which way do you want to—" I begin, just as Andrew
says, "Can we talk for a second, before we get started?"

I nod, holding back a sigh. "Go ahead." I know what he's
going to say, now that it's just the two of us. He's going to
apologize for last night. Which is nice of him but doesn't
mean a whole lot. Whether or not he intended to say what

he did about me never becoming a professional dancer—the words are out there. I know what he thinks of me. There's a lot of truth in the things people wish they could take back.

Sure enough: "I wanted to tell you I'm sorry, again."

"It's okay," I say, waiting for this moment to be over. For us to move on.

"I'm gonna make it up to you. Getting off on the wrong foot like that."

"You don't have to—"

"Yeah. I do. I want to. I will. So . . . friends?"

I say, brightly, "Friends! Great." My smile is on full wattage. And it does its job. Andrew looks relieved.

"So do you want to be blindfolded first? Or do you want me to start?"

"Um. You go." I want—I need—to see what he looks like, so I'll know what to expect when it's my turn. So I can glimpse what he'll see of me. I wish I could go a step further. See what my body looks like through outside eyes. Without the filter of my own head, and without the inner voice that mocks and shouts and hisses.

Andrew ties the blindfold around his head. In the sunlight, his wavy hair is the color of wet sand. It falls over the blue blindfold like one of those sand-in-a-bottle sculptures you can make at a kiosk in the mall. But not ugly.

Frankly, nothing about Andrew is ugly. He's not my usual type—if one serious boyfriend counts as a type—but I like what I see. He's taller than me, and while he's not made of muscle, he looks like he takes care of himself. Last night he was working the farm-boy thing in a T-shirt and faded jeans, but today he's a little more dressed up—I guess because he's in "peer adviser" mode. He's wearing a deep-green polo shirt tucked into a pair of khaki pants. And he—

"Uh, Sam? You have to say something."

I feel my face flush.

Nice. You're checking him out, and he just wants to get on with it.

"Sorry!" I say, with a little laugh that rings wrong in my ears. But thinking about how Andrew is cute in a different way than Marcus is cute has me doing exactly what I don't want to be doing—thinking about Marcus—and now I'm feeling wobbly. Wobbli*er*. It's like I'm walking a tightrope, and on one side is outer me and on the other is inner me, and if I fall, the whole circus tent is going to collapse.

Everything's already collapsed. You're delusional if you think otherwise.

"Sorry," I say again fast, almost to myself. I look in all directions and then choose the sidewalk that cuts around the side of the house, past the row of pine trees, heading toward the campus woods. "Turn to your right."

Andrew swings right and almost walks into the lamp-post at the foot of the stairs.

"Whoa, stop!" I run to his side, grabbing his arm. His bicep tightens under my grip like he's surprised I touched him. I let go and step back, feeling even more flustered. "Um. Turn back to the left." Andrew inches left. "A little more. A little more. Now walk straight."

He takes a step, arms extended in front of him. Another

31

step. And another. Like each time, he's not sure whether the ground will rise up to meet him. When we get into a rhythm, he starts making conversation. "So, where are you from?"

"Outside Chattanooga," I say. "You?"

"North Georgia. Small town. You won't know it. Trust me."

We turn the corner and I start describing what's in front of us, like Dr. Lancaster instructed. "We're going around the side of the house. By the woods. There's a big grassy field, and then a bunch of redbrick campus buildings. You can see the mountains in the distance."

Perform at Your Peak is in North Carolina, which means my home is on the other side of those mountains. So is the ballet intensive I'll start three weeks from today.

If they don't kick you out the moment they see you.

"There's a greenhouse to our right," I continue, trying not to let my inner voice derail me. "With a vegetable garden. And there's a gazebo in front of us. Set back in the woods a little. Looks like no one's gone over there yet."

"Oh yeah, the gazebo. Let's go check it out."

His words make me pause. He's been here before. I'd forgotten. "This is weird," I tell him.

"What's weird?"

"I'm describing stuff to you that you've already seen."

"It was three years ago," he jokes. "I barely remember."

"Still."

"It's not really about the landscape, Sam," he says, his

voice growing earnest. "It's about learning to trust each other."

"Right. Okay." I guide him off the path and across the lawn. Andrew keeps his arms held stiffly out in front of him. That, plus his polo and khakis and his slow progress forward, makes him look like a preppy zombie.

"So, what year are you?" he asks.

"I'll be a junior. What year are you?"

"I'll be a junior too. But in college, obviously."

"Oh. Right." The age difference between us: another thing that separates Andrew from Marcus.

Stop thinking about Marcus. He dumped you. Get over it.

"So, do you like college?" I ask Andrew, wincing right away at how young the question makes me sound. "I mean, do you like the University of Georgia?"

"Yeah, it's great."

"Even after you quit football?"

"Yeah. It has a lot more to offer than that. Though it's a great football school, for sure. You a football fan?"

The question is so absurd that I actually laugh out loud. "Um, no."

"Your loss." Andrew flashes his warm smile in my direction. But since he's blindfolded, it looks like he's smiling at the trees over my left shoulder. "Anyway, I still like watching football. I go to all the home games. I just didn't want to play anymore."

"How come?" I ask. "I heard what you said in there, but . . ."

"I spent way too long letting my dad run the show. With him, I never had a choice. He put me in peewee when I was nine—that was the earliest my mom would let me play—and we never looked back. Playing in high school and college was a given. But when I got to UGA, it was like a lightning bolt: I *did* have a choice. Dr. Lancaster said something similar to me when I was here, but I didn't really *get* it until I wasn't living at home anymore, you know?"

"So you were just . . . done? Just like that?"

"You make it sound so easy. But believe me, there was time between deciding and quitting. Took me all of fall semester to get up the nerve."

As he's been talking, I've been studying his features, framed by that sandy hair. The furrow in his brow above the blindfold. A small, white scar on his chin, just off center. Thin lips, which he presses together tightly before going on:

"You said last night your mom was a dancer?"

"She was in the corps de ballet at a small company in Virginia. But not long after she met my dad, she broke her ankle."

"It ended her career?"

"Yeah. It didn't heal properly."

"Too bad."

"It's scary, how one wrong move can screw everything up." I shudder a little. "But then my parents got married and my mom got pregnant. As soon as I was old enough, she put me in ballet classes, and I turned out to love it as much as she did."

"It's good she's supportive of your dancing."

"She totally is."

"As long as she supports you in whatever you want to do. When I quit football, my dad about had a heart attack. Threatened to stop paying my tuition. My mom changed his mind on that one real fast."

I can't imagine what my mom would do if I decided to quit ballet. Luckily, I plan to never find out. "So why did you decide to come back and be a peer adviser here?"

"Fall of sophomore year, I took Intro to Psychology as a gen-ed. It made me remember being here, working with Dr. Lancaster, so I thought, why not major in psych? And then this past spring, Dr. Lancaster emailed and mentioned that she was looking for a guy and a girl to work here this summer, so I signed up. I'm actually getting college credit. I have to write a paper about this place." He turns his head in my direction. "Everything I talk about with y'all is confidential, obviously. My essay is more about Dr. Lancaster's methods."

We keep walking and chatting until we reach the gazebo. Then I get back to describing what he can't see. The white paint, peeling, with the natural wood showing through. The three stairs leading up to the center platform. The rail around the platform that looks like a picket fence. The high ceiling with abandoned birds' nests in the eaves.

He listens, and he walks, running his hand along the side of the structure. Just as I'm describing how there's a path that goes back into the woods, he reaches up and pulls off the blindfold.

"Hey! No cheating." I say it like a joke, but the truth is, the instant he can see me again, I'm nervous. It was so much easier to talk to him with his eyes covered.

"I'm not cheating. It's your turn." He waves the bandanna at me, grinning.

I grin back, even as my anxiety bubbles up. I take the bandanna from Andrew and lift it to my face. The world goes dark. I have trouble tying the knot at the back of my head. My fingers fumble with the fabric.

"Here. I got it." Andrew's hands brush mine as he takes the blindfold. I drop my arms and stand totally still as he ties the ends together. He's right behind me. It's a little unnerving, and a little . . . something else. I feel his breath at the back of my neck—or was it the wind?

I wonder what I look like to him right now. How he's looking at me when I can't look back. What he thinks when he sees my body up close.

Your enormous thighs. That muffin top you think you're hiding. The way your bra pinches in, giving you back fat. Fat fat fat fat—

I want to curl inward, to shrink. But I force myself to stand tall.

"Okay!" I say, and again my voice rings out like a sour note. "I'm ready!"

He's staring at you. He's disgusted by you.

I make fists, digging my nails into my palms.

"Turn around halfway," Andrew says.

"Halfway? Like, a hundred and eighty degrees?"

"What is this—math class? Yeah, a hundred and eighty degrees. Give or take."

I rotate my right leg out at the hip until my feet are in a perfect first position: heels together, toes pointed in opposite directions. Planting my right foot, I rotate to face it.

Andrew lets out a snort of laughter.

He's laughing at you he's laughing at you he's laughing at you he's laughing—

"Why didn't I think of that?" he says. "Note to self: ballet feet. Nice." I hear him move away, the crunch of weight on twigs getting softer. "Okay, ten steps toward my voice, straight ahead. We're going around the other side of the gazebo. It, uh, looks the same as the part you showed me earlier."

We move like that, a few feet at a time, his deep voice pulling me toward him. The dirt and twigs of the woods give way to mown lawn. A breeze brushes my face and a blade of grass tickles my ankle. I feel the sunlight on my shoulders.

Just as I start to think this isn't so bad, I take a step forward and my foot doesn't meet the ground—not right away. I land, hard, a few inches down. I feel the jolt in my knee, in my hip, in my teeth.

At first, I'm stunned. Then—the flip of a switch—I'm freaking out.

I hear Andrew's voice: "Whoa, are you okay?"

I rip off the blindfold. "What was that?"

"A step down I should've warned you about?" He squats

37

to look at the dip where I'm standing. "Sorry, I totally missed it. Looks like a groundhog hole or something."

"Do you know what could've happened?" Now I'm panic-breathing, in-out-in-out-in-out-in-out, thinking about the possibilities: a sprained ankle, a stress fracture, a broken toe, a torn ACL, a pulled hamstring. "I just told you that an injury ended my mom's dance career. And then you drop me into a huge hole and say 'sorry'?"

"Are you hurt?" He stands, reaching toward me.

I step back. "I'm not. But I could've been! And it would've been your fault!"

I know I'm overreacting. But once the panic breath starts, it's all downhill. My mind is racing. I can't control it.

It doesn't matter if you get injured. Your dance career is a fantasy. It's a joke.

I need to go somewhere quiet. Somewhere no one will see if I lose it completely.

Your dreams are a joke. Your body is a joke. You are a joke.

There's no time to get away. No time to hide. I crouch, wrap my arms around my body, and squeeze everything. My forearms across my chest. My knees together. My eyes closed.

You're a joke. A disappointment. You should be so ashamed of yourself—

"Sam! Sam!"

That snaps me out of it.

I look up. Andrew's eyes are wide.

"I'm going to get Dr. Lancaster," he says. "Stay here.

No, wait—come with me. Can you walk? Never mind, you should probably stay here. Or—"

"It's okay," I say, taking in a shuddering breath. "I'm okay now."

You're not okay you're not okay you're not okay.

"Really." I muster a smile and sit in the grass. "Can we stay here for a bit?"

"I—um—I guess, yeah." He looks back at the house, clearly conflicted, and then plops down next to me. A few beats of silence pass. Then he asks, his voice gentle, like he's talking to a skittish wild animal, "Was that a panic attack?"

I look over at him. I want to pretend it was nothing. I want to laugh it off. But now he's seen what happens. Now he knows why I'm here. And he isn't laughing at me. He doesn't look shocked or disgusted. Rattled, but that's about it.

Because of that, I trust him enough to say, "Yes."

"For me, it was chest pain. Like an elephant was sitting on my ribcage. For you, it's trouble breathing?"

I nod.

"Is it always that sudden? And that bad?"

I answer the second part first. "Sometimes it's worse." And as for sudden—if I'm honest with myself, that's been building in me since last night. A full-out, sweat-drenched ballet class this morning might have warded it off. Maybe. But between Zoe and Jenna and Andrew and thinking about Marcus and wearing the blindfold and stepping in that hole and just *being here* . . . the tightrope snapped.

I unspool another length of cord. Stretch it back across the chasm inside my head.

"Please don't tell anyone."

He blinks at me. "You know I have to tell Dr. Lancaster."

"Let me tell her." It's only delaying the inevitable, but this feels important. "I'll even say I asked you not to tell her before I could, so you don't get in trouble. Please?"

After an excruciating pause, he nods. "Only because I owe you for last night."

"Thanks."

I look around the grounds, taking everything in. Katie is leading blindfolded Dominic toward the gazebo. Omar is with Yasmin by the vegetable garden. Zoe and Jenna are nowhere to be seen. I can't even imagine how they're interacting. I think about last night, in the Dogwood Room: Jenna's precision and chill versus Zoe's chaos and fire.

"So can I ask what that was about?" Andrew asks. I must look alarmed—I *feel* alarmed—because he adds, "I'm curious what's going on inside your head. That's all."

That's all. That's. All.

"I freaked out when I stepped in that hole. You saw it happen."

We're so close, I can see that he has sandy eyelashes to match his sandy hair, and that his brown eyes have flecks of gold. His gaze makes me want to scoot away fast. But because he's looking at my face, and not at the rest of me, I'm able to stay.

"I have a lot on my mind right now," I tell him.

"Like what?"

"Like . . . my ballet intensive, where I'm going next. If everything goes well there, I could get asked to train at that school year-round. And that could lead to them offering me an apprenticeship, which could lead to a professional company position."

Andrew listens. Then he says, slowly, "Don't take this the wrong way, but that's a lot of 'coulds.'"

My heart rate picks up again. I pull my knees into my chest and hug. "I know," I admit. "But it's the only plan I've got."

"What else is on your mind?"

"What do you mean?"

"You said 'a lot.' So what else?"

"Oh." I don't want to tell him what else. "Just . . . stuff."

"Stuff. Got it." To my surprise, he doesn't push it. He sits next to me, in silence, until his watch alarm beeps. "Time to go back in," he says. "Packed schedule today."

"Okay." But before standing, I lie flat on my back and stare into the clouds. I picture myself as light and breezy as they are. I picture floating away.

four

BACK IN THE DOGWOOD ROOM, DR. LANCASTER asks each of us to tell the group about our experience with the blindfold exercise. When it's our turn, Andrew talks about walking to the gazebo, and how I described the landscape clearly and didn't let him run into anything. He talks about how it was obvious I'm a dancer, because of how aware I was of my body when I was blindfolded. True to his word, he *doesn't* talk about my panic attack—though he does shoot me a meaningful look when he's done.

"How about you, Sam?" Dr. Lancaster asks.

"It was nice to be outside," I say, after a long pause. I know that's a cop-out answer, but just because I'm sort-of-kind-of willing to confide in Andrew now, it doesn't mean I want to bare my soul to my fellow campers.

"Anything else?" Dr. Lancaster prompts.

"Um." I drop my gaze to the floor. "Pass."

I'm not the only one who's holding back. Zoe and Jenna answer Dr. Lancaster's questions in single syllables. Their body language couldn't be more different—Jenna is sitting up ramrod straight, hands clasped in her lap, lips pursed, while Zoe slouches in her seat, arms folded across her chest—but it's clear that they both want out of this room. Omar, who was paired with Yasmin, fidgets and stammers out his answers. Dominic and Katie are the only two who seem remotely comfortable with each other.

"Dominic was a great guide," Katie says.

"*Yeah* I was," Dominic congratulates himself.

"I wasn't nervous at all," Katie goes on. "But stuff like this isn't what makes me nervous."

"And Dominic, how about you?" Dr. Lancaster asks. "Did you trust Katie? And do you feel like you might be able to open up to her now?"

Dominic snorts, shaking his head. "You mean, like, talk about our feelings or whatever? No, thank you. Not my thing."

Katie looks thoughtful. She sticks her hand in the air. "Dr. Lancaster?"

"Yes?"

"Can I talk about my feelings?"

Zoe laughs, and Dr. Lancaster shoots her a look.

Katie pales but keeps going. "I want to say why I'm here. I want to get it out of the way. Rip off the Band-Aid, you know?"

Dr. Lancaster nods. "Of course. Each of you can tell

your story when you're ready. And if you're ready now, Katie, we're ready to listen."

Katie clears her throat. "So, about eight months ago, I fell off the balance beam. I was working on my new dismount—a roundoff double back—and my foot slipped going into the roundoff. But I had too much momentum to stop. My hand missed the beam and I just . . . crashed. I slammed into the beam and then hit the floor. I broke my collarbone in two places. I was lucky it wasn't a lot worse."

She lifts her hand, running her fingers across what I can see, when I squint, is a slight bump on her collarbone. "It took about three months to heal. And then I got back to training. But now, every time I get on the beam . . ." She blinks, her eyes wet. "When it happened for real, I didn't know it had happened until it was over and I was on the ground. It was so fast. But now I see it in slow motion. I see my hand slide and the mat get closer and closer. I hear my coach gasp. I watch myself land on my head, snap my neck. I look down, and I'm curled up on the floor. I can't move or breathe."

"Whoa," Omar says.

Katie sends a watery smile in his direction. "Yeah. So anyway, a few months ago, I started doing these rituals. Like, making a deal with myself. If I coat my hands and feet with extra-strength deodorant—twice—before my routine, I won't slip and fall. If I always listen to the same song before I get on the beam, I won't fall. If I take the right number of steps to get there, and if I breathe the right number of times before I touch the beam, I won't fall."

Everything she's saying—I get it. I have my own set of rules. Only eat at certain times of day. Sip water constantly, to fill my stomach up faster. Count calories, count servings, count bites. I can't help asking, "Do the rituals make a difference?"

Katie makes a face. "They used to? But now I have to do more and more of them, and I still don't feel anywhere close to how I used to feel." She sniffles. "I really want to get past this. I want to feel normal again."

Normal, my inner voice sneers. *Maybe she can go back to how she was before, but you're living your new normal. Welcome to the rest of your life.*

"Thank you, Katie," Dr. Lancaster says. "Does anyone want to respond?"

I shake my head. So do Omar and Jenna and Dominic. And Zoe's eyes are closed, chin dropped to her chest. She's faking being asleep, which is almost more obnoxious than *actually* being asleep.

"Then we'll break for lunch," Dr. Lancaster says. "You'll each have your initial private session with me this afternoon. Sam, you're first, with Omar on deck."

I nod. And I look at Katie. She seems calmer now that her secrets are out in the open. I envy her a little bit.

That still doesn't mean I'm ready to talk.

* * *

THE KITCHEN ISLAND is set up buffet style for lunch: first a big pot of spaghetti, then a pot of tomato sauce, and finally a platter of meatballs and a bowl of grated Parmesan. It looks—and smells—amazing. It also looks—and smells—incredibly fattening.

And I'm back to thinking about eating in front of everyone. Their eyes on my plate, on my fork as it travels from my plate to my mouth, on my face as I chew and swallow. The hunger I've been ignoring since I woke up—it's replaced by butterflies. Lead butterflies, clanking around and scratching my insides with their wings.

I step out of line, swallowing past a thick lump in my throat. "I'll be right back . . . ," I say to Katie, behind me, and I head for the stairs. I'll hide in my room, or in the bathroom, and eat when everyone else is done. It's a foolproof plan.

But Dr. Lancaster appears out of nowhere. "Sam," she says. "You must be starving; I know you missed breakfast. You're going to love this spaghetti."

"Great," I say, giving her my everything's-totally-fine smile. "I just, um, need to go to the restroom first."

"Go right ahead. I'll make you up a plate and leave it at the table for you."

"You don't have to do that. I can make my own plate when I get back."

"It's my pleasure. See you in there."

I do end up going to the bathroom, for appearance's sake. Then I head back to the dining room, feeling dread settle in over my shoulders like a woolen blanket.

It's not that I'm worried about having another panic attack. They don't usually happen right on top of each other. But as I stare at the plate of spaghetti in front of me—a huge serving, and way too heavy for lunch—I just. Don't. Want. To eat it.

So I turn to talk to Katie instead. She's sitting next to me, and Dominic's across from her, and they're both chowing down like it's the easiest thing in the world.

"That was brave, how you opened up back there," I say, twirling pasta around my fork. I twirl. And twirl. And twirl.

"Thanks. It wasn't as hard as I thought. You should go next!" Katie squeaks. Then, like she realizes that might've been too pushy, she adds, "If you want. If you're ready."

"Maybe," I say, even though I don't mean it.

Honestly, I don't know where I'd begin. I don't have a cut-and-dried story like Katie's, where one awful thing happened and everything changed. Would I start with the Saturday in February when Tabitha saw me holding a sandwich after ballet class and asked, all fake concern, "Are you sure you need to eat that?" That's when I stopped eating in front of other dancers. I'd rather snack in the bathroom, perched on the toilet, than let them see me with a single almond or grape.

Or I could talk about that rehearsal in March, when the guest choreographer patted my stomach and poked at the wobbly part of my upper arm and said, "Work on this"—in front of everyone. I barely made it to the janitor's closet before breaking down.

Or I could go straight to the panic attack that sent me here. It was April. Backstage before *Paquita*. I put on Lauren's tiny tutu by mistake and caught sight of myself in the mirror, and all the air left the room.

Or should I describe how I feel every day? The storm in my stomach. The mocking voice that fills my thoughts. The way my skin crawls when people look at me for more than a few seconds. The tears trapped behind my smile.

"It might make you feel better to get it off your chest," Katie says, slurping up a strand of spaghetti with a satisfying smack.

The only thing that makes me feel better is keeping it in. Acting like nothing's wrong. Fooling everyone.

But I say, "I'll think about it."

Katie looks pleased.

I've been twirling my spaghetti the whole time Katie and I have been talking. The pasta spirals out from my fork, and a large meatball teeters at the edge of the plate. I use my knife to tip it back into safety and start slicing it into bite-sized chunks.

"Hey, Ballerina Barbie's making progress!" Zoe says.

I look over at her, startled. "What?"

"You think I didn't notice that you're not eating?"

I say the first lie I can think of. "It was hot. I was letting it cool down."

"Hot. Huh." Zoe opens her mouth and crams in an entire meatball. "Nope!" she says as she chews. "Try again."

"I'm eating!" I stab a cube of meatball and stick it in my mouth. It's every bit as delicious as it smells, perfectly seasoned and sprinkled with melting Parmesan.

Now take the rest of your lunch and stick it around your waistline—

Zoe applauds. Then her tone turns conversational. "So are you here because you're anorexic? Or are you going to go upstairs and throw up the one bite you ate?"

"Zoe!" Katie exclaims. "You can't say things like that. It's in the rules. And it's not nice."

"This isn't group. I can say whatever I want," Zoe says. "Unless you wanna stop me? I'd like to see you try. How old are you, anyway? Eleven? Did you bring your teddy bear here with you?"

"I'm fourteen," Katie says, reddening. "And no, Mr. Bear stayed home."

Zoe cracks up. "Mr. Bear! I knew it!" She turns her attention back to me. "Eating disorder—yes or no? I'm living with you; I need to know what I'm dealing with. You show me yours, I'll show you mine." She wiggles her eyebrows suggestively.

I'm chewing my second bite of spaghetti, trying to savor the rich tomato tang—and to look like all this is just rolling off my back. But Zoe is getting dangerously close to the thing I won't ever, ever, ever say, not to anyone, and it's

49

making my heart pound. "I don't have an eating disorder," I tell her.

"Sure you do. I saw *Black Swan*."

I stiffen. "Not every ballet dancer has an eating disorder."

But you've thought about it. A lot. And what about those times you—

I take another bite, a bigger one. It probably counts as bites three *and* four. As I swallow, I imagine my nasty inner voice getting quieter and quieter, being choked and smothered by deliciousness. I think about covering the noise in my head with food. And then I think about how fat that would make me, and I have to put my fork down.

Omar has been watching the back-and-forth between me and Zoe like a Ping-Pong match. His eyes are wide and he's drumming his fingers on the table. "Please stop," he says. "Dominic, make them stop."

"Not my fight." Dominic's leaning away from us, looking uncomfortable.

Zoe stares me down as I eat bites five and six.

This—*this*—is why I don't eat in front of people. I'm either eating too much or too little. I can't make anyone happy. No matter what I choose, I choose wrong.

Jenna finally breaks the silence. "If the two of you are done, I'd like to finish my lunch in peace."

"Roger that, Michelle Kwan," Zoe says.

"Michelle Kwan," Jenna repeats, in a voice like dry ice. "Because I'm Asian. How original. Does that mean I can call you Venus or Serena?"

"Come on. I'm obviously Anna Kournikova." Zoe tosses her braids like she's in a shampoo commercial. "So do you skate like Michelle Kwan, too? Isn't she the one who never won a gold medal?"

"Isn't Anna Kournikova a glorified underwear model?" Jenna shoots back.

"Hey—if you've got it, flaunt it." Now Zoe strikes a model pose in her chair.

Jenna opens her mouth to say something more, but Zoe cuts her off.

"Seriously, do any of you have a sense of humor? Or did they forget to put that on the Crazy Camp packing list?"

"Crazy Camp?" Katie echoes.

"Yeah," Zoe says, in a voice that screams *duh*. "As in, a summer camp for teenagers who are crazy."

"We're not crazy," Jenna argues.

"Ri-i-i-i-ight." Zoe says, "Tell me more about how not-crazy you are."

Instead of answering, Jenna picks up her plate and walks away.

A second later, Yasmin comes into the dining room with her plate and sits down in Jenna's empty chair. "Looked like a lively discussion over here!" she says. "Sorry I missed it. Dr. Lancaster was talking to me and Andrew in the kitchen. Who wants to tell me something they learned about one of their fellow campers during lunch?"

I expect Zoe to point an accusing finger at my plate.

Instead she says, with glee in her voice, "Katie still sleeps with a teddy bear."

"I didn't say that!" Katie yelps. "He's, like, a good-luck charm. For meets."

"Sure he is," Zoe says.

"Anyone else?" Yasmin asks. "Sam?"

I'm saved from answering by Dr. Lancaster, who comes over and puts her hand on my shoulder. "Sam, I have to whisk you away. We need to start our private session."

"Oh. Okay." I stand, glad not to have to force down any more food. I had six bites. Barely enough to get me through the afternoon, but maybe I can grab a snack later.

"Good luck!" Katie squeals. "Tell me how it goes! If you want. . . ."

I nod, and I square my shoulders, and I follow Dr. Lancaster through the kitchen. We pass Andrew, who's filling his plate at the buffet. He gives me that same meaningful look from earlier. The don't-forget-to-tell-her-about-your-panic-attack look. I avert my eyes. Dr. Lancaster leads me down the hall to her office. She holds the heavy wooden door open. I step inside.

five

"TAKE A SEAT, SAM," DR. LANCASTER SAYS, POINTING to the couch at one side of the room. She circles around the large wooden desk to get a yellow legal pad, then settles into a wood-and-leather armchair across from me. She smiles. It's the same gentle, welcoming smile she's been giving us since we got here. It's so consistent, I'm starting to wonder whether she practices it. I picture her standing in front of her bathroom mirror in the morning, doing her exercises: smile, and release. Smile, and release.

That's what I do sometimes. Just to make sure it still works.

"Are you getting settled in all right?" she asks. "Do you need anything?"

"I'm fine."

You're not fine. You're nowhere close to fine—

"Wonderful. I know it can be difficult being away from

home, especially in a situation like this. Please know that you can always come to me, Andrew, or Yasmin with concerns." She writes my name on the top page of her pad in loopy cursive. When she sees me looking, she angles the pad up and away from me. "Before we get started, I wanted to remind you that after dinner, I'll be collecting everyone's cell phones."

She mentioned this at orientation last night. How in order to really dig into our work here, we need to be untethered. Her word, not mine.

"Your mother knows to call the main number if she needs to reach you. You'll have this afternoon to send any messages you want to friends. Or a significant other."

That last part is almost a question. She looks at me, raising her eyebrows, and I shake my head. Nope. No significant other. Not anymore.

"Part of the benefit of being here is the isolation," she goes on, while I try to wipe Marcus's face from my mind's eye. "You've all been removed from the intense training and competing environments where your anxiety manifests most strongly. Here, you'll get perspective, as well as a chance to—"

I stop her midscript. "I'm not going to fight you for my phone. Don't worry."

She leans forward in her chair. "You won't feel disconnected from your friends and family?"

Trust a therapist to read too much into every comment. "Like you said, my mom knows how to reach me. And I told my friends I wouldn't be in touch much, if at all, until I get to my ballet intensive in three weeks." Only a few people outside my immediate family even know I'm here. Miss Elise. The director of the intensive in Nashville. Bianca. And Marcus—because we only just broke up. I doubt he's planning to call or write. Everyone else thinks I'm on a road trip out West with my dad. Noncustodial-parent bonding time, complete with limited internet access and bad cell reception. "I'm not that tied to my phone, anyway."

She makes a note on her pad. Then she looks at me intently. "So tell me, Sam. What do you hope to get out of your stay here?"

I gulp and give her the answer I've been rehearsing. "I would like to learn how to stop having panic attacks."

"We'll certainly work on coping mechanisms for your anxiety," Dr. Lancaster says, "and I'm glad you're open to doing that work. But we also want to tackle your anxiety issues at their source. Can you tell me a little about the circumstances that surround your panic attacks?"

This is the perfect time for me to mention what happened earlier, with Andrew, but I can't help deflecting. "My mom and I filled out your giant questionnaire a month ago. Don't you already have a file on me or something?" I don't mention the fact that I wasn't entirely honest in that questionnaire. How could I be, with my mom looming over my shoulder?

Dr. Lancaster smiles patiently. "I'd prefer to hear it in your words. Maybe you can describe a recent panic attack.

How you felt just before it hit. Where you were, what was going on."

I think about Andrew's promise to let me tell Dr. Lancaster in my own way. He put a lot of trust in me by agreeing not to talk about what happened until I did. "There is something. . . ."

Stop. She doesn't need to know. No one needs to know.

Dr. Lancaster waits.

"Earlier, during the blindfold exercise, I kind of had . . . okay, I did, but it wasn't that bad, not compared to . . . and Andrew was there, so I was fine, and anyway, it was over fast." I stare at my hands. They're shaking. I tuck them under my thighs.

Dr. Lancaster lets the silence stretch out, until every other sound is amplified. The ticking of the clock on the wall. The whirring buzz of her computer. The branch of the tree outside blowing in the breeze and knocking at the window.

After what feels like an eternity, she says, "Sam, are you trying to tell me that you had a panic attack this morning?"

I force myself to nod. And I parrot what I said earlier: "I would like to learn how to stop having panic attacks."

"What were you doing when it happened this morning?"

"Um. I was blindfolded. Andrew was leading me across the lawn. And he—I stepped in a hole. And it set me off."

"Set you off?"

"I started thinking about what would happen to me if I got injured. That's how my mom's dance career ended, and

56

for me, I'd be done before I even got started. This summer is really important. For my future."

"And what happened when you thought about all that?"

"I—I couldn't breathe."

Dr. Lancaster writes something down. "How were you feeling before you stepped in the hole?"

"Okay, I guess."

"Describe 'okay.'"

I look at her. "What do you mean?"

"What does 'okay' mean to you? What does it feel like?"

"Oh. Um, anxious, but not terrible."

Her pen *scritch-scritch-scritch*es on her notepad. "Can you tell me why you were feeling anxious during the blindfold exercise?"

I remind myself that this is her job—and that mine, right now, is to *stop having panic attacks*. But my heart is beating faster. And I'm sweating, despite the office's arctic AC. I shiver and wipe the beads of moisture from the back of my neck.

Dr. Lancaster is still watching me.

I blurt, "Can you turn around or something?"

"I'm sorry?"

"I can't think with you staring at me. Or writing things about me."

She puts the pad on her desk and turns to look out the window. "Is that better?"

Now I feel stupid. But it does help. "Sure."

"So, why were you feeling anxious?"

"I, um, didn't like the blindfold. He could see me, but I couldn't see him."

"What do you mean by that?"

"I don't like it when people look at me behind my back. And this felt like that. It made me . . . uncomfortable."

"Uncomfortable?"

"If I can't see someone's face, I don't know what they think of me. I can't see if they're judging me, or whatever."

"Do you generally feel that when people are looking at you, they're judging you?"

"I guess so, yeah."

Because they are.

"Even when you can see their faces?" She turns to look back at me, meets my eyes, and then returns her gaze to the window.

"I just don't like being looked at, okay?"

"Do you want to say anything more about that?"

"Nope." I want this to be over.

And I'm drowning in memories.

I auditioned for a bunch of summer intensives this year. There was one audition I knew I'd aced. I danced so well. Everything felt effortless. I was practically levitating in the final series of leaps across the floor.

And then, in the hallway outside the studio, I got that neck-prickling feeling you get when someone's looking at you. I thought maybe I was being paranoid, but I turned around anyway. And someone *was* staring. Two someones. The teacher who'd led the class I just took, and the director of the summer intensive. They were frowning. At me. The program director shook his head, and the teacher shrugged and said something I couldn't hear.

That's when I knew I wasn't getting in.

At my next audition, we had to fill out a form with our personal information—including our current weight. Below that question, there was an asterisk: *Dancers who are deemed over- or underweight may be put on probation.* But how heavy was too heavy? What was the exact right number? If I told the truth, would they discount me before I even got a chance to dance? If I lied, would they know right away? Would they laugh me out of the building?

I decided to lie. And I had a terrible class, worrying the whole time about whether the number I'd written matched what the adjudicators saw in front of them. Whether I'd made the right choice. I didn't get into that program, either.

Both of those auditions were in February. Four months and eight pounds ago.

Imagine if they could see you now.

The audition for the program I'm going to attend was in January. Five months and eleven pounds ago—

"Sam? Is there anything else you'd like to get out of your time here?"

"Not unless you can help me lose fourteen pounds. . . ."

It's a joke. Sort of.

Dr. Lancaster doesn't laugh.

"But since that's not going to happen," I add quickly, "at least, not without me doing something drastic . . . not having panic attacks is enough."

"Something drastic. Like what?"

"Um. You know, like starving myself, or whatever."

"Have you ever tried doing something drastic?"

"No. I mean—no. Of course not."

She glances at the notepad on her desk, and then at me, without responding. Her silence only makes me more nervous.

"Other than—"

Shut up. Shut up, shut up, shut up!

I make myself study Dr. Lancaster instead of speaking. Her oatmeal-colored cardigan is paired with a white top and crisp khaki pants. Her gray-blond hair is pulled into a low bun and wrapped in an off-white scrunchie. Her wardrobe, on top of her calm, soothing voice and her gentle, reassuring expression—she's the definition of bland. But maybe that's on purpose. So we focus on ourselves, not on her—

"Well, our time is almost up. I think we're off to a great start. We have a lot to unpack, and it won't be easy, but I know you can handle it." My skepticism must show on my face, because she goes on, "You're training to be a professional ballet dancer. Is *that* easy?"

"No."

"I'm confident that we'll find some of those answers you're looking for. But I need you to work with me. I can't offer you coping mechanisms that are specific to your needs until I know what those needs are. It's like cross-training—not every type of exercise is right for every person. If it makes it easier, you can think of me as your emotional personal trainer."

I wonder how long she's been saving that line.

She stands, so I do too. "Thank you for talking with me today. Can you send Omar in next?" She guides me to the door.

Hand on the knob, I remember something else I need to say. "Dr. Lancaster—about this morning. When it happened, when I had my . . . you know. Andrew wanted to get you right away, but I asked him not to. I wanted to tell you. Well, I didn't *want* to tell you, but I wanted *me* to tell you more than I wanted *him* to. . . . Anyway, I thought you should know that."

"Thank you, Sam."

I escape out into the hallway. I lean against the wall, closing my eyes. I am so, so tired. It's early afternoon, but I feel like I'm at the end of a marathon dance day. And I can't rest now. I have calories to burn. It won't do me any good to fix my panic problem if I'm so fat by the time this is over that my dance dreams are done.

They already are. You know that, right? You're kidding yourself if you think, with how you look, you can—

I push myself to standing and go to find Omar. After I track him down—on the front porch, showing Yasmin how to play a game on his phone—I stop in the kitchen to grab a granola bar. Then I head upstairs to change into yoga pants and a T-shirt.

My bedroom is empty. I peek out the window and spot

Zoe outside, lying on the lawn in a hot-pink two-piece. Off to the side of the house, Dominic is teaching Katie how to hold a football. He guides her arm back, then steps away and lets her throw. It almost hits the tree she was aiming at. To celebrate, she does a roundoff back handspring and then gives Dominic a high five.

I'm wondering where Jenna is when I hear strains of classical music coming from the next bedroom. I press my ear to the wall. It's Tchaikovsky, muffled but unmistakable.

I consider going over to knock on her door. She'd probably dance with me again, even if she doesn't care to know a thing about me as a person. But she left lunch so fast, after Zoe insulted her. Maybe she wants to be alone.

I know something about wanting to be alone.

I put in my earbuds and crank up Prokofiev's *Romeo and Juliet*. I drop to the floor and start doing Pilates exercises. When my muscles feel warm, I do a ballet barre, holding on to the closet door for balance. Then I go into the center of the room and jump: sautés in first, second, and fifth, then changements, then échappés, and on and on and on. I do every exercise I can think of that fits into a three-by-six-foot space, including a mega crunch series, push-ups, and jumping jacks. I don't stop to rest until I'm pouring sweat. Until I'm gasping and my muscles are screaming.

It's not just about staying in shape. It's also that, after the day I've had so far, I need the release. Only when my body is sore and tired and trembling can I turn off my overactive brain.

I skip to the track for the balcony scene, where Romeo whisks Juliet away to dance in the moonlight. I mime Juliet's breathless leap into Romeo's waiting arms. He catches her, lifts her, guides her through a series of pirouettes en pointe, and pulls her into a passionate embrace. Of course, I'm embracing myself, and the only thing to catch me when I fall out of my pirouette is Zoe's bed. I bounce off it, bumping my thigh on the corner of her nightstand. That hurts enough to knock me back to the here and now.

You're not Juliet. And you never will be.

DINNER IS WAY more subdued than lunch. Other than Andrew and Dominic, who are debating college football coaching strategies at the end of the communal table, nobody seems to want to talk. Even Zoe is silent. She stabs at her food like it's the face of someone she hates, and when she catches me looking at her, she shoots me a glare that could melt glass.

I stare down at my grilled chicken and green beans and potatoes. I cut everything up into bite-sized pieces before starting to eat. I count the bites: fifteen cubes of chicken, thirty green beans, and six spoonfuls of mashed potatoes. Manageable. Especially with no one distracting me. I put the first bite in my mouth.

It's good. The potatoes are buttery and salty, and the chicken is tender. But when I'm about two-thirds of the way finished, I look up to see Dr. Lancaster watching me from the head of the table. She gives me an encouraging nod.

I take the next bite. I chew. Now it tastes like dirt.

We're supposed to have free time before lights-out, but no sooner do I sit down on the couch in the Dogwood Room with Katie to watch TV than Yasmin comes to find me. "Sam," she says, touching my shoulder. "You have a phone call."

I follow her to Dr. Lancaster's office and pick up the receiver that's been left on the desk. Yasmin steps outside, shutting the door behind her.

"Hello?" I say.

"Samantha?"

It's my mom. Even though she can't see me, I sit up straighter and suck in my stomach.

"I wanted to discuss your first day. How did it go?"

"Good. It was . . . good."

"What did you talk about?"

"Um, things that make us anxious?" I say, keeping my voice light.

"Samantha. That was a serious question."

"I know, Mom," I say quickly. And I also know, now, what kind of mood Mom is in. She can be my biggest cheer-leader and my biggest critic. Sometimes both in the same sentence. Since she started working at the ballet studio a few months ago, it's been more of the latter, but I was hoping today she'd cut me a little slack. "So far, it's been mostly introductory stuff. Getting to know each other, and Dr. Lancaster, and our peer advisers. Those are—"

She doesn't let me finish. "Do they have a plan to address your . . . issues?" Mom says *issues* like it's a dirty word. I can practically hear her wrinkling her nose through the phone line.

"Dr. Lancaster says it's not one-size-fits-all. She wants to get to know me first."

"Well, I hope she figures it out soon. You'll want to be at your best at the intensive. It's only three weeks away, you know."

Right on cue, my stomach knots up. "I know, Mom."

"Did you work out today?"

"Yeah, for about two hours this afternoon."

It's not enough. It won't make a difference.

"Hmm," Mom says. "What are they feeding you?"

"Spaghetti and meatballs for lunch. Chicken and vegetables for dinner."

"*Meatballs*," Mom says. Another dirty word. "Ask if they can make you a salad tomorrow."

"Okay." My knee is bouncing up and down. I put my hand on it to stop it.

"I know I can count on you to make good choices," Mom says.

"I will. I promise."

"This is just a bump in the road. You're still my beautiful ballerina."

No, it isn't. And no, you're not.

I need to get off the phone. I'm a ball of electricity, shaking in my seat. But I can't tell her that. Especially not after she says, "I miss you already! The house feels so empty. I hate being by myself."

So I pretend to yawn. "I miss you too, Mom. But I need to get ready for bed. It's been a really long day." Understatement of the year.

"All right," Mom says. "I'll speak to you tomorrow."

"Tomorrow?" I echo.

"Tomorrow," she confirms. "Good night, Samantha."

I sit there for a second after I hang up the phone. I love my mom. She cares about me and my future. I should want to talk to her every day, right?

I leave Dr. Lancaster's office, walk back down the hall, and sit next to Katie on the sofa. She glances at me and opens her mouth, but I must have a *Do Not Disturb* sign on my forehead, because in the end, she doesn't say a word.

six

I'M IN THE WINGS, TUCKED BEHIND A CURTAIN, staring out onto the brightly lit stage. It's *Nutcracker*, Act II—all gumdrops and sparkles. Clara is sitting on the Sugar Plum Fairy's throne. She claps her hands with delight as Mother Ginger's gingerbread children cartwheel and somersault in front of her. The music is building to a crescendo.

I roll through my feet, pressing over onto one pointe, then the other. I run my hands over the bodice of my costume, stopping at the delicate pink lace draped across my hips. I shake my head a few times to make sure my tiara is securely pinned in.

Onstage, Mother Ginger's children are bowing and curtseying.

The audience is clapping.

I'm next.

Bianca, still dressed in her tutu from the Spanish

variation, leans in close to wish me good luck: "*Merde*, Sam-a-lam-a!" From the opposite wing, my mom gives me a radiant smile and a thumbs-up.

In the moment of silence before the orchestra begins to play "Waltz of the Flowers," I hear my pulse and my breath. Time slows down. Then the music starts.

I rise up onto my toes, let my arms float up like a breath. I run onstage.

It's my last performance as the Dewdrop Fairy. I give it everything I have. I spin and soar through space. I feel free and effortless and perfect. For seven and a half minutes, nothing exists but the beautiful, magical *now*.

I pirouette into my final pose, with the corps de ballet fanned out around me. The applause is like thunder. It almost brings tears to my eyes. We move into a straight line. At center stage, I curtsy deep, touching my hand to my heart. I—

I wake up.

And then I do start crying, because I'm not onstage, after the performance of a lifetime. I'm *here*. The place my awful roommate won't stop calling Crazy Camp.

Zoe stirs in the bed across from me. The last thing I want to do is talk to her, so I jump up and gather my towel, my toiletries, and a sundress to change into after I shower. I slip silently down the dark hallway to the bathroom. It's empty; I'm safe. I step into the shower stall, leaving my pajamas on the floor. I turn the faucet. And then I stand there, with water running down my back and tears running down my face.

The joy I felt in my dream—the joy I felt onstage that night, back in December—I want to feel it again. I want that with every fiber of my being.

You won't get it back. You can't.

I pull myself together and finish washing up. I shut off the water. The bathroom is still empty, still quiet, so I'm able to dry off and get dressed in peace.

When I go downstairs to the kitchen, Andrew is standing in front of the open fridge. "Hi! You're up early."

"So are you," I say, climbing onto one of the stools at the kitchen island.

"Ah, but I have a reason." He gets out a massive fruit bowl and a cling-wrapped cookie sheet laden with unbaked cinnamon rolls.

Don't even think about it.

"I have to make breakfast for you guys."

"Dr. Lancaster's really putting you to work, huh?"

"I don't mind. Believe it or not, I'm a morning person."

I pretend to grimace. "Ugh."

He laughs. "I know, right? But I like being up when the rest of the world is still sleeping. It's, I don't know, magical or something."

"Magical," I repeat, shaking my head. "To me, the only good thing about getting up early is having the bathroom to myself."

"That is another perk," he says. "Though I bet my morning routine is a lot more stripped-down than yours." He sets the oven to preheat, then starts washing grapes in the sink, dropping them one by one into a colander. "That's the great thing about being a guy."

I laugh.

"Um, so about yesterday . . ." He keeps methodically separating grapes from their stems, but I can see his shoulders tense up. "I'm glad you told Dr. Lancaster what happened. And thanks for telling her I wanted to run and get her immediately."

"I promised I would," I say quietly.

"I know. But thanks anyway for following through. I want to be here. I'd hate to screw it up." He tosses the stems in the garbage, swirls the grapes around in the colander one last time, and turns the faucet off. "And I'm sorry, again, for that whole thing. For not being more careful with you." Now he turns to face me, putting the dripping colander on a paper towel on the counter.

"It's fine. I was . . ." I gulp. "I was a little bit of a basket case yesterday."

"You seemed okay to me. Until . . ."

"Yeah, well." That's what I do. I seem okay, *until*.

"Was it anything I did? Was it what I said on Sunday?"

I shake my head, even though that's not entirely true. "It's this whole thing. This place. I'm—I'm kind of a mess."

Now it's Andrew's turn to shake his head. "Nope. I don't accept that."

"You don't accept that I'm a mess?"

"I do not. In fact, I think you're pretty great."

His words—and the sincere smile on his face—almost

70

knock me over. I have to grip the sides of the stool to stay upright. "Oh," I say, my voice coming out weaker than I want it to. "Thanks, I guess."

"You're welcome. And just so you know—" Andrew shuts his mouth abruptly as Dominic walks in. He's in plaid pajama bottoms and a white T-shirt, and his dark hair is sticking out in all directions.

"Hey," he says, yawning. "I'm starving. What's for breakfast?"

Andrew snaps into action. "Cinnamon rolls—about to go in the oven. And there's fruit salad. Want to help? It'll be ready faster if you do."

"I guess," Dominic says. "What do you need?"

Andrew sets him up slicing strawberries. Then he looks over to me. "Can you help me out by peeling some clementines?"

I nod, and he pushes the bowl my way.

"Thanks," he says.

"No problem."

"Oh, and I should've asked earlier. Do you drink coffee? I made a pot." He points at the coffeemaker.

"Sometimes." The problem is, I like it light and sweet—and that's how the calories get in.

Andrew pulls a mug out of the cabinet. "I'll get you some. How do you take it?"

"Black."

When he hands me the steaming mug, our fingers brush. The brief touch gives me goose bumps up and down

71

my arms. I take a sip of the black coffee, trying not to cringe at the bitter liquid as it hits my taste buds. Then I get to work on the clementines.

Andrew puts the pastries in the oven. Within minutes, the smell of cinnamon sugar is overwhelming. Intoxicating.

I lift a peeled clementine to my nose. I breathe in the bright citrus scent. I tell myself, *This* is what I want. Fresh fruit. Not butter and dough and icing. I pull off a segment and pop it into my mouth, biting down. The juice is sweet and tart.

I set the rest of the clementine aside on a paper towel. Every time the cinnamon roll smell threatens to overwhelm me, I eat another segment.

And bite by bite, I make it through the next hour.

THE MORNING'S GROUP session is about anxiety triggers and symptoms. Dr. Lancaster has us call out how we feel in stressful situations. She writes down our ideas on the big whiteboard that appeared in the Dogwood Room overnight.

"I can't breathe," Katie says. "And my heart beats so hard."

"I get dizzy," Omar adds.

"Upset stomach," Jenna says primly.

After a long pause, Dominic says, "*If* I get really freaked out—and I'm not saying I ever do, but, like, hypothetically—my palms get all sweaty. I can't grip the ball." He slouches in his seat and repeats, "Hypothetically."

"Good," Dr. Lancaster says. "Anyone else?"

"The voice in my head gets really loud," I murmur.

Dr. Lancaster writes *Negative self-talk* on the whiteboard. "Zoe?"

"Like I told you yesterday," Zoe says, looking bored, "I don't have a problem with anxiety. Psychoanalyze me all you want. You won't get anywhere."

Dr. Lancaster nods. "Okay then." She starts talking about how when we experience those initial symptoms, we can anticipate the anxiety taking over. And using the techniques we're going to explore while we're here, we can defuse the tension and prepare to compete or perform more effectively.

I lean forward in my seat, paying close attention. If my mom quizzes me about this tonight, I want to have something to tell her. Never mind how much my life would change if the techniques Dr. Lancaster is talking about actually work.

They won't work. Nothing will work. You're stuck like this—

I raise my hand. "When will we start practicing?"

"Practicing what, Sam?"

I list off a few of the things she mentioned. "Breathing. Mantras. Redirecting our nervous energy. All of it."

"Every day that you're here, you'll be picking up new tactics to battle your anxiety. To become a stronger you."

A stronger you. Ha! Every day that you're here, you're getting weaker. Softer. Fatter—

"What are we learning today?" I ask, talking over the voice in my head.

"We're going to do another activity that might help you

express what you're feeling, in the event that talking about it is too hard. Have you ever heard the expression 'A picture is worth a thousand words'?"

"Obviously," Zoe grumbles. "We're not idiots."

Dr. Lancaster ignores her. "You'll have the next hour to create a collage that represents a situation that makes you anxious. Yasmin has turned the dining room into an art room for you, complete with scissors, glue, magazines, and more."

Now Zoe bursts out laughing. "It's arts-and-crafts time at Crazy Camp!" Then she stops laughing, turning her face into a mask of concern. "Are you sure we're allowed to have scissors? Isn't that . . . dangerous?"

"Zoe," Dr. Lancaster says sharply. "What did we discuss yesterday?"

"I know, I know: don't make fun of the process," Zoe singsongs.

In the dining room, we spread out, grabbing magazines and other supplies. Katie sits down next to me, and we both start flipping glossy pages.

Jenna pulls out a chair across from us. "Sam?"

I tense up but keep my expression calm and pleasant. "Yes, Jenna?"

"I'd be interested in doing a ballet barre with you later. If you don't mind."

"Even though you're not here to make friends?" I say, surprising myself—and Katie, who lets out a little squeak.

Jenna gives me an appraising look. "Yes."

I have to exercise anyway. But I can play it just as cool as she is. "Find me after your session with Dr. Lancaster."

"Okay. I will."

I turn back to Katie. "What are you going to make?"

She's already cutting out a long strip of brown construction paper. "A balance beam, of course. How about you?"

"I don't know yet." I flip page after page, looking for inspiration. And then I reach a perfume ad where the model seems to be staring right at me. Through me. Into me. I stare back, an idea forming. I cut out her eyes and put them off to the side.

The hour of cutting and pasting passes in a flash. When Andrew touches me on the shoulder to give me a five-minute warning, I startle, as if I'm waking up.

"That's really interesting." He's staring down at my collage.

I study what I've made. There's a single small figure, in silhouette, floating in a sea of eyes. Blue eyes and green eyes and brown eyes. All shapes and sizes. It's . . . weird. Uncomfortable to look at for too long.

"Is interesting good?" I ask, smiling like I don't care one bit. Like his opinion doesn't matter. Like his presence behind me isn't enough to throw me for a loop, after what he said to me this morning about thinking I'm pretty great.

"Yeah. I can't wait to hear more about it."

"Andrew? A little help?" Yasmin calls from the other

side of the room, where she's trying to peel off several pages that have been glued to the dining table.

Zoe looks pleased with herself. "You didn't say I had to make my collage on *paper*," she drawls. "I was just expressing my feelings."

"If this damages the wood," Yasmin says, "Dr. Lancaster may have to call your parents."

"Do it," Zoe growls, eyes flashing. "Call 'em."

Dr. Lancaster walks in, glancing at the clock on the wall. "Time to— Oh, Zoe." Her face drops in disappointment. "Everyone, please take your collages to the Dogwood Room."

"My collage can't be moved," Zoe says grandly. "Does that mean I get to skip the next session?"

"No." Dr. Lancaster leans in close to the table, picking at one of the glued-on pages. "Yasmin, Andrew, can you take care of this?"

They nod.

"Zoe?" Dr. Lancaster steps to the side, extending her arm. Zoe stares her down. Dr. Lancaster doesn't budge. And finally, with an exaggerated sigh, Zoe trudges out of the room. The rest of us follow.

"Do you think she'll get sent home?" Katie whispers to me, once we're back seated in our folding-chair circle.

"On the second day? She'll probably get a warning or something."

I look over at Zoe. Dr. Lancaster is speaking to her in a low voice. Zoe rolls her eyes. "Whatever," she says.

Dr. Lancaster addresses all of us. "Zoe would like to say something."

"Would I?"

"Yes, Zoe, you would."

"Oh, fine. I'm sorry for disrupting arts and crafts. I won't do it again."

She doesn't sound sorry. She sounds like she's plotting her next attack.

But Dr. Lancaster says mildly, "Thank you, Zoe. I know it can be difficult to adapt to being here, even if you came by choice—"

"Oh, I'm not here by choice."

Dr. Lancaster gives her a considering look. "You filled out the paperwork, along with your parents. Are you telling me you didn't consent—"

"Yeah, I filled out your stupid questionnaire. I signed the forms. It was this place or tennis camp. I chose to come here. But that doesn't mean I want to be here. Or that I *need* to be here."

The way she says "need"—like the rest of us are irreparably screwed up in a way that she isn't—makes me cringe.

"Does anyone want to respond to Zoe?"

No one speaks except for Jenna, who says, "Pass" in a voice that's like a slap of icy air to the face.

"I know Zoe will appreciate your support, just as you'll appreciate hers."

Zoe snorts.

"Now, let's discuss your collages. Katie, would you mind going first?"

"I guess not." Katie holds up her picture. It's a balance beam over a red mat. There's a crying baby sitting on the beam, and lots of people around the edges of the page, watching. "This is, um, exactly what it looks like. It's what I told you yesterday. How I'm afraid of falling." She pauses. "I'm not exactly an artist."

"No kidding," Zoe says, and Katie shrinks back into her chair.

"Zoe." Dr. Lancaster closes her eyes for a second, breathing in and out through her nose. "Apologize to Katie."

"Sorry, Katie," Zoe says.

"Thank you. Katie, great job. Do you want to say anything else?"

"No," Katie says quietly. "That's it."

Dr. Lancaster moves on. "Sam?"

I prop my picture up in my lap, looking down at it. "I guess I went more abstract. The person in the center of the picture is being stared at." I hesitate, then add, "She doesn't like it."

No one speaks for a second. And it's such a long second. With their eyes on me. Eyes upon eyes upon eyes.

"Weird," Zoe says.

"It's cool?" Omar says, like he's not sure. "But it also kind of freaks me out?"

"It's very evocative, Sam," Dr. Lancaster says. "Nice

78

work." The way she's looking at me, at my picture, I know we'll be talking about it in my private session later. But for now, thank goodness, the focus moves off me. I put the picture under my chair and breathe in deep to stop the shuddering in my chest.

Jenna created a scoreboard out of precise black and white squares. When Dr. Lancaster prompts her, she explains, "Figure skating has such a complex scoring system. It can come down to hundredths of a point." She bites her lip. "I spend a lot of time thinking about those hundredths."

Dominic used pictures of people: professional football players, but also executives in suits and men driving expensive cars. "It's, like, the future," he tells us. "Where I wanna be. Where I'm *gonna* be."

Omar filled his page with cameras and theater seats and bright lights. "It's supposed to be about the first time I got really anxious, and I didn't know what was happening to me," he says, frowning at it. "It's not very good."

"It's great, Omar. All of you did a wonderful job," Dr. Lancaster says, ignoring Zoe's silent, gagging face. "Can everyone hold your pictures up one more time?"

I pull my collage back onto my lap.

"Take a look around. What can you learn from your fellow campers' artwork? Is it possible that you have more in common with each other than you realize?" Dr. Lancaster smiles. "I promise, it will be easier to make the most of your time here if you consider yourselves allies rather than adversaries."

Jenna narrows her eyes. "But we compete alone."

"Not all of you," Dr. Lancaster counters. "Remember, Dominic's on a team."

"Yeah, but I'm QB," Dominic says, grinning. "So I'm kind of a big deal."

"How is what's helpful for Dominic possibly going to help me?" Jenna asks. "And how will arts and crafts help *at all*? This isn't why I'm here."

"Would you like to tell us why you are here, Jenna?"

She opens her mouth and then slams it shut. "No, thank you. I don't see how it makes a difference if *they* know"— she gestures at all of us—"when you and I will be talking about it in private every afternoon."

"Your fellow campers can empathize. They can make you feel less alone, even if you'll be competing alone when you return home. They can brainstorm with you. Support you." Dr. Lancaster finishes, her voice gentle, "The whole point is that you don't have to go through what you're going through by yourself."

"No one here can help me," Jenna mutters darkly, so quiet, I barely hear her.

No one can help you, either, my inner voice whispers. *Enjoy being alone.*

seven

INSTEAD OF WAITING TO GET TRICKED INTO EATING lunch with everyone else—in front of everyone else—I slip into the bathroom the moment Dr. Lancaster lets us leave the Dogwood Room. I wait a few minutes, then poke my head out the door to check that the hallway is empty. I sneak into the kitchen, relying on all my dancer's grace not to make a sound. I grab a six-inch turkey sub and head outside to sit on the front porch.

I down it in nine huge bites. It's the first thing I've eaten since I got here that's actually satisfying.

But then Dr. Lancaster finds me. "Sam," she says. "We need to discuss why you're avoiding meals."

"I'm not—"

"Did you eat?"

I show her my empty plate, complete with bread crumbs.

"Then we'll start your afternoon session a few minutes

early. Come with me."

We go to her office. She shuts the door and points at the couch. I drop into it, the feeling of peace I got from my private lunch evaporating.

"You need to eat, Sam—in the dining room, with everyone else."

"But—"

"It's not negotiable. Part of my job here is to keep all of you safe and healthy. For you, that means making sure you're eating."

"I eat! I promise, I do."

Too much. And too often.

"I don't have a problem with food." Frustrated tears prick at my eyes, and feeling those tears makes me even more frustrated. "Why do I have to prove it? Why can't you trust me?"

"Because—" For a second, I think Dr. Lancaster is going to pull a *Because I said so*, but instead she says, "I see your reluctance to eat. I see you counting what's on your plate. Forcing yourself to eat more than you want—or less."

The fight drains out of me. Shame settles in. "You see all that?" I whisper.

"I'm trained to see it," Dr. Lancaster says patiently.

I curl up on the couch, the sandwich I wolfed down becoming a knife in my gut.

"Do you want to tell me about the eyes?" She pulls out the collage I left under my chair in the Dogwood Room. "What do they symbolize?"

"You're the therapist. You tell me."

"Can you tell me about a time when someone was looking at you and you didn't like it?" She's quoting my own words back at me.

"Want me to make a list?"

Dr. Lancaster looks thoughtful. "Actually, yes."

I sit upright. "I was being sarcastic."

She smiles. "I know. But you're all going to get journals tomorrow anyway. Maybe I'll give you a head start."

"Great." I wait a beat. "That was also sarcasm, by the way."

Dr. Lancaster rummages around in a desk drawer and pulls out a selection of spiral-bound notebooks. "Blue, green, or purple?" she asks, fanning them out.

"Um. Green, I guess."

"Excellent choice." She hands it to me. "Before tomorrow's session, I want you to write about at least three instances when you struggled with being looked at."

"Three? By tomorrow?"

"You don't have to write a novel about each one. A few paragraphs will do." She crosses her legs, giving me a keen look. "Do you want to go ahead and get started, or would you rather keep talking to me?"

An easy choice. "I'll take the extra writing time."

"All right. But I need you to take this assignment seriously. And I think *you* need you to take it seriously too." She motions to the door. "I'll let you get to work."

* * *

I SET UP camp in the gazebo Andrew and I explored yesterday. I lean back into a corner, legs extended out on the wooden bench, ankles crossed, with the notebook in my lap. There's a breeze blowing. I feel it rustling my ponytail. And while the sun is blazing down, it's cooler in the shade of the gazebo's roof. I can see waves of heat radiating in the distance, but I'm not even sweating.

I doodle a flower in the margin of the paper. I add some swirly spirals around it and then shade in the petals.

I don't know what to write.

Andrew and Dominic come out the back door. Dominic has a football in one hand. He laughs at something Andrew says and then gives Andrew a friendly shove. Andrew shoves him back. Then they go to opposite ends of the lawn and start passing the ball back and forth. I watch the way Dominic launches the ball into its smooth arc. I watch it spiral through the air. I watch Andrew jump to catch it, cradling it close. It's like a choreographed dance: pas de trois for two men and a football.

You're stalling.

"I know," I tell my inner voice.

So get on with it. Write out each and every humiliation. Live it all over again.

I tap my pen on the page, thinking. Remembering.

Then I start to write about the day the cast list went up for our spring performance. At my studio, we do a mixed-rep show in the early fall, *Nutcracker* in December, and then alternate between a full-length story ballet and a mixed-rep show every other spring. This year we did the variations from *Paquita*, a Spanish-infused classical tutu ballet, along with two new ballets by guest choreographers.

I got a solo in *Paquita*. The variation that begins with all the leaps from the upstage left corner and has the arabesque and attitude pirouettes in the middle. My favorite, the one I'd always dreamed of performing.

I wasn't so lucky with the other ballets. I was cast in the corps de ballet in one and was an understudy in the other.

This was mid-February—my body was already well on its way to being the disaster it is now—but I was still surprised. Still hurt. And then I went upstairs to the lobby, where I found my mom talking to Tabitha's mom.

"Are you disappointed?" Mrs. Hoyt asked.

"Of course. Samantha and I had obviously hoped for more this spring," my mom said. "But Giorgio's piece is going to be in unitards."

It took me a second to realize what she was really saying: that the choreographer didn't want my body, in a skin-tight costume, dancing his work. But did Mom know for a fact that that was why I wasn't chosen? Or was she guessing?

Both options hurt—just in different ways.

"In the meantime, I've already adjusted Samantha's diet," Mom went on. "We'll have her unitard-ready by the next show."

"It's great that Sam has you on her side, with all of your experience," Mrs. Hoyt said. "Tabitha looks up to you so much."

"That's so sweet. Your daughter is a beautiful dancer with a bright future. And—" That's when my mom noticed me standing there. "Samantha!" She stood up. "A *Paquita* variation! Well done! I danced that one in school too."

"Thanks." Better to pretend I didn't hear a thing. Otherwise I'd never make it out of here without falling apart.

"Are you ready to go?" Mom asked.

"Are you?" This was before Mom had started working at the studio, but it still felt like she was there as much as I was. Never mind her full-time job—

"Hey. Aren't you supposed to be with Dr. Lancaster?"

I jolt out of my memories to discover Andrew standing outside the gazebo, leaning against the railing next to me. I close the notebook fast, hiding my scribbled words. "I, uh . . ." I feel breathless. Off balance. "She gave me homework."

"Ouch. So much for summer vacation."

I let out a small laugh at that. "Like any of this counts as summer vacation."

"So how's it going?" He walks around the corner and up the steps. Sits down on the wooden bench across from me.

"Okay, I guess."

"You looked like you were concentrating pretty hard. I didn't want to interrupt you. But then I realized what time it was, so I figured I'd check in."

"Oh." I wait for him to go away, now that he's done his peer-adviser duty. But he doesn't. And when I look out into the yard, Dominic is now playing catch with Katie.

Andrew follows my gaze. "He'll make a wide receiver

out of her yet," he jokes.

I laugh again. This time, it's a little louder. A little more real. "I'd agree with you, except I have no idea what a wide receiver is."

"Oh. It's the guy who catches the pass and runs it in for a touchdown."

"Got it."

A few silent seconds go by. I look down at my notebook, thinking about my unfinished story—and the two I still have to write. And then Andrew clears his throat. He leans forward, elbows resting on his knees. "This morning, when we got interrupted—I just wanted to tell you I think you're doing great here so far."

Sarcasm. Lies. Great is the last thing you are.

I stare at him. "Yesterday I had a panic attack right in front of you. Today Dr. Lancaster chews me out for not eating in the dining room and then gives me extra work to do as punishment. I don't think I've earned a therapy gold star."

"Chews you out?" Andrew says, cocking his head to one side. "For not eating?"

I snort. "Yeah, no pun intended."

"But seriously," Andrew goes on. "You're trying. Not everyone is. I'm working on Dominic, and Zoe's a whole other situation, but—" He checks himself, like he realizes he shouldn't be talking about them to me. "I remember what it felt like, the first few days here. It's tough. Emotional."

"Yeah," I say, looking down at my knees.

"I hope this isn't presumptuous or crossing a line to say,

but—I feel like I *get* you, Sam. What makes you tick. With your mom and my dad, I think we have a lot in common. So I want to help you make the most of your time here."

"Okay."

He's looking at me. His eyes should scrape at my skin. They should bruise me. They have before. But in this moment, they aren't.

He's totally judging you. What is he looking at right now?

I duck my head again, second-guessing. Does sitting like this make my stomach pooch out? And what about my thighs and butt, squishing into the wooden slats of the bench? I can't bring my knees to my chest or sit cross-legged in this sundress, so I swing around to place my feet flat on the floor. Problems solved.

But changing positions doesn't make me any more comfortable.

"Um, I have to get back to work." My voice is too loud. "Thanks for the pep talk!" I give him my best stage smile. Lips pulled wide, showing all my teeth.

And then I flip my notebook open and frown at it, pretending to think. I wait. I hear him stand and walk down the gazebo steps. When I finally lift my eyes, he's back with Dominic and Katie, talking animatedly, one hand on each of their shoulders.

I put my pen to the page. I try to pick up where I left off.

JENNA FINDS ME an hour or two later, when her private session is done. She knocks on the side of the gazebo. "Ready?"

I look up, surprised to see that she's been crying. Her eyes are red and she has a raw spot on her lower lip, like she's been gnawing on it.

When I don't answer right away, she starts smoothing her already-slick hair back from her face. "You don't have to dance with me. Never mind." She turns to go.

"Wait. I want to." I close the notebook and get to my feet.

Those are the only words we say to each other, aside from coming up with barre exercises. And honestly, that's fine by me. I don't want to talk. I just want to *move.*

I head into dinner feeling okay. I burned enough calories to justify eating a proper meal. Dancing did its job. Dr. Lancaster will be thrilled that I'm not running away from the fajita buffet Yasmin has set up. I watch Jenna make her plate and copy her exactly: two fajitas, three chicken strips in each tortilla, no cheese or sour cream or guacamole. As I'm spooning a bit of fresh salsa over each fajita, I realize that this could be my new plan to get through mealtimes. Jenna looks like she lives low-cal, and yet no one's accusing her of having an eating disorder. If I eat what she eats, maybe Dr. Lancaster—and everyone else—will leave me alone.

But when I talk to my mom later that night, she stops me as soon as I say "fajita."

"You know you shouldn't be eating tortillas, Samantha," she says. "Did you ask for a salad alternative, like I told you?"

The guilt hits—I totally forgot. I lie: "I have to eat what they provide, Mom."

"Well, then you need to do a better job of adapting." It's the start of a lecture I've heard so many times over the past few months. One I'm usually able to sit through. Even tune out. But tonight, by the end of it, I'm crying silently into the phone.

"Samantha? Are you there?"

"Yes."

"Were you listening?"

"Yes."

Mom's voice softens. "I love you. I'm so proud of you."

"I love you too, Mom." I wipe my eyes with the heel of my hand and smile into the phone, because I don't want her to hear the tears in my voice. I'm supposed to be better than this.

There is no "better." Not for you.

eight

ON WEDNESDAY MORNING, I GET UP EARLY SO I CAN shower and get dressed in peace. I head down to the kitchen, where Yasmin is setting out bagels and muffins and other things I'm not supposed to let tempt me. I help her chop fruit. I peel clementines, and I eat one, slowly, because that worked yesterday. And then I sit in the Dogwood Room and listen to Dr. Lancaster lecture about not being so hard on yourself.

You should *be hard on yourself,* my inner voice sneers. *You deserve it.*

"And on the topic of giving yourself a break, I have a surprise for you!" Dr. Lancaster announces. "I'm so glad the sun is out, because we've gotten permission from the campus to spend the rest of the morning swimming in the lake."

She keeps talking, but I don't hear a thing after "swimming."

I can't.

I won't.

I'll say I don't know how. Or that I forgot my suit. Or that I'm afraid of fish.

I'll say anything.

But not right now, because everyone looks so happy. I force myself to smile. To cheer along with them. When the others run upstairs to change into their swimsuits, I go too. I'm on autopilot, rooting around in my suitcase until I find the black one-piece my mom bought me last week. I never intended to wear it. I almost didn't pack it.

I rip off the tag with my teeth.

I change in a bathroom stall. Slowly.

"We'll see you downstairs!" Katie calls, letting the door slam shut behind her.

I count to sixty once. Twice. Three times.

And then I open the bathroom stall to look at myself in the mirror.

No no no no no no no—

"It's not any different than a leotard," I whisper. I spin, taking in all the angles.

Cellulite. Stomach rolls. Boobs that are about to escape from their halter.

Suck it in. Suck it up.

The suit is getting tighter and tighter. The ties are strangling me. I'm tingling all over, losing circulation, losing air.

I want to curl up in the fetal position on the floor. That's what I did last month, the last time I put on a swimsuit.

Bianca decided to have a pool party to celebrate the end of the school year. An hour before the party, I tried on last year's swimsuits, one after another, growing more and more anxious. The bottom one in the stack was a high-waisted, bright yellow, polka-dotted two-piece. I loved that suit. I thought I'd saved the best for last.

But no. I was a sausage escaping its casing, skin and flesh bulging out all over.

I turned into a puddle of tears and snot on my bathroom floor. It wasn't as bad as the *Paquita* incident . . . but it was close. I called Bianca and told her I was sick. I asked whether I could take a pool-party rain check. Not that I ever planned to cash that check.

Now I stare at myself in the mirror. When my mom handed me this swimsuit, she told me, "Black is slimming."

If this is slim, *imagine what you'd look like wearing a color—*

"Sam?" Katie calls from downstairs. "You coming?"

I poke my head out the door. "Almost ready!"

Why are you doing this? What's wrong with you?

I'm fine. I don't even have to get undressed when we get there. I'll just sit in the sun and watch everyone else swim. It'll be fun.

Liar liar liar liar—

I throw on shorts and a tank top and force myself out the door.

The whole walk across the lawn, along the trail through the woods, toward the lake, I'm a ball of nerves. But I keep my face neutral.

Everyone can tell. They see everything you're hiding.

I rub my hands up and down my arms, suddenly cold despite the typical North Carolina heat and humidity. My teeth are chattering. I clench my jaw shut to muffle the sound. The fabric of my swimsuit feels like a cheese grater on my skin. Everything hurts.

This is going to end badly. You know it is.

I push forward, feeling like my feet are stuck in cement blocks.

I can get past this. I'm stronger than this.

No, you're not.

We reach the lake. I hear the splash first. Dominic's in the water. Omar jumps off the dock next, followed by Andrew.

Jenna is undressing. So is Katie. So is Yasmin. I stare at them, unable to avert my eyes even though I know I should. Jenna's reed-thin silhouette. Katie's compact body and defined muscles. Yasmin's flat stomach.

I don't have any of those things.

Bianca does. Her body is amazing. And she's talented, which would be infuriating if she weren't also so nice. We've been friends for eight years, since she moved to my hometown from California. We used to have sleepovers where we'd watch ballet movies and flip through my mom's back issues of *Dance Magazine*. We talked about joining American Ballet Theatre together one day. We'd be roommates in a tiny apartment in New York City and rise through the company ranks side by side.

It didn't seem too far-fetched. We were both good

dancers, but with different strengths. Bianca loves adagio work, moving through space with slow control. I love turns and jumps, spinning and soaring. But then my body changed, and hers didn't. The unitard piece I was cast as an understudy in? Bianca was one of the leads.

As I stare at Katie and Jenna and Yasmin in their swimsuits, and as I think about everything that now separates me from Bianca—and from our shared future—my vision gets cloudy.

You'll never look like them. You'll never feel *like them, at ease in your skin—*

"Okay over there, Ballerina Barbie?" Zoe is leaning against a tree, tucking her braids up under a swim cap. She smirks at me.

I open my mouth and close it, like a fish.

"Seriously, you look like you saw a ghost. You know this isn't one of those haunted summer camps, right?"

I can't breathe. I can't breathe. I can't breathe.

I sink to the ground. I close my eyes and put my hands over my ears. I rock back and forth, willing my pulse to slow down and my lungs to work.

I hear, through the pounding in my skull, someone shouting my name. I feel hands touch my shoulders, jerk away, touch me again.

I ignore it all. I go into my tiny, dark, quiet place. The place I discovered the first time this happened. Where I'm small and safe. Where no one and nothing can reach me or hurt me.

Arms around me. Thin. Bony.

A voice, soft and close, in my ear: "Hey. Sam. You're okay. Shh. Shh."

I open my eyes and am vaguely surprised to see that it's Jenna who's got me. Our eyes meet, and she gives me a small nod.

"Excuse me, Jenna." Dr. Lancaster comes into my field of vision. She sits in the dirt next to me. Jenna scoots away. Dr. Lancaster leans in close. "Do you think you can walk with me back to the house?"

I look around. At Katie's scared eyes and the furrow between Jenna's brows. At Zoe's wrinkled nose—like what just happened to me smells bad. At Dominic, who's gaping, and at Omar, who's bouncing in place and muttering to himself: "I don't like this. I don't like this. I don't like this."

Me neither.

I nod in answer to Dr. Lancaster's question, and it's like the blood and the air rush back into the vacuum of my body. It feels so overwhelming and amazing that I start crying. Loud, gulping, heaving sobs.

Dr. Lancaster stands and lets Andrew help me to my feet. His grip is firm, solid. "I've got you," he says. It makes me cry harder.

"Let's go." Dr. Lancaster wraps one arm around me. "Andrew, Yasmin, do you have everything under control here?"

"Yes, ma'am," Andrew says, and Yasmin echoes him.

I go with Dr. Lancaster, leaving a shocked silence in my wake.

THE PANIC FADES fast.

Usually, after something like this, I'm so drained that I can barely function. But this time, it's different. Maybe it's Dr. Lancaster's arm across my shoulders, weighing me down with her concern and care. Or maybe it's the fact that I am now, indisputably, the craziest person at Crazy Camp. I can feel anger building inside me. It's a hot, sharp, vicious thing.

I want to throw something. Or hit something. I want to lash out.

This is new.

It feels horrible and satisfying, all at once.

"Can you tell me what happened back there?" Dr. Lancaster asks.

"You tell me." I drop onto the sofa in her office, arms crossed like a shield.

"What do you mean by that?"

"Oh, so *yesterday*, you're somehow able to see every little thing about me, but today, you completely fail to notice when I'm about to have a meltdown." My voice is jagged. "Excellent therapy camp you're running here."

"Can you tell me what triggered the panic attack?"

"If I could tell you, I wouldn't have to be here!"

"You seem angry."

I jump to my feet. "Yes! I'm angry! I'm angry at you for not realizing that I might not want to wear a freaking swimsuit when I hate how I look. When all I can think about 95 percent of the time is how people are staring at me and judging me."

"Who else are you angry at?"

I start to pace the room. "I'm angry at everyone who saw what just happened. Nobody should get to see me like that. Nobody. And I'm angry at my dance teacher for convincing me to talk to her about how I was feeling and advising my mom to send me *here*." I infuse that last word with as much contempt as possible.

"Anyone else?"

"The costume designer who made my new tutu too tight, on purpose, so that I'd have a reason to lose weight. Like I wasn't trying to do that already. And all the girls at ballet who gave me diet tips with these fake-helpful smiles, like they were doing me a favor. And the choreographer who wouldn't cast me in his piece because of how I might look in a costume. Like he couldn't possibly pick a different costume direction. Like his *vision* was more important than the dancing." I pause. "I would've kicked butt in that piece."

"I'm sure you—"

"And I'm angry at George freaking Balanchine!"

"Because?"

"Because it's his fault the ballet world is obsessed with who can be the skinniest. It's his aesthetic. He's the reason girls like me can't—of course, he was a genius, but this is all his fault. If I could time-travel, I'd make it so ballet was always about the best dancer, no matter what she looked like."

Dr. Lancaster is nodding. "Who else?"

Marcus. His name floats into my mind, taunting me. I shake it away.

Bianca. No, that doesn't make sense. She's my closest friend.

I'm not angry with either of them. They've actually been there for me through most of this—at least, until Marcus dumped me. So maybe I am mad at him. But not Bianca. And anyway, I don't want to tell Dr. Lancaster about my breakup.

"I'm angry at my brain for not being able to handle, like, *life*," I finally spit out. "For screwing up *everything* I care about. I am so, so mad at myself." Saying it out loud makes me shake with emotion.

"All of this is good," Dr. Lancaster says.

"Good?" I turn on her. "Nothing about this is *good*."

"Expressing your anger is good."

"How does it help me?" I answer my own question. "It doesn't. At all."

"It will. I promise."

"I don't want promises. I want results." Now I sound like my mom. And thinking about how she'd feel, seeing me like this, makes my voice crack. "You're supposed to fix me. Not make me even more of a wreck! Two panic attacks in three

99

days—at therapy camp!"

"So what can you learn from those two panic attacks?"

"Not to trust you! Or this place. To keep doing what I was doing, because that works better than anything you can tell me."

"Do you really believe that?"

I nod fiercely. But the anger is dying down. I drop back onto the couch, hugging the nearest pillow to my stomach.

"I'll tell you one thing I think you can take away from what just happened."

She waits for me to respond. I don't.

"You need to tell someone when you feel overwhelmed, rather than bottling it all up. If you'd mentioned to me, or Yasmin, or Andrew, or even one of your peers that you were having anxiety about swimming, we could have done something to prevent that anxiety from becoming a full-blown panic attack."

I grunt at her.

"Also, now that your panic is out in the open with your peers, I think you'll find it easier to talk to them and rely on them going forward. You don't have to be a brick wall. You're allowed to be vulnerable."

"Being vulnerable won't help me become a professional ballerina."

"What about Juliet?" she counters. "What about Giselle? What about Ophelia?"

"Ophelia?"

"From *Hamlet*."

"Oh."

"Or Odette," she goes on.

"I wasn't talking about that kind of vulnerability," I argue. "I can be strong in real life and still dance a sad role."

"Yes. Exactly. I agree."

"So why do I have to let everyone see how I'm feeling all the time? What if I want to keep my anxiety to myself?"

"There's a difference between being a private person and being so bottled up that it's harmful to you." Dr. Lancaster leans forward in her seat. "Picture yourself as a two-liter bottle of Diet Coke that is tightly sealed, and someone starts shaking it. And shaking. And shaking. The minute you open the bottle, even if you turn the lid oh so slowly, it's going to explode, right?"

I nod.

"You don't have to share everything with everyone. But you have to know when to let some of that fizz out."

"Fizz. Right." I yawn, suddenly incredibly tired.

"Would you like to lie down until the group comes back from the lake?"

"Yes, please." I get to my feet. Stumble to the door. I pause in the doorway. "I'm sorry I yelled at you."

"Don't be sorry, Sam. I'm happy you yelled. You needed to yell."

"I guess."

"You can even yell again, if there's more to yell about."

101

Dr. Lancaster smiles. "I'll wake you up for lunch, okay?"

"There isn't any way I can . . . eat in my room?"

"I'm afraid not. But it won't be as bad as you think."

It will be exactly as bad as I think. I know it. But I just say, "All right." I'm too worn out to fight.

nine

I SLEEP, DEEP AND DREAMLESS. I WAKE UP WITH matted hair and pillow folds etched into my face. I sit up. Stretch. Yawn.

I don't feel much better than I did before. I'm no longer so exhausted that I can barely stand, but the anxiety is still buzzing away in my belly. There's only one reliable cure.

I spend the next twenty minutes doing a series of relevés, using the closet door for balance. I lift my heels high and lower them to the floor, with control, twenty times each in first, second, fourth, and fifth positions. Then I do twenty relevés on each leg, with the other foot lifted in coupé. I finish with an extended balance on each foot, trying to distill my focus down to a pinpoint on the closet door in front of me.

By the time I'm done, my calves are burning. I have to pace back and forth between the two beds to loosen the muscles up again. But my pulse and my breath are calm. The repetitive up, down, up, down of the movement did its job.

I still don't want to go downstairs. I'm afraid of what's waiting for me.

Stares. Whispers.

I've been here before: my first day back at my dance studio after my *Paquita* panic attack. I walked into the room and everyone went silent. I thought that was something that only happened in movies until it happened to me. Then Miss Elise came in, clapped her hands, and cued the accompanist to begin playing our plié music. Bianca stood next to me at the barre, but everyone else gave me a wide berth. Like they thought anxiety was contagious.

And how much worse will it be here, where all of us are battling the same demons? I now represent everything Katie and Jenna and Dominic and Omar and maybe even Zoe don't want to be: a weak, sobbing failure.

But when Dr. Lancaster comes to get me, I go with her. I get a small scoop of pasta salad. I walk into the dining room, plate in hand, and brace myself. I dig my feet into the floor and clench my muscles, like I'm preparing for a tidal wave to hit me.

The only thing that hits me is Katie. She barrels into me, wrapping her arms around my waist. "I'm so glad you're okay!"

I stagger back a step, trying not to drop my meal. "Yeah, I'm okay."

Not a chance——

"I didn't know what to do. I froze. I'm so sorry. But then Jenna jumped in, and . . ." Katie finally lets go of me.

Jenna's standing a few feet away. "Are you all right?" she asks, her tone formal.

"Yeah. Thanks for . . ." I fade out, still not sure exactly what she did. All I know is that when I came back to myself, she was hugging me. The last person I'd expect to be doing that, aside from Zoe.

"No problem." Jenna smooths back a lock of her hair, turns, and walks away.

Katie keeps talking. "Jenna knew just what to do. Dr. Lancaster was still walking over from the house, and Zoe went running to get her, and then the guys got out of the water, and Andrew was ready to carry you, but Jenna waved him off and, like, cocooned you, and . . . it was intense."

I manage a weak smile. "It was intense for me, too."

Katie blushes. "Right. I didn't mean—I'm sorry, we don't have to talk about it."

"Thanks." I follow Katie over to the dining table and sit down across from Omar and Dominic. Omar gawks at me, then shuts his mouth so fast that it makes a snapping noise. Dominic is staring at his food like it's the most fascinating thing in the room.

"Look who it is!" Zoe calls out. She's sitting way off to the side with Yasmin, like she's in time-out. "Feel better, Sleeping Beauty?"

"I'm fine," I say automatically. I spear three elbow macaroni and a cherry tomato and pop the bite into my mouth. Delicious. But I don't think I can stomach any more. Not when I'm the center of attention like this. I start counting the pieces of pasta and veggies on my plate. Moving items from one pile to another. Separating out the little feta cheese cubes.

"Are we going to talk about what happened?" Zoe says into the awkward silence.

Dr. Lancaster sits down at the table. "It's up to Sam." I'm glad she said that, but I also kind of wish she hadn't, because now I feel even more in the spotlight.

Everyone looks at me.

"Um," I say.

"Come on," Zoe groans. "You can't seriously expect us to focus on anything else right now." She says, slowly and distinctly, "Sam, just say you're anorexic, or whatever, and we'll move on with our lives——"

"Zoe!" Dr. Lancaster says.

Zoe doesn't even pause. "Is it really that big a deal? So you don't like how you look. You and every other teenaged girl on the planet——"

Dr. Lancaster pushes her chair back. "My office. Now."

"Make me." Zoe grips the seat of her chair like Dr. Lancaster might try to forcibly remove her.

"Okay," Dr. Lancaster says. "You can stay right where you are. Andrew, Yasmin, would you mind taking the rest of the campers outside to finish lunch on the back porch?"

We all get up fast, collecting our plates and cups. The last thing I hear as I leave is Zoe's unrepentant voice: "You said we're supposed to be opening up to each other about our issues. I'm just trying to speed up the process——"

Andrew holds the door open for me. "Are you all right?"

"Yeah. Thanks." I sit on the steps next to Katie. Andrew sits on my other side. "I'm not gonna freak out again." I say that part louder, so everyone on the porch can hear.

We eat in silence. And I feel the silent seconds tick by. It's like they're landing on me. Each moment stings.

I want the stinging to stop.

So I finally blurt, "I have panic attacks. The whole thing about people looking at me, that collage I made yesterday— it's about my body. I gained some weight recently, and I'm . . . I'm . . ." I should have planned out what I was going to say. It would have sounded better than this. But now that I've started, I can't stop. "I'm having a hard time dealing with it. How I look now. So, um, that's what that was about."

Andrew gives my shoulder an encouraging nudge. I sneak a glance his way and he's smiling. "Good job," he says under his breath.

I exhale, hard.

And I wait for someone else to say something.

To my surprise, Dominic's the first one to speak. "Man, Zoe's gonna be mad she missed your big confession." I can't tell if he's serious, or joking, or making fun of me until he adds, "That girl needs an attitude adjustment."

Jenna blinks up at him. "An attitude adjustment? How old are you again?"

Dominic laughs. "That's what Coach calls it. He basically

means you're about to have to do stadium sprints."

"I don't think working out would help her," Katie says, sounding uncharacteristically sour. "She's just . . . awful."

"Well, yeah," Dominic says, "but honestly, you need to not give her so much attention. If you quit egging her on, she might stop doing what she's doing."

"How do you know she'll stop?" Omar asks.

"It's just a guess." Dominic shrugs. "But I have five little brothers and sisters. I know when someone wants attention."

"So why can't she get our attention by being nice?" Katie asks.

"I didn't say she wanted *our* attention."

"She's going to get kicked out," Omar says.

"Maybe that's what she wants," Dominic answers. "Maybe she doesn't want to be here."

"You don't want to be here, either," Katie says. "You told me yourself."

"Yeah, but I know when I need something. And I need to be here. I'm . . ." He sighs. "I'm stupid-anxious, and it's gonna mess up a lot of things for me. So do I want to be here? No. Am I gonna tough it out? Yeah. Because that's what you do when you need something."

"Ditto," Jenna says. She and Dominic share a look. She gives him a brittle smile.

"Do any of us really want to be here?" Omar asks. He puts a finger beside his nose. "Not it."

"You might feel that way now," Yasmin says, "but I

promise, by the time you leave, you'll be so grateful. . . ."

I can't believe they're not obsessing about my panic attack. I don't know whether they're trying to respect my feelings and my privacy, or if Zoe's just a more interesting topic of discussion. But I don't mind. I'm happy to be in the background. I manage to swallow a few more vegetables before Dr. Lancaster summons Yasmin. They chat just inside the doorway, and then Yasmin comes back out onto the porch.

"Change of plans for this afternoon," she says. "Until Dr. Lancaster is done talking to Zoe, you're supposed to each work on an aspirational collage."

"A what?" Omar asks. "How am I supposed to do it the right way if I don't know what that word means?"

"A collage that represents an ideal day doing your activity," Yasmin says, smiling at him. "Whatever that means to you. There's no one answer, Omar, so you don't have to worry about getting it 'right.'" She makes air quotes. "You'll talk about your image with Dr. Lancaster in your one-on-one later. Dominic, can you help me get the supplies?"

"Sure," he says, getting up. "I know you need a big strong guy to carry it all."

Yasmin laughs. "Yeah, that's totally it, hotshot."

"Lucky I'm here to come to your rescue." Dominic follows her inside.

"I'll help too!" Omar jumps to his feet and runs after Dominic. Something about it—their size difference, Dominic's swagger versus Omar's eagerness—makes Omar look like a puppy chasing a German shepherd.

"Arts and crafts again," Jenna says, sounding disappointed. She smooths her ponytail and then gets to her feet, brushing invisible crumbs from her shorts.

I think about what Dominic said about toughing it out. "Whatever works, right?"

"Right," Katie says firmly.

I SPEND THE afternoon making a ballerina out of weightless things. Ethereal and graceful things. Floating and soaring and spinning things.

I start with a picture of a dancer in arabesque—a lucky find in an entertainment magazine article about a new TV show with a ballerina main character. But she's just my template. I cover her body with photos that represent everything beautiful about ballet. Her torso and arms are made of water and bubbles and clouds. Her feet and ankles become tree roots. Her calves and shins are blades of grass bending in the breeze. Her chest is a dandelion puff. Her fingers are rays of light, shining out.

"Wow," Yasmin says when she sees. "That's gorgeous, Sam."

I actually agree. And so does Dr. Lancaster, when I show it to her.

"This is what you want to be?" she asks. "Your perfect dancer?"

"Yeah. She's light, but grounded. She moves like water, like a reed, like the wind. She shines onstage. . . ." I realize

I'm doing it again, the thing that made Zoe laugh at me during our first group session, when I said dancing the Dewdrop Fairy made me feel light and sparkling. But Zoe isn't here now. It's just me and Dr. Lancaster.

"Do you feel like this collage represents you, at your best?"

"I—yes? No. Sometimes." I chew on my lip. "I guess I might *move* this way, but I don't *look* this way."

That's it in a nutshell—and it's the thing I can't seem to change.

ten

AFTER MY SESSION WITH DR. LANCASTER, I HEAD upstairs to my bedroom. My plan is to work out more. The twenty minutes of relevés I squeezed in earlier aren't going to cut it. Not in terms of my fitness goals, and not in terms of shaking off the residue from my panic attack earlier.

But when I swing the door open, I hear: "Go away."

Zoe's curled up in a lump on her bed. She's under the covers, just the top of her head poking out.

"It's my room too," I tell her.

"Go away!" she shouts.

"No!" I shout back, surprising myself.

I think about everything she said to me at lunch. Everything she's said to me since I got here. Then I think about what Dominic said: we have to quit giving Zoe attention. So although I could yell at her more—I probably have every right to, and it might feel good—I don't.

I crouch next to my suitcase and start folding the clothes I dumped on the floor during this morning's marathon what-am-I-going-to-wear session. Every day I do this. Rumple the clothes in the morning, fold them back up later. I know I could fold them again right away, but I kind of like waiting until it's a big project. I like restoring order to the mess I've made.

I've just tucked the last tank top back into my suitcase when Zoe says quietly, "They said no."

I glance at the door to our bedroom. I could just walk out. There's no reason for me to talk to Zoe.

But then she repeats, even softer, like she can't believe it: "They said no."

I lean back against my bed. I ask, even though I'm not sure I should, "Who?"

"My parents."

"What did they say no to?"

"Coming to get me."

"So you *were* trying to get sent home?" I know I sound skeptical. But I'm not ready to give her the benefit of the doubt.

She sits up, eyes blazing. "I'm not like you. Don't think for a second that I'm anything like you!"

I keep my voice calm, even though my pulse has quickened. "Not like me how?"

"I shouldn't be here. This is all wrong."

"You said you chose to come here."

"I made a mistake." She flops down in the bed and pulls the covers over her head.

"Um, okay." I pick up my workout clothes and get to my feet.

Zoe doesn't speak again until I'm at the door. "I lied," she says, her voice muffled by the blankets. "I wanted to quit tennis, so I lied and told my parents it was giving me panic attacks. I thought it was a great plan. But they went online and found this place."

I pause with my hand on the knob. "But you still had to agree to come here."

"Like I said yesterday. I had a choice: here, or elite tennis camp. I thought if I came here but got kicked out, oops, it's too late to sign up for tennis camp. But—my parents—they won't—" Her voice cracks. "My dad told me to 'straighten up and fly right.' Like he's some 1950s sitcom parent. My mom wouldn't even come to the phone. She couldn't be bothered to talk to me. They don't listen." She takes a ragged breath. "They never listen."

I think about my own mom. I only tried to tell her once how bad I was feeling. The rest of the time, I worked so hard not to let her see. Because she didn't need to see that. She was finally acting like herself again after splitting from my dad two years ago.

When Dad first filed for divorce, I was Mom's lifeline. My dancing made her happy when nothing else could. And when the curvy genes on Dad's side of the family finally caught up with me, I became more than her lifeline. I turned into her project.

I didn't mind. I don't mind.

But there was one night in late March, about three weeks before our spring show, when I thought I was finished. I couldn't handle it anymore. Mom had reserved the small downstairs studio for a private coaching session, just the two of us. She'd brought a list of technique issues she wanted to address. My extensions could be higher. I was sickling my feet when I pointed really hard. My shoulders were lifting in my pirouettes. I was holding too much tension in my hands.

"I'm tired, Mom," I told her when she wanted me to repeat an exercise for the fourth time. Really, what I was feeling wasn't exhaustion. It was pinpricks all over my skin and a sick swirling in my stomach and tightness in my chest. By that point, I knew where those sensations could lead. And I didn't want to break down in front of her.

"You're not too tired to do the exercise correctly."

"Mom, I—" I walked over to lean on the wall-mounted barre, resting my head in my hands. "I don't think this is good for me." That was the only way I could say it. It was the most honest I was able to be. And she didn't hear me.

"What was that?"

"I don't think . . ." I couldn't get it out a second time. "Never mind." I walked back to the center of the studio. I did the exercise again, trying to incorporate all her feedback, trembling with the effort and barely keeping the tears in.

When I was through, I looked at Mom. She was standing by the stereo. Hands clasped in front of her heart. Eyes moist. Sad smile dancing on her lips. "That was beautiful," she said.

The weight lifted a little. "Really?"

"Oh, yes. If we can get rid of those pesky extra pounds, you'll be unstoppable."

And the heaviness settled back in. "I need to go to the bathroom," I told her.

"Go ahead and get changed. I'll wait for you upstairs. We have to go to the store on the way home, so don't dawdle."

I nodded and went to my favorite toilet stall. The one where I ate my lunch and snacks on long rehearsal days. The one where I found my breath when I'd lost it. The one where I cried hot, silent tears. I didn't do any of that that night. I sat on the closed toilet lid, pulling my knees up to my chin and wrapping my arms around my legs. I stared at the peeling gray paint on the stall door. I practiced my smile.

I had to make it home, to my own bedroom, before I could let go.

Now I look at Zoe balled up on her bed. I could tell her about my mom. She might get it. "Zoe—"

"Didn't I tell you to go away?" she says from under her blanket. "I want to be alone. Don't you have a twinkle or a toe touch to do somewhere? Anywhere that isn't around me?"

I leave without saying good-bye.

* * *

AFTER DINNER, I'M sitting on the back porch, watching the sun set over the mountains, when Andrew sits down next to me.

"How's it going?" he asks.

"I'm fine."

My inner voice doesn't even have to chime in. We both know I'm not fine. It's no longer a secret.

"Maybe it has to feel worse before it feels better?"

"I hope it doesn't feel much worse than this." As soon as I say it, my eyes fill up. Because of course it can feel worse.

"Penny for your thoughts?"

Since talking to Zoe, I haven't been able to stop thinking about my mom. If some of why Zoe is so obnoxious is because of how her parents treat her, does some of my anxiety come from my mom? Obviously, there have been times she's made me anxious—but she's not the reason for it, right? My anxiety's on me. Because it's my body that betrayed me.

"When you were here, did you and Dr. Lancaster talk about your dad?" I ask Andrew.

"It's one of the things we talked about."

"How he put pressure on you, and it made you anxious?"

"Yeah. But it wasn't just about him. I'm a people pleaser. I don't ever want to let anyone down. In high school, that was my dad, my coach, my teammates, my school—even my hometown."

"You really felt like you'd let your entire town down if you didn't play well?"

"I was the star of the team. Regional MVP. I was on the front page of the local sports section just about every Saturday morning." He says that last part with a snort of self-deprecating laughter, and I can't help but laugh with him.

"I get it. You were kind of a big deal."

"I was." He pauses. "But I never loved football as much as my dad loved it."

"Oh." Now it's my turn to pause. "I love ballet as much as my mom loved it."

Andrew lets a few seconds go by. "Are you telling me that, like a fact, or are you trying to convince yourself?"

"I'm telling you," I say firmly. "I love ballet."

"Good. I think you have to love something if you're gonna make sacrifices for it."

Sacrifices. My stomach rumbles.

I'm starving right now. I had a clementine for breakfast, a few forkfuls of elbow macaroni and raw veggies for lunch, and half a turkey burger and five asparagus spears for dinner. I could totally have a snack without going over my calorie limit. But it's 8:17 p.m. Not eating after eight o'clock is one of my biggest rules, ever since I read that article online about how the time of day you eat is almost as important as what you eat when it comes to losing weight.

Plus, Katie, Yasmin, and Omar are baking cookies. I couldn't go into the kitchen even if it was 7:59. Cookies are too tempting. Better to stay away.

"Just make sure you're not sacrificing your happiness," Andrew continues.

"I'm not. Why would you say that?" I look at him out of the corner of my eye.

"Caring about something can make you do things you shouldn't."

I gasp and then try to hide the fact that I gasped by coughing.

He knows. How could he possibly know about that—

It's obvious. You're not hiding anything—

He pats my back, between my shoulder blades, like he's trying to dislodge whatever's choking me. "Anyway," he says, "I'm sorry today was rough."

I gulp. I breathe.

He doesn't know. No one does.

"I brought you something. Thought it might cheer you up."

He holds out a single Hershey's Kiss, flat on his palm. Its little flag waves in the evening breeze. "It's dark chocolate. That means it's healthy, right?"

I laugh, even as my eyes threaten to overflow. "That's what the chocolate industry wants you to think."

"No, there are studies about it. It's . . . science," he finishes, laughing with me.

"Oh, well if it's *science*." I take the candy from him. I haven't had chocolate in . . . I don't know how long. Mom won't let it in the house. I swear, if I ate some in secret, even here, she could smell it on me. But I don't want to say no to Andrew.

Instead I say, "Thanks."

"You're welcome." He stands. "I have to get back inside. I promised Dominic I'd talk to him about what college scouts are really looking for. He wanted to watch ESPN with me, but Dr. Lancaster has it blocked, since it might trigger your anxiety."

"Not mine," I say, my voice deliberately dry. "Bring on the college football."

He laughs, softer this time. He squeezes my shoulder. "Don't stay out here alone too long, okay?" He walks away, leaving me with the chocolate in my hand and a humming-bird in my chest.

Marcus used to bring me gifts.

Little things. Inexpensive—and sometimes downright cheap. But always personal. Meaningful. About me, or about him, or about *us*.

A flower from the park where we'd shared a picnic at a free outdoor concert—our first official date. He'd tried to dry the flower and press it flat, but it had ended up kind of shriveled and brown. I loved it anyway.

A Pacific Northwest Ballet refrigerator magnet, from when his family went on a trip to Seattle over fall break. He said since he couldn't take me to see the company, he'd bring a little bit of the company to me.

A tiny Erlenmeyer flask on a key chain. Marcus was in our school's science club and spent hours helping me with my chemistry homework before final semester exams.

A homemade gift certificate for unlimited concession-stand popcorn at his baseball games in the spring. I never used that one, but I kept the certificate folded in my wallet. I liked imagining him on his computer, picking out just the right fonts.

Marcus wasn't perfect. It bugged him that I had to spend so much time at the ballet studio, that I couldn't go out with him and his friends and their girlfriends every Saturday. And he didn't always know what to say to me, especially when I saw him after something bad had happened at ballet. Comforting words weren't his thing. But then I'd get a trinket in my locker, or tucked into the front pocket of my backpack, and I'd know he was there for me.

I study the Hershey's Kiss Andrew gave me. I turn it over and over in my hands.

It reminds me of Marcus, and that hurts. But it also feels like the start of something new.

I tuck the Kiss into my pocket as the last rays of sunshine fade.

eleven

IN EIGHTH GRADE, BIANCA WENT THROUGH A climbing-as-cross-training phase. She got her parents to buy her a ten-class card at the local indoor rock wall for her birthday, and she convinced me to join her for her first session. She was a natural. I . . . was not. But she stayed by my side until I made it to the top of the wall, and she cheered louder than anyone when my feet landed back on solid ground.

I can't help thinking about that ill-fated climbing lesson on Thursday morning. Instead of starting the day with our usual chat in the Dogwood Room, we hiked across campus to a ropes course. First we did low ropes—like moving a plank between a series of ever-smaller wooden platforms until we'd all reached the other side—cooperative problem-solving activities. Then we jumped into the high ropes. Now I'm dangling from a cargo net, wearing a harness and a dopey-looking helmet. Sweat is dripping down my face and back.

For the first time since arriving at Perform at Your Peak, I wish Bianca was here.

"Go, Sam! You've got this!" Yasmin calls from below me.

The net is loose, like a diagonal hammock. It's taking all my upper-body strength to hold on. Still, I'm doing okay until Zoe starts up behind me, and Katie follows her. Then it's like the net gets a mind of its own. Taut ropes become slack in an instant. I miss a step and find myself hanging by my arms. I'm surprised to feel, after a second of flailing, a hand under my right foot.

I look down, ready to say thanks, and Zoe grimaces at me. "Can you try not to fall on my head?"

I make a face back. Yesterday afternoon I actually felt a little sorry for Zoe. She seemed genuinely upset. But this morning, when I woke her up, she cursed me out and threw her pillow at me. And while we were getting harnessed to start the high ropes, she called out, "Hey, Sam—be honest, does this outfit make me look fat?"

When I reach the top of the net, the ropes-course facilitator pulls me up onto the platform. I sit, feet dangling, to catch my breath. Zoe's the next one up. "Little help?" she gasps. I think about pretending I didn't hear her. But she was there for me when I lost my footing, even if she won't admit it, so I give her a hand.

"Thanks," she grunts.

"No problem."

The ropes course is supposed to be helping us continue to build teamwork and trust. Dr. Lancaster also said we'd see, in action, how people have different natural strengths. It's supposed to give us perspective. Help us see that even though there will be things other people do better than us, there are also things we do better than them.

And it's supposed to be fun. I'm not yet convinced. At least I'm burning calories.

Andrew's waiting by the next obstacle: a suspension bridge with slats missing, straight out of an Indiana Jones movie. It's swaying in the breeze. But there's a cable across the top that we hook our harnesses to, so I guess there's no chance we can fall.

Still, just before I take that first step, I freeze.

You're too heavy. You're going to break it.

I can see it in my mind's eye. The plank snapping under my foot. Me dangling, helpless, from the harness. Everyone pointing and laughing.

I look over to the other side. Dominic is already there. He's bigger and heavier than me, by a lot, and he didn't break the bridge. So why can't I move?

"All right, Sam?" Andrew asks.

I nod. I'm being an idiot. I take a deep breath and race across the bridge. On the other side, I wait next to Dominic. He's looking out over the ropes course. With his resolute face and the way his dark curls are fluttering in the wind, he looks like the captain of a ship. Then I notice how tightly he's gripping the safety railing.

"Are you okay?" I ask him.

He startles, like he didn't realize I was there. "Huh?

Oh. Yeah, I'm great."

I look down at his hands.

"I don't like heights. So sue me." He points across the course at a set of suspended balance beams. "But I was looking at that. Think Katie knows it's coming?"

"Should we warn her?"

"I dunno. Maybe it's part of the deal that she's not supposed to have time to obsess."

When Katie crosses the Indiana Jones bridge and comes to stand next to us, I make a decision. I wouldn't want someone to thrust me into a dance studio filled with fun-house mirrors with no warning. "Katie . . ." I point, and she looks.

"Yeah," she says quietly. "Dr. Lancaster and I talked about it yesterday."

"Are you going to be okay?"

She nods. "I think so."

I give her arm an encouraging squeeze. "You'll do great."

"Totally," Dominic says from my other side.

Next, the guy in charge of the course has us cross a suspended-tire bridge. Then we follow him down a rock wall, across a low tightrope with a cable above it to help us balance, and up again, via a series of platforms and movable ladders.

I'm sweating so much. My hands are cramping. So are my quads. But I am having a pretty good time. It's nice to be outside, in the sunshine, getting exercise. And I see what Dr. Lancaster meant about different people being good at different things. I have good balance; when I stop thinking about how I'm going to break them, I can cross the wobbly bridges and planks with ease. Dominic's a fast climber, when he doesn't look down. Zoe seems fearless, but she's slower. Katie's upper body is stronger than her lower body; she pulls herself up the obstacles using more arm than leg. Jenna is agile and quick, though not as strong. And Omar—I think his specialty might be "anything that is not a ropes course." He's bringing up the rear, but Yasmin stays by his side just like Bianca did for me back in eighth grade.

When we reach the highest platform in the whole course, we take a group photo and then break for lunch. Yasmin and Andrew hand out water bottles and brown paper lunch bags. I eat my sandwich fast, my back turned to everyone else, and wash it down with gulp after gulp of cool water. I wish I had another bottle to dump over my head.

Andrew squats next to me. "Hey, Sam. Having fun?"

"Surprisingly, yes. And it's a good workout, too." I pluck at my sweat-drenched shirt. "Though I'm pretty sure I'm starting to stink."

Andrew sniffs the air. "Nope. I smell nothing."

There are a lot of things that leave me a nervous, self-conscious wreck, but body odor isn't one of them—I guess because even skinny people can smell bad. "It smells like nature out here," I say, laughing, "so you can't smell me."

Andrew laughs too. "I doubt you ever have serious BO."

I shake my head. "Ballet dancers are gross."

"Really?"

"You think we sweat rose petals? My dance bag smells

like something died in it. With baby powder on top."

"You're shattering my illusions." Andrew shakes his head. "But I maintain that you do not stink. Not right now, anyway."

"Aww, thanks." I try to think of a silly compliment to give him in return. "You know, I think the ropes-course look works for you. Helmet and all."

He laughs. "You don't look half bad yourself."

The hummingbird in my chest is back. After the Hershey's Kiss last night . . . this is totally flirting, right? He's flirting with me, and I'm flirting back.

Which is ridiculous. You're ridiculous.

You just got dumped, remember? And Andrew's too old for you. He's basically your camp counselor. It's his job to act like he likes you.

Plus, there's no way someone as cute as him would flirt with someone like you.

No way—

"What's wrong?" Andrew asks. "You're frowning."

"Nothing. Sun in my eyes," I say quickly, shading my face with my hand. Luckily, he leaves it at that.

We maneuver through a few more obstacles as a group before we reach the side-by-side balance beams. They're just far enough apart for two people to walk on them with arms outstretched.

I look at Katie. She's gone completely ashen.

"So all you have to do before you get to zip-line down," the ropes-course facilitator says, "is walk across these beams to that platform, holding hands with a partner. Who's first?"

Dominic steps up. "I'll go. Get it over with."

Zoe joins him. "Me too." She looks back at Katie and then says to Andrew, "You're not seriously going to make her do this, are you?"

"Katie doesn't have to go if she doesn't want to," Andrew says. "Katie, let me know if you want to get down a different way."

"Okay," Katie says softly. "But I think I can do it." She looks determined. Also like she's about to puke. And I notice her hand rhythmically tapping her thigh.

On impulse, I reach out and grab her other hand. "I'll go with you, okay?"

Andrew hooks up Dominic's and Zoe's harnesses to the cables. When they're both secure, they step out onto the beams. Zoe immediately lets out a stream of curse words. "This thing moves!" she yells.

"It moves?" I look closer and see that the beams aren't nailed to the platforms; they're connected by thick chains. With each step forward, Dominic and Zoe cause the beams to wobble from side to side. Dominic walks slowly and stiffly. I want to tell him to loosen up—that's the key to finding a tough balance. Not being a solid block of wood, but letting different small muscles take over. Adapting.

When they make it to the other side and step off the beams onto the platform, I see Dominic's tension melt away. Zoe, meanwhile, is jumping up and down. "Yes!" she shouts. "That was awesome!"

Katie's palm is sweaty, but I don't let go. She's started counting under her breath. "One two three four. One two three four."

Jenna and Omar make the crossing. "And last but not least," Andrew says. He takes Katie by both shoulders, looking her right in the eyes. "Are you sure?" he asks. "I can cross with Sam. You can go down with Yasmin and wait with Dr. Lancaster at the end of the zip line."

Katie nods her head. It's small, almost imperceptible.

"We can do this," I tell her. "Just don't look down."

"We have to"—she gulps—"we have to take four steps up to the beam. And then we have to breathe in and out four times. Dr. Lancaster said I could if I needed to. Just this once."

We take four steps forward. We breathe in, out, in, out, in, out, in, out. Katie's grip on my hand tightens. It hurts a little, but no way am I going to ask her to let go.

She's where I was yesterday, staring at my swimsuit-clad body in the mirror. I see it in her eyes. She's walking that mental tightrope, millimeters from falling apart.

We move forward. One step. Two steps. And I immediately understand why Dominic became a block of wood and why Zoe was cursing. We're a good twenty feet off the ground, and the beam is anything but steady. I know we're strapped to cables—there's no way we can fall—but I still feel unsupported. Unsafe.

If that's how I'm feeling, I can't imagine how Katie is feeling.

I peel my eyes away from the beam in front of me to look at her. She has tears rolling down her face. Her shoulders are shaking. Silent sobs are hitching her chest up and down. She takes another step and then stops.

"Katie?"

"I can't."

"You can. I know you can."

Katie shakes her head. "I can't. I can't. I need to get down. I have to get down." Her breath is coming faster. Her fingers feel like ice. "I have to get down. Please!"

"It's just a few more steps, and then we'll get down, okay?"

"I have to get down *now*!"

"Come on, Katie!" Yasmin shouts. "You've got this!" Everyone else joins in. "We're here for you! Go, Katie, go!"

Their voices sound really far away. I feel like Katie and I are in a bubble.

I rotate my body, slowly, to face Katie head-on. "Katie. Look at me." I hold out my other hand.

Katie meets my eyes. There are tear tracks down her face.

"Can you turn to face me?"

She pivots on the beam, biting her lip. She takes my hand.

"We'll go sideways. Hold on to me, and don't look away. Feel with your feet." I don't know where this new version of me is coming from—this take-charge, calm-in-a-crisis, comforting person. I just know that it's who I have to be, right now, for Katie.

We inch toward the platform where the others are waiting. Katie's eyes bore into mine. Her fingers grip my wrists.

Now I'm crying too. I look over my shoulder. "We're close."

Katie nods.

Finally I feel my left foot hit the solid platform. I step up and pull Katie up after me. Katie collapses, wailing, into Dominic's arms. He looks a little freaked out at the wave of emotion, but he pats her on the back. "Hey, you did it," he tells her. "Good job. Good hustle."

Zoe is pacing on the tiny platform, confined not only by its size but also by the fact that she's hooked up to the cable, ready to zip-line. She looks furious.

"Are you insane?" she yells at Andrew and Yasmin, who are crossing the beams, and then at Dr. Lancaster, who's waiting on the ground. "You *know* she has a thing about balance beams and you make her go on, like, the King Kong of balance beams? How are you even allowed—"

"Zoe!" Dr. Lancaster calls, cupping her hands around her mouth. "Enough!"

"This place isn't just Crazy Camp," Zoe rants. "It's, like—" She sees me staring at her. "Why are *you* crying? Is part of your body-image problem having a problem when your body isn't the center of attention? Welcome to the real world, Ballerina Barbie. It doesn't revolve around you."

I take a step back, stung. I wipe my face with one hand. Zoe resumes pacing.

"Um, I'd really like to not be here right now," Omar

says. He's bouncing in place again. He adjusts his glasses and fusses with his harness and scratches his head and shifts from foot to foot, like fidgeting is the only thing keeping him from freaking out too.

One by one, we ride the zip line down to the ground. I thought I would enjoy it—the wind in my hair, the scenery rushing by, the weightlessness—but all I can think about is Katie's face, and all I can feel is the tears drying on my cheeks.

twelve

WHEN WE GET BACK TO THE PERFORM AT YOUR PEAK house, Dr. Lancaster takes Katie to her office. Half an hour later, after we've had time to clean up and change clothes, we meet in the Dogwood Room. "I want to talk about everyone's experience with the ropes course," Dr. Lancaster says. "But first, Katie wants to tell you all exactly what happened."

"Um, okay. So, I had a total panic attack on the beam. You all saw that." Katie's voice wavers a little, and her eyes are on the carpet, but she doesn't stop. "I was determined to make it across, and I thought I could. A regulation balance beam is narrower than those were, and I do handsprings and stuff on that. Without a harness. I told myself, *You can do this*. But then we paused out in the middle, and it was like—it was like I remembered I was supposed to be scared. And my body just shut down. I couldn't take another step."

She looks at Dr. Lancaster.

"How did you feel in that moment?"

"I was so freaked out. I—I don't know what I would have done without Sam there." Katie gives me a grateful smile.

"And how do you feel now?"

"Um. This is going to sound stupid, but—"

"Nothing you say in here is stupid, Katie," Dr. Lancaster says.

"Oh." Katie makes a face. "Sure. Anyway, now that it's all over and done, I feel like—like, wow, I did it. Like it doesn't matter that I panicked, because in the end I got across. I didn't give up." She looks at me again. "Thanks to you, I got across."

"And?" Dr. Lancaster prompts.

"And I feel like maybe that's what I needed. The first step. It was scary, and it sucked, but I did it."

"So you think you could get up there and not have a panic attack, if you tried again?" Dominic asks. "It's that simple?"

"I think," Katie says slowly, "that maybe I have to think about the fact that I *can* do it, because I already have. The number of times I've been on a balance beam without falling is so many more than the number of times I've fallen." She pauses. "But who knows? Maybe I'll still be screwed up after this. Maybe today means nothing."

"Or maybe it means a lot," Dr. Lancaster says firmly.

Katie nods. "Can we go back to the ropes course? So I can try again?"

"I'll check our schedule, and the course's availability."

"You should all come," Katie says. "Even Zoe."

For a second, Zoe looks wounded. But all she says is "Party at the ropes course."

"Now," Dr. Lancaster says, "if you don't mind us moving on, Katie, I'd like to spend some time talking about everyone else's experience on the course."

"I don't mind. I'd love to hear about someone else's problems!"

"Uh, yeah, about that . . ." Omar has his hand in the air. His knees are jiggling rapid fire, and he's blinking a lot.

"Yes, Omar?" Dr. Lancaster says.

"It's not about the ropes course."

"That's okay. What would you like to talk about?"

"Why I'm here, I guess. Can I?"

"Of course. Go ahead."

"So, I get stage fright," he tells us. "Really bad. Which is so dumb, because I started doing commercials when I was, like, three. I've been acting my whole life. But for the past year, ever since *Our Town*, it's like . . . I look out at the audience or whatever, and I want to throw up. I used to love acting. But now it makes me feel sick. Even memorizing lines makes me want to puke."

"So quit," Zoe says. "I don't get what the big deal is."

"I don't want to quit. At least, I don't think I do." Now he's wiggling in his seat like a toddler who has to go to the bathroom. "But I'm so anxious, all the time. Onstage and offstage. I'm anxious because I'm anxious, if that makes sense. Obviously I can't sit still. My girlfriend told me I'm like one of those hairless dogs that shake all the time?" He barks out a laugh that makes all of us jump. "And every decision feels huge. Like, what to have for lunch feels like it matters *so much*. So how can I know if I'm supposed to quit acting?"

"Did you try taking a break from acting?" Katie asks. "To see if you missed it?"

"Yeah, but then I was anxious that acting's the thing I'm supposed to be doing, and I couldn't focus on school and my grades were slipping. . . ." He scratches his head. Fixes his glasses. "Maybe I'm just burned out. Or the pressure's getting to me. It's hard going from cute-kid jobs to real jobs. There aren't that many roles for people who look like me. I'm a short, not-that-good-looking, brown kid who wears Harry Potter glasses and has allergies. Casting directors aren't busting my parents' door down. So anyway," he finishes. "That's why I'm here."

"What made you feel ready to open up?" Dr. Lancaster asks.

"Katie and Sam. You guys were so honest. It kind of inspired me."

"Thanks, Omar," Dr. Lancaster says. "Does anyone want to respond?"

Dominic clears his throat. "Hey, if Omar can do it, I guess I can too." He crosses his arms, leans back in his chair, and talks to the ceiling. "So, I'm here because there were all these college scouts at our spring practices, and my coach kept pointing them out and introducing me. He'd stop our workouts and call me over and put me on the spot. And it started getting inside my head. I'd set up for a pass, and then I'd look over at Coach So-and-So from the University of Wherever with his clipboard and I'd totally screw it up."

"Who had the idea for you to come to Perform at Your Peak?" Dr. Lancaster asks.

"Coach. And me, I guess. He found you. I signed up." Dominic looks around the circle. "I'm good. Really good," he says, and for once it doesn't sound like cockiness. "And I want to play professional ball, so I need to go to the right college. But wherever I end up, I need a full ride. I'm *here* on scholarship. And I'm not ashamed of it. I've got five siblings. My dad's a mechanic and my mom's a nurse. They work hard, and they expect me to. Which is why I gotta stop psyching myself out, like yesterday." He exhales in frustration. "Plus, the guys on the team, they've, uh, been ragging on me. Calling me a pussy, or whatever."

"What?" Katie jumps in, indignant. "That's so mean!"

Dominic laughs. "I've heard worse. I'm more worried about going to college."

"Thank you so much for sharing that, Dominic," Dr. Lancaster says. "Does anyone else want to share something?"

Jenna's the next domino to fall. "I suppose it's my turn." She pats down her perfect ponytail, laces her fingers together in her lap, and sits up even straighter than she already was. "I'm kind of a perfectionist," she begins. "I get caught up in doing everything exactly right. Which shouldn't be a problem—it should make me better. Stronger. Striving for perfection should make me a champion." I get the feeling this is an argument she's had with herself many times.

"But . . . ?" I say softly.

Her head whips in my direction. "But it's causing some *issues*." She says the word the same way my mom does. I wonder if someone says it like that to her, or if she does it all on her own.

"Issues like what?" Omar asks.

"I'm not sleeping very well. I can't turn my brain off." Jenna's tone is clipped, like she's reciting a rehearsed speech. "And I'll watch videos of myself skating and jot down notes and corrections for hours and hours and hours, without realizing how much time has passed. And when practice doesn't go well . . ." She clears her throat. "The harder I work, the more I practice—the worse I skate. I'm screwing up the easiest components, and my artistic scores are terrible. I hate what I look like on the ice right now. So I'm here to fix it. To fix myself."

It's the same thing I told Dr. Lancaster yesterday—I want this place to fix me. It sounds like we all do.

Except for Zoe. "In case you think I'm about to spill my guts," she says loudly, "I'm not. Get your gawk on somewhere else."

Dr. Lancaster sighs and rolls her eyes the tiniest bit. I think I'm the only one who sees it. The gesture makes her look human. And it makes me like her a little more.

Then the placid therapist smile reappears. "This has been such a good session," she says. "Thank you all for participating, and for supporting each other. I want to touch base with each of you privately for a few minutes. Sam?"

I get to my feet. As I pass Jenna's chair, she taps me on the arm. "Barre later?"

"Okay." I hesitate, then add, "We don't have to be friends if you don't want to. But it seems like we have some things in common."

She just looks at me. I can't read her expression.

"So . . . maybe we should compare notes."

"Maybe." She sounds wary. But it's not a no.

"I'M PROUD OF you, Sam," Dr. Lancaster says.

"Proud?"

"I just heard you reach out to Jenna. And you were such a strong support for Katie on the elevated beams. You're becoming a vital member of our little community."

"Oh. Thanks."

"I promise, leaning on your fellow campers—and letting them lean on you—will enhance this whole experience." She goes on about the benefits of bonding with each other. It's nothing she hasn't told us before. Honestly, I zone out until I hear her say, ". . . message from your mother this morning."

I sit up straighter. "Mom? What did she want?"

"She was concerned that you didn't return her call last night."

"Oh. I forgot." Yasmin told me that Mom had called, but then Andrew sat beside me on the porch and gave me chocolate and made me feel like the world wasn't such a bad place after all, and calling Mom back wasn't even on my radar. "Was she mad?"

Dr. Lancaster gives me a keen look. "Do you expect your mother to be angry?"

I squirm under her gaze, wishing she'd look somewhere else. "Um. No. I guess more . . . disappointed?"

"Why?"

"She said she wanted to check in with me every day while I'm here."

"Do you feel like it helps you to speak to her every day?"

"I don't mind talking to her. It makes her feel better."

"Let's talk about how you feel, Sam. Not how your mother feels."

"It's fine. I'm fine. Mom and I are fine."

"Do you want to call her now?" Dr. Lancaster pushes the phone on her desk toward me. She's giving me that look I don't like again. The one where she's trying to see inside me.

"No. I'll do it later. If that's okay."

"It is." Dr. Lancaster jots down a note on her pad.

"What are you writing?" I don't know why I'm suddenly so jittery. Her pen's scratching is like nails on a chalkboard. I'm tempted to snatch the pen away from her and stuff it down into the couch cushions.

"Just notes for my records."

"Why are you asking me about my mom?"

"You seem agitated, Sam."

"My mom supports me," I tell her. "She cares so much about my career. She wants me to succeed. She's helping me fight for it. We're a team. Since my dad left, it's just Mom and me."

Dr. Lancaster makes an *mm-hmm* noise. She doesn't sound convinced.

"Can we talk about something else?" I pull out my notebook. "I did my homework assignment."

She nods. "Of course, Sam. Go ahead."

I flip past the story about my mom and Mrs. Hoyt and the unitards. Instead, I share the pages I wrote about my first costume fitting for *Paquita*.

Miss Elise rented tutus from a nearby ballet company, but none of the soloist costumes were my size. So my mom put her in touch with a tutu specialist who could create a new one for me. Which sounds nice in theory, but costume fittings are bad enough when it's only a matter of trying on different tutus until you find the right one. When there's no *right one* in the box and you're the only person getting a costume made from scratch . . .

"The costume designer has me put on the largest tutu, even though we know it won't work," I read to Dr. Lancaster. "She wants to see how big I am, compared to the size I should be. The tutu gapes open in the back. She tugs at it until I can barely breathe, and still it won't fasten."

While all my classmates admired their reflections in their tutus—while they practiced pirouettes and fouettés and applauded each other—I stood there having my

141

measurements taken. Bust, waist, hips, and on and on. The costume designer didn't speak to me or look me in the eye. I wasn't a person to her. I was a collection of wrong-sized body parts.

When she was done, she told Miss Elise, not even bothering to lower her voice, that this wasn't going to be easy. Or cheap. She'd have to find lace and sequins that matched the existing tutus. She'd have to create a new pattern based on my measurements. "I'll send an invoice," she said, and then it was over.

And that wasn't even the worst part.

"When my finished costume arrives, it's so tight I can't inhale fully," I read. "The boning in the bodice digs into my skin. I wince as the costume designer hooks me in, and she frowns at me. 'Something to aspire to,' she says."

I close the notebook and look at Dr. Lancaster.

"Did you tell Bianca how you were feeling?" she asks.

"No."

"Why not?"

"I don't think she'd understand. Her body is *perfect*. She's like Sylvie Guillem."

Dr. Lancaster raises her eyebrows, so I clarify.

"Super skinny, but not unhealthy. Long legs. Arch-y feet."

"So you think she wouldn't be able to empathize with you?"

"I guess she'd feel sorry for me."

"You don't want her to feel sorry for you?"

"I don't want things to change between us."

They already have. You know that. Bianca knows that.

"If she's your friend, she'll—"

"I don't want to tell her, okay? It's embarrassing. It's bad enough that I look the way I look, but . . . the fact that I'm having panic attacks about it?"

"Has Bianca ever seen you have a panic attack?"

I scowl. "Yeah. The, um—the same one everyone else saw."

"Ah. And how did she respond?"

"She was . . . pretty great, actually." I mutter that last part, irritated at having been called out. "But it's still my choice who I tell about what's going on inside my head."

Dr. Lancaster nods. "It is. But when you go home, you're going to want to surround yourself with a strong support system. I'm trying to get you to think about who those people are, in your daily life. What about your teacher?"

"Miss Elise? What about her?"

"She seems quite invested in you."

"What makes you say that?"

"She recommended that you come here, right?"

I nod.

"And based on the story you just read me, she was willing to have a new costume custom-made for you, despite the expense."

"None of the others fit me. She didn't have a choice."

"There's always a choice, Sam."

Realization hits me like a brick. Miss Elise could have

given someone else my solo. She didn't have to feature me—especially when featuring me was costing the studio money.

"Oh," I say.

"What about your mom? Did you tell her that the costume fitting made you upset?"

"No. I told her everything went well."

Dr. Lancaster opens her mouth, but I speak before she can.

"Mom and I don't talk about that sort of thing."

"Why not?"

I don't have an answer. Or maybe I have too many answers, and I can't pick one.

I leave Dr. Lancaster's office thinking about my support system. Have I been hurting myself by hiding from Bianca how much I'm hurting? Has Miss Elise been on my side all along? Would my mom understand what I've been feeling if I broke down and told her?

Maybe I should.

But I don't call home that night.

I tell myself it's because I'm busy. First, Jenna and I have to do a ballet barre. Then we have an hour for dinner, and then we all decide to watch a movie in the Dogwood Room before bed. Even Dr. Lancaster joins us. I'm technically free to go make a phone call, but the night feels too normal—like we're just hanging out—to spoil it.

I'm sitting on the couch between Katie and Andrew. And maybe I'm a few millimeters closer to him than to her, or maybe I'm imagining it. The space between our arms and our legs feels magnetic. But Andrew doesn't look my way.

Not once. In fact, he and Zoe keep shouting about what's going to happen next—which redshirt is going to die, whatever that means.

I don't know how I feel about Andrew joking around with Zoe. She's acting like a human being, and if it's his influence that's doing it, that's a good thing. But I want him to be joking around with me. Flirting, like on the ropes course. Staring at me like I'm the only person that matters, like last night.

You like him.

No, I don't.

Yes, you do.

I lose track of the plot. Which alien ships belong to the good guys and which ones we're trying to blow up. I fidget in my seat, moving a fraction of an inch closer to Andrew. Our hips bump, and he finally looks in my direction.

"Hey. You like the movie?"

"Yeah."

"Cool. This is one of my favorites." He grins and turns back to the TV just as a starship explodes in a shimmer of light.

This is a bad idea, and you know it. The last thing you need is to fall for someone who's so far out of your league. He'll hurt you, just like Marcus hurt you—

That's what shuts up my inner voice.

Whatever's going on between us, I honestly don't think Andrew will hurt me.

thirteen

WE START FRIDAY MORNING OFF WITH A GROUP
yoga class, which should make me feel great. I like yoga. I'm
good at it. And burning calories before lunch is a total win.
But as I move from downward-facing dog into plank pose,
lower myself to the floor, and arch my back into upward-
facing dog, I can't quiet my mind.

I'm thinking about talking to Dr. Lancaster about my
mom.

I'm thinking about Andrew. Why I can't shake the feeling that he likes me back.

I'm thinking about Marcus, and how I shouldn't be falling for Andrew right after Marcus dumped me.

And I'm thinking about my body. Always and forever
my body.

Your hips and thighs look enormous in these leggings, my inner
voice taunts me as I return to downward-facing dog. *When*

you're upside down like this, your top rides up, and your stomach hangs out. Look at all that fat! We hop our feet into forward bend, and I try to surreptitiously pull my leggings up and my shirt down. *Too late.* I close my eyes and I roll up to standing, hands in a prayer gesture in front of my chest.

If I keep my eyes closed, I won't have to see the looks on all their faces.

Yasmin opened our session by sharing her journey from yoga newbie to fully certified instructor. Then she led us in thirty minutes of breathing exercises, to help us learn how to regulate our breath when the anxiety comes. We breathed lying on our backs with our hands on our stomachs. We breathed folded into child's pose, foreheads pressed to the floor. We breathed sitting cross-legged and we breathed standing like we are now. It was nice. Soothing.

But now, in motion, I can't get that calm back.

We start another Sun Salutation. I bend forward and then jump my feet into downward-facing dog. I drop my head and look through my legs. Andrew is sitting behind me. I try to follow the line of his eyes. It's hard to tell upside down, but I think he's looking at Yasmin. Petite, gorgeous Yasmin, whose perfect makeup and blown-out waves and toned body look straight out of a fitness-wear ad. Of course he's staring at her. I huff in frustration, blowing a stray hair out of my eyes. I watch Yasmin help Omar transition from downward-facing dog into a long lunge. She lunges forward with him. She's almost as flexible as I am. And she looks way better in spandex.

I bring my right foot forward into a runner's stretch, feeling my left hip flexor lengthen. I flatten my spine. Lift my chest. I glance back at Andrew a second time.

Now he's looking at me. He smiles.

I turn away fast. I wish I hadn't seen him looking. I'm glad I did.

I sneak another peek. Now he's looking toward Yasmin again. Or maybe at Jenna.

It makes me think about when Marcus stopped by the ballet studio to pick me up after a Saturday rehearsal, back in April—about a week and a half before spring show. I came up from the dressing room to find him chatting with Lauren and Tabitha and Becca. They were kind of fawning over him. He didn't look like he minded. And when Tabitha turned away, I swear he checked out her butt.

The stab I felt then—the utter certainty that Marcus found those other girls so much more attractive than he found the new, not-so-skinny me—I feel it now, with Andrew.

"Step back into downward-facing dog, and then roll forward into plank," Yasmin intones. "Drop your knees, chest, and chin to the mat, keeping your heart open. . . ."

I lower into the pose, trying not to think about whether Andrew is looking at me right this second, or about whether Marcus liked me less after I gained weight. I focus on arching my back. I feel my abs stretch.

Then I hear a wolf whistle. "Lookin' good, Ballerina Barbie! Show off that butt!"

I flatten myself to the floor. A split second later, I'm standing, and I'm angry. "No!" I say loudly, just a note below a shout. Out of the corner of my eye, I see Dr. Lancaster coming toward me and Zoe. I know I should let her handle this, but I can't stop. "No more!"

"No more what?" Zoe looks amused by my outburst.

Her twitching lips only make me madder. "You can't say things like that to me. To any of us. You have to stop."

"Jeez, Ballerina Barbie, it was a compliment. Hand to God."

Dr. Lancaster crouches down between the yoga mats. "Up, Zoe."

"Come on. I was doing her a favor, letting her know everyone's staring at her butt." Zoe looks at me, amusement turning to annoyance. "I said your butt looked *good*. What is your problem?"

"Up," Dr. Lancaster repeats. And something in her tone, in her eyes, makes Zoe actually do it. I watch them leave the room, and then I deflate. I look around. My stomach begins to churn.

Everyone's staring at you.

If they weren't looking at your butt before, they are now.

You have to get out of here.

"Sam," Katie starts, sounding impressed. "That was—"

I don't wait for her to finish. I run for the door.

HERE'S WHAT HAPPENED at the end of April.

It was opening night for our spring show. I was

149

excited—but more than that, I was nervous. I couldn't stop thinking about the audience watching me dance. Or really, watching my new, heavier, curvier body dance. Most of them were probably at *Nutcracker*. They'd seen me as Dewdrop. Would they recognize me now? Did I even look like the same person?

I didn't feel like the same person.

After a jittery warm-up onstage, I headed back to the soloists' dressing room to finish getting ready. I styled my hair into a braided bun. I pinned my *Paquita* headpiece into place. I did my stage makeup: thick black eyeliner, fake lashes, rosy cheeks, red lips. The ritual of it all started to make me feel better. More prepared. More normal.

And then I tried to put on my tutu.

Something was wrong. The leg holes were too tight; the elastic cut into my thighs. The basque wouldn't fasten around my hips. The bodice was inches from closing.

I saw my reflection. My worst nightmare had happened overnight.

You are too fat for your costume.

I staggered forward, leaned against the counter, tried to catch my breath. The tutu flapped open at my back, but I felt like I was being squeezed from the inside. My heart was in my clenched fist. I discovered that I was crying when I looked up and saw makeup streaking down my face. I sat down on the floor. Fell, really.

That was when Lauren came into the dressing room and asked, "Um, why are you wearing my tutu?" That was her question, before: "Are you okay?"

I was not okay. I was shaking and sobbing and wheezing and scratching at my skin like after a decade of dancing, I'd suddenly become allergic to tulle and sequins. My chest felt like it was going to explode. I genuinely thought I was dying.

Lauren's shouts brought all the other girls running. Bianca pushed through the crowd, saw me, and pushed back out into the hallway. She returned with Miss Elise and my mom, who was assisting backstage. Miss Elise helped me stand. She guided me out of Lauren's tutu and back into my sweats. She unlaced my pointe shoes. She wiped the smeared makeup from my face.

My mom watched all this happen, stunned into silence. Eventually Miss Elise ushered her outside. Asked her to check on the rest of the cast. To report back when it was ten minutes to curtain. My mom left.

Miss Elise sat with me. She got me to talk.

And I ended up here.

That panic attack led to this moment—to me sitting on the girls' bathroom floor, back against the wall, crying because my mean roommate paid me a sarcastic compliment, and I can no longer tell when people are laughing at me and when they're being serious, or even nice.

This is what I've become.

You're pathetic.

Realizing how pathetic I am just makes me cry harder.

There's a knock at the door. I don't answer. Another knock.

"Go away!"

But the door creaks open.

"Sam?"

I look over. Andrew is standing in the doorway. He's leaning in, but his feet are still planted in the hall.

"Can I come in?"

"No." I turn my back on him, resting my cheek against the cold tile.

"Can I get you to come out?"

"No."

"Do you want to talk about it?"

"I think I've humiliated myself enough for one day. Thanks anyway."

"You didn't humiliate yourself—" Andrew begins, but I cut him off.

"I just want to be normal. Why can't I be normal?" That feeling I had two days ago of wanting to hit something—it's back. Simmering in my belly, alongside the hum of anxiety that lives there. I want to hit something, and I want to keep crying, and I want to give up, and I want to fight. All at the same time.

A noise behind me. The door clicks shut. For a second, I'm sure Andrew's gone.

You scared him away. Nice work.

And then he's sitting next to me, hand on my back. He rubs a circle between my shoulder blades. He doesn't say a word, but he's telling me he's not going anywhere.

Without thinking about what I'm doing, what it might

mean, I lean into him. I feel his body tense up, like he's surprised, and then he relaxes. A little. Not entirely. But he also doesn't move away. After another moment, he puts his arm around me. I can feel his chest rising and falling. His inhales are my inhales, and my exhales are his.

I fit into his arms differently than I fit into Marcus's. It's weird, and it's wrong, and it's right. I don't know how much time passes, whether it's just a few minutes or much longer. But eventually he clears his throat.

I pull away from him. "Sorry. I—"

"Ready to leave the bathroom now?"

"Yeah. I think so."

I scramble to my feet and catch sight of myself in the mirror. I'm a disaster. Red-faced from yoga. Messy ponytail. Wet, puffy eyes.

And Andrew's still here.

"ARE YOU ALL right, Sam?" Dr. Lancaster sits across from me, leaning forward in her chair. "I've talked to Zoe. Again. I've called her parents again as well."

I picture Zoe, a ball of misery in her twin bed.

"This is strike two," Dr. Lancaster goes on. "I won't take no for an answer from them a third time. Your well-being is too important—"

"I'm okay. I promise."

"Do you want to talk about what happened?"

"You saw what happened. And you know how I feel about people staring at me."

Except Andrew, my inner voice mocks. I ignore it.

"I guess I'd just . . . had enough. I'm sorry I disrupted the class."

"You weren't the only person to disrupt the class," she says gently.

"Do you think Zoe was telling the truth?"

"About what?"

"About what she said being a compliment. About my—about my butt. Do you think she really was trying to be nice?"

"I think," she says, seeming to choose her words carefully, "that Zoe didn't consider the fact that what she said might upset you."

"She's always saying obnoxious things. To all of us."

Dr. Lancaster doesn't agree or disagree. She waits for me to continue.

"So how was I supposed to know if this time it was a compliment, not a joke?"

Still no response.

"Was I supposed to ignore her?"

"Why was her comment today so hard for you to ignore?"

"I guess because I'm . . . I'm sensitive about my"—I make a disgusted noise—"my butt. I don't like it."

"What if she had commented on something about your body that you do like? How might you have responded then?"

"I—I don't know."

"What's something you like about your body?"

"Um. My feet?"

"Why?"

I slip out of my right sandal and point my foot to show her. "I have high arches and long toes, so that gives me a really nice line. My feet look good in pointe shoes."

"Lovely. What's something else you like about yourself?"

Now I pause. "I, uh—can I think about it for a second?"

"I want to try an exercise with you," Dr. Lancaster says, after a few awkward moments of silence. "Make some lists for me: what you like and dislike about your body. And I want you to try something. Make the lists the same length. For every dislike, add a like."

I'm not sure that's even possible, but I don't argue. I pick up my notebook and head for the door.

fourteen

THAT EVENING, AS A REWARD FOR A LONG, HARD, productive week, we all go into town.

If you can call it a town.

The small college campus where Perform at Your Peak is housed is about fifteen minutes away from a strip of cutesy shops and mom-and-pop restaurants that's literally called Main Street. Andrew parks the van at one end of the road and we all pile out.

"So what's the plan?" Zoe asks. "Meet you back here in a few hours?"

"No," Dr. Lancaster says, taking Zoe by the arm. "You're staying with me."

"Oh, good." Zoe nods. "Didn't want this to be fun or anything."

"We have dinner reservations at Loretta's at seven o'clock. But since we're early, I thought we could spend some time in the general store."

"Yee-haw," Zoe shouts. A couple walking by turns to stare. She waves and bows. "Don't mind us. Just a few *cra-a-a-zy* kids out for a night on the town." She turns to us and stage-whispers, "They don't know you all are actually crazy!"

"Give it a rest," Dominic says. He and Andrew start walking down the sidewalk. I grab Katie and follow, and then we're all on our way.

Walking into the general store is like stepping into a time machine. There's fishing equipment and mason jars of all different sizes and a whole section of overalls. Babies' overalls and kids' overalls and grown-ups' overalls, in denim and camo print.

"Sam!" Katie models a Davy Crockett raccoon-skin cap. "How do I look?"

"Awesome," I tell her. Weirdly enough, she's making it work.

"You're ready to kill a bear, for sure," Omar chimes in.

"Ew," Katie says. "What?"

"You know, the song?"

"Do you know what he's talking about?" Katie asks me.

I vaguely remember learning a song about Davy Crockett in elementary school. "Kind of," I say.

"Sing it, Omar!" Katie says. She's flipped the hat so the tail is off to the side, draped over her shoulder, where she can pet it.

Omar clears his throat and launches into the first verse. His voice wavers at first but then comes out clear and strong and deeper than I'd expected. When he reaches the chorus, Yasmin appears next to him, harmonizing in a sweet soprano: *"Davy, Davy Crockett! King of the Wild Frontier."*

Katie and I applaud, and from behind us, Dominic says, "Nice."

While he sang, Omar stood tall. But the moment he stops, he shrinks. "Thanks," he mutters, and then runs off to another part of the store. Yasmin follows him.

Katie and I find Jenna looking through a rack of T-shirts airbrushed in neon colors. "Do people really wear these?" she asks, running her fingers over a tie-dyed, pink-and-purple shirt that says "JEN!" across the chest. She looks up at Katie, eyes widening. "*What* is on your head?"

Katie pets her hat. "I'm totally buying this. And you should get that shirt." She turns to me. "Sam, what are we going to get you?"

The challenge is on. We spend the next half hour looking for the weirdest things in the store. I reject the camo-print pashmina and hand the old-timey shaving kit to Dominic when he joins our hunt. Omar shows up wearing a straw fedora he says makes him look like Bruno Mars. And then we see the wall of aprons. Katie makes me try on a few before we settle on a blue flowered one trimmed with white ruffles.

I spin, holding the edges out. "What do you think?"

"It's perfect."

I don't look at myself in the mirror. I don't want to ruin the moment. Instead, I look for Andrew. He's at the front of the store, flipping through a coffee-table book about the Smoky Mountains.

"Hey, Sam!" he says when he sees me. "I like your apron."

"Thanks. We all decided to buy something random."

"That blue brings out your eyes." He smiles and turns back to his book. "Did you know the Great Smoky Mountains National Park has 244,000 acres in Tennessee and 276,000 acres in North Carolina?"

"Um, no. I did not." I take a step closer, looking at the pictures of waterfalls and hiking trails with him. Not because I'm interested in the mountains. Because I want to be near him. I feel so much better when he's around. He makes me feel like *before*. Like the past seven months never happened and I'm still a whole, happy person.

After this morning, I know I still have a long way to go.

When Dr. Lancaster gathers us by the register to pay, I realize that Zoe's been sitting in a folding chair, wedged between the door and a humming mint-green refrigerator, this whole time. She has her chin in her hands, elbows on her knees.

"Nice apron, Ballerina Barbie," she says. Her words lack some of their usual bite.

"Thanks." I take it off and hand it to the cashier. And then—I don't know exactly why—I grab a key chain from the closest rack. It says, "I'm part of the Wolfpack!" on one side, with the North Carolina State logo on the other. "This too," I tell the cashier.

"That's a dollar extra."

159

I place the bills on the counter and toss the key chain to Zoe.

She catches it in one hand. "What's this for?"

"We all got something. I'll take it back if you don't want it."

She looks at both sides and then says, "Whatever." But she keeps it.

LORETTA'S IS AN old-school Southern meat-and-three place: you get chicken, roast beef, or catfish, a choice of sides, and a biscuit or cornbread muffin for a set price. I stand in front of the array of options, feeling the fun I had earlier fizzle away. Everything's cooked in butter. Most of the vegetables have bacon in them. I have no idea what I'm supposed to eat.

I let Jenna go ahead of me. She orders fried chicken, collard greens, green beans, and red-skin potatoes, so I do too. She gets cornbread, but I skip it, even when the woman at the buffet—Loretta herself?—tries to insist. I tell her I'm allergic, and she says, "Oh, sweetie," like that's the saddest thing in the world.

I sit down at the table and start peeling the skin off my chicken and separating the bacon out of my greens. I'm dividing a potato into four equal bites when Katie leans in close and whispers, "What do you think Dr. Lancaster's story is? Do you think she has a family?"

"She doesn't wear a wedding ring," Omar says.

"Okay, but do you think she's divorced, or never got

married? Do you think she's with somebody now?" Katie looks toward the other end of the table, where Dr. Lancaster is talking to Yasmin and Dominic.

"Why are you so interested in Dr. Lancaster's love life?" Jenna asks.

"It feels weird that she knows so much about us, but we don't know anything about her," Katie answers. "Like, does she have kids? How old do you think she is?"

"About my mom's age?" Omar guesses. "Maybe a little older?"

"I bet she has kids," Katie says, nodding. "Maybe college age. That's why she can stay here with us for three weeks."

"Or she never had kids." Omar lowers his voice and adds dramatically, "We're the teenagers she never got to raise. We make the sacrifice worth it."

"The sacrifice?" Jenna asks, arching an eyebrow.

"Yeah," Omar says, back in his normal voice. "She always wanted kids, but she put her career first, and before she knew it, life had passed her by."

"Actually, the opposite." We startle. Dr. Lancaster is now standing behind us, wearing a wry smile. "I had children young, then went back to school. And"—she holds up a hand to stop Katie's next question—"that's all I'm going to tell you. Ready to go?"

THAT NIGHT, AFTER we've all gone to bed, Zoe gets up and grabs the tote bag she carried into town. "Come on," she whispers, shaking my shoulder.

I roll over. "What?"

"Come with me."

"Where?"

My eyes have adjusted to the dark enough that I see her put her finger on her lips. "It's a secret."

I roll back over. "No."

"Yes." She pulls on my arm. "Trust me."

"Why would I do that?"

"I'm sorry I said that thing about your butt, okay? So . . . come with me?"

I groan. "Fine." I wait while she looks down the hall in both directions. I pad behind her on the thick carpet to Dominic and Omar's door. She knocks.

Dominic answers. "What's up?"

Zoe holds up her tote bag. "I come bearing gifts."

"What could you have in there that I want?"

"Just let us in."

"Hey, Sam." Dominic opens the door wider. "Omar, make yourself presentable. We've got company."

Omar sits up in bed as Zoe drops her tote bag on the floor. It clanks when it lands, and she says, "Whoops!" Then she leaves again. "BRB."

Dominic points to the desk chair between his and Omar's beds. "Wanna sit?"

"Sure. Thanks." I do, crossing my arms in front of my stomach. I look around the guys' room. It's surprisingly neat. Both of their suitcases are closed and zipped. Other than some energy-bar wrappers on Dominic's nightstand and a dog-eared graphic novel on Omar's side, you can barely tell anyone's staying here.

"What's going on?" Omar asks, yawning.

"No idea. Sorry to barge in."

"We weren't asleep." Dominic leans back into his pillows, lacing his fingers behind his head. The position makes his biceps bulge—and judging by the way he's smiling, he knows it.

Zoe returns with Jenna and Katie, shuts the door, and turns off the overhead light. Then she opens the curtains to get maximum moonlight and flops down on the floor. Jenna sits on the edge of Dominic's bed, and Katie sits cross-legged next to Omar. And we stare at one another.

"So?" Jenna asks briskly. "We're here. What's so important?"

"This." Zoe dives into her tote bag and emerges with a beer. She sets it on the floor in front of her.

"Where'd you get that?" Dominic asks.

"Took it from the general store."

"You stole a beer."

"Not just *a* beer." She pulls out five more and sets them in a circle. "One for each of us. Welcome to the first meeting of"—dramatic pause—"the Secret Society of Crazy Campers."

Omar frowns. "We're not crazy—"

"We can workshop the name later."

"I can't believe you stole beer!" Katie scoots away like she's going to get in trouble just for looking at it.

"I can't believe you did it without Dr. Lancaster finding out," Jenna says.

"She went to the bathroom. Left me with Andrew. Thanks for distracting him, Ballerina Barbie." Zoe picks up a beer, pops off the cap, and gives me a cheers. "Who wants one?"

Dominic leans down and takes a bottle. "Me."

Katie frowns at him. "You shouldn't."

"It's not like she stole a keg. It's one beer."

"I guess it can't hurt," Jenna says. "We can pay the store back next time we go into town."

"Barbs?" Zoe waves a bottle at me.

"No, thanks." I don't drink—and even if I did, it wouldn't be beer.

"Worried about the calories?" Zoe taunts.

It's pointless to deny it. Everyone knows I am.

"I hereby declare this a therapy-free zone!" Zoe announces. "No talking about your issues, or whatever. I don't want to hear it." She takes a gulp of her beer.

"I'll drink to that," Dominic says. He takes a drink and groans. "You couldn't have stolen the good stuff?"

"Sam didn't flirt long enough for me to be choosy."

I shoot Zoe a sharp look. Does she know how I feel about Andrew?

She winks at me, which isn't reassuring.

"Okay, give me one," Omar says. Zoe does. He opens it and takes a huge drink—which he promptly sputters and coughs all over his bedspread. Katie squeaks and dives out of the way. "Ugh, that's disgusting!"

Dominic laughs. "Omar, is that your first beer?"

"Yeah. So?" Omar says, defensive.

"That's kind of how I looked after my first taste. You get used to it."

"I didn't really want one anyway," Omar grumbles.

"So why'd you take it?" Jenna asks, sipping at her beer like it's a fancy cocktail.

"Because—because Dominic did." Omar looks like he's sweating a little.

"Hey, I so did not peer-pressure you," Dominic says.

"Aww, someone's got a crush!" Zoe grins. "Young love is so cute."

"I do not have a crush on Dominic!" Omar protests.

"It's okay. You're an actor, we get it—"

"I told you yesterday, I have a girlfriend." Omar pulls out the photo he's using to mark his place in his book. "See?" It's him with a cute brunette, both dressed up in Victorian outfits. We pass it around the circle.

"Whoa, are you at the Renaissance Faire?" Zoe asks. "Dominic, you've got your work cut out for you."

"Helena and I were in *My Fair Lady* together," Omar says. "That's how we met."

"Zoe, you're awfully interested in who likes me." Dominic's finished his beer and is leaning back in bed in that *look at my biceps* pose again. "Maybe you're the one with the crush? Wouldn't be the first—"

"Uh, no. You're not my type."

"Not into tall, dark, and handsome?"

"Not into dudes."

"You're gay?" Katie asks.

Zoe turns on her. "Got a problem with that?"

Katie wilts under Zoe's glare. "No, of course not."

"I had a huge crush on my skating partner, when I used to do pairs," Jenna says. "He turned out to be gay."

"What about you, Sam?" Zoe asks. "Isn't the ballet world full of gay boys?"

"And straight ones. It's a stereotype that all male dancers are gay, just like . . ." I was going to remind her of what she said at lunch on Monday, about all ballerinas having eating disorders. But I don't want to go there. It's too close to what I try never to think about. "Anyway," I say, "the only guy at my studio's straight."

"And are you two . . . you know . . ."

"No." I think about tiny, goofy Theo and can't help but laugh. "No."

We sit there, talking about random stuff, for another few minutes. We learn important facts such as Dominic's favorite color—orange—and how old Jenna was when she broke her first bone: three, and it was her pinky finger, and it happened when she was jumping on the bed after her parents told her not to.

Then we hear a creak in the hallway.

"Shh!" Zoe hisses. Like any of us was going to make another noise in that moment. When we're not busted, Zoe says, "All right, losers. Back to bed." She gathers up the bottles and walks out of the room without another word.

Jenna and I look at each other. "That was weird," she says in a low voice, motioning toward Zoe's departing back.

I nod.

"But also not terrible."

I nod again.

Jenna brushes some imaginary dirt from her pajama top. "Well, good night, Sam."

"Night." I wave at the others and follow Zoe down the hall.

fifteen

ANDREW HAS A MUG OF BLACK COFFEE WAITING FOR me on the kitchen island at seven thirty Saturday morning. "Just the way you like it," he says with a smile.

I actually am starting to like it this way. You can taste the richness of the coffee, without the sugar and cream masking it. Or maybe I just like that this is something between me and Andrew. He knows how I take my coffee. Sort of.

I help him cut up fruit for the fruit salad. I eat my daily clementine, thinking that if nothing else, by the end of Perform at Your Peak, I'll be caught up on my vitamin C. And then I ask Andrew some of the questions from last night's Secret Society meeting.

"What's your favorite color?"

"Green," he says, rinsing out the fruit bowl. "What's yours?"

"Blue. Like a deep teal."

"Nice." He pours in the sliced strawberries and the clementine segments and the halved grapes. "Like, after-sunset blue?"

I nod fast. "Yeah, exactly." He gets it. He gets *me*. I need to know more. "Do you have a favorite number?"

"Forty-two," he answers without hesitating.

"That's, um, random."

He leans in close, putting on a solemn face. "It's not random. It's the answer to life, the universe, and everything."

"Okay . . ."

He steps back, and I miss him right away. "It's from a book," he says. "*The Hitchhiker's Guide to the Galaxy*. I take it you haven't read it?"

"No."

"You should pick it up."

"I will." I don't read much for pleasure, but if Andrew recommends it, I'll find it.

"Good morning!" Zoe saunters into the kitchen and throws open the fridge door. "I need a Bloody Mary. Hair of the dog, and all that . . ."

Andrew laughs. "Party too hard last night?"

"You know it."

I laugh weakly. Because no, she didn't party too hard last night. Obviously. But those stolen beers are still under her bed, in our shared bedroom.

"Here." Andrew hands her a mug. I'm jealous—until he

says, "Let me know how you take it." Then I sip my black coffee and let myself smile for real.

DR. LANCASTER ASSEMBLES us in the Dogwood Room after breakfast. "You are not your talent," she says to start the session. "You are so much more. So today, you're each going to teach a fellow camper a new skill. But"—she holds up a finger—"not your primary skill."

"What do you mean?" Omar asks. He already looks anxious. He's doing the fidgeting thing again.

"You could be considered experts in your respective fields—but you're beginners at other activities. And that's okay. You can still have fun regardless of your skill level."

She breaks us into pairs: Jenna and Dominic, Zoe and Katie, and me and Omar.

"Jenna, you'll be teaching Dominic to tie a balloon animal. Dominic, you'll be teaching Jenna to jump double Dutch—with assistance from Andrew and Yasmin on the jump ropes."

Jenna's mouth drops open and Dominic laughs out loud.

Dr. Lancaster continues, "Zoe, you'll be teaching Katie how to construct an Ikea side table. Katie, you'll teach Zoe to program an old VCR."

Zoe shakes her head. "Oh, Katie, you are in for it."

"And finally, Omar, you'll teach Sam how to build a house of cards, and Sam, you'll teach Omar how to fold an origami flower."

I look at Omar. "I've never done origami in my life."

"How hard can building a house of cards be?"

It turns out: pretty hard. Especially with all the other activities going on. Yasmin and Andrew bring a folding table into the Dogwood Room for us. I'm given a new deck of cards and Omar's given a sheet of instructions. I'm not allowed to look at his paper, and he's not allowed to touch the cards.

"Lean a pair of cards against each other to create an apex," Omar reads. "That's an upside-down V. Like a tent." He raises his voice to be heard over Zoe, who's already barking at Katie about separating different-sized screws and finding the Allen wrench.

I follow his instructions. "Done."

"Make five more like that, in a row, touching one another."

I set up tents two and three and am carefully pulling my hands away from tent four when Dominic pops a balloon and curses loudly. I jump and my cards scatter.

Zoe curses back at him. "Can you not do that?"

"Sorry," Dominic says, and blows up another balloon.

I start building my house of cards again. I focus on my hands. On not breathing too hard. I tune out Katie's hammering and the teeth-grinding squeaks of Dominic's balloon twisting.

This time, I'm on the second level when everything comes tumbling down.

"Um, it says that if you use glossy cards, they can slip against one another. Maybe these cards are too glossy?"

Omar is tapping his hand against the table. When I start rebuilding, he moves the tapping to his thigh.

"Maybe," I murmur, dropping a pair of cards into place.

"I don't like watching you do this," he confesses. "It's making me anxious."

I glance at him. "Can you try to breathe, like we practiced yesterday?"

He nods at me. "Yeah. Okay."

"But don't breathe at the cards."

"Right." He turns sideways.

I keep building. Card after card, each set gently against its neighbor. While Omar is taking in gulps of air, I'm holding my breath. When my hands start to tremble, I rub them together to make the trembling stop.

All of a sudden, it's really important for me to finish this tower. Such a delicate thing. So hard to construct, and so easy to topple.

I lay a card flat across the top of two tents and sit back, taking in a ragged breath.

"Are you okay?" Omar asks.

I nod. "Mm-hmm."

"You look upset."

"I'm fine." I look at his worried face. "Okay, yes, I'm upset. And it's stupid. This—" I gesture at the half-finished tower. My hand moves the air, and the structure wavers. I gasp. But it stays up. "It's a metaphor, right?"

Dr. Lancaster is walking over, looking interested.

"You did this on purpose," I tell her.

"What's that?"

"The house of cards—it's a metaphor. It's me."

"How so?"

I glare at her, and then at the tower. "Isn't it obvious? Everything about me is shaky. I'm barely holding together. Breathe too hard, and I fall apart."

As if on cue, Dominic accidentally pops another balloon. Katie shrieks in surprise, and I jump and bump the table, and my tower collapses.

I put my head in my hands. "You couldn't at least let us work somewhere quiet and calm?" I say to Dr. Lancaster, through gritted teeth.

"We don't always get to choose where we build our towers," she says.

More metaphors. Great.

"Sometimes there are distractions. There are setbacks. How do you proceed?"

"I can build it again," I say. "Start from scratch. But . . . it's just going to keep falling down. It's the same tower. The same cards."

"So how can you improve your chances of having it stand?"

I know we're not really talking about the house of cards anymore, but I can't resist saying, "I don't know. Glue?"

She smiles. "Interesting. I'll get some." She leaves the room.

That's when I realize no one else is doing anything. They've been watching. Listening. Having their attention on me brings back the skin-crawling feeling I hate. "Can you all not look at me right now?" I ask, mortified.

"Sure," Dominic says. "Back to my balloons. My baby sister's gonna flip when she finds out I can do this."

"I don't think *that*"—Jenna points at the squiggle in his hands—"counts as a balloon animal."

He waves it at her. "This is totally a poodle. Use your imagination."

"Okay, break's over, back to work," Zoe tells Katie. "You need to find eight screws that look like this." She points at a tiny metal piece.

Omar and I sit, not looking at each other. But by the way he's wiggling in his chair, I can tell he has something to say. "What is it?" I finally ask.

"How can you not like people looking at you?" His eyes are wide behind his round glasses. "You and me—we're performers. We do what we do to be seen, right?"

"I guess."

"Is it because you gained weight?" He says it without malice, just repeating what I told the group a few days ago. Still, I flinch. "I know a little bit about the dance world," he goes on. "The musical-theater side of it, but still. It must suck."

"It does, yeah."

"Type matters for me, too. People don't want an actor with my skin color, or they want a brown kid, but it has to be a guy who's more conventionally hot. And sometimes it feels like it doesn't matter whether I'm any good. You know?"

"I know."

"Is that why you're anxious? Because you feel like it doesn't matter how good you are?"

It's so simple. So true. "That's part of it."

"Do your parents support you?"

"My dad's not around. My parents are divorced. But my mom . . . yeah, you could say she's supportive."

"My parents were supportive of me acting when I was little. But my dad's a physicist and my mom's an anesthesiologist, so you can imagine how well it went over when their only son told them he wanted to be on Broadway, like, as a career."

"My mom used to dance, so she gets it."

"Wow. Lucky."

"Yeah. Lucky," I echo.

A minute later, Dr. Lancaster returns with a bottle of Elmer's. "What does the glue represent?" she asks, handing it to me.

I unscrew the cap. "Maybe . . . new coping mechanisms for anxiety? Like, what I was doing before wasn't working, so let's try something new?"

"That makes sense. Anything else?"

I think for a moment. "We talked on Thursday about my support system. That's kind of like glue, holding me together when I can't do it myself. Right?"

"Right." Dr. Lancaster looks like she wants to be smiling even bigger than she's letting herself smile. It's embarrassing. I'm glad when she says, "Well, knock yourself out. We have fifteen minutes before we trade partners."

I think about holding the cards in place while the glue

dries. "I know Omar's not supposed to help me," I say, "but I'm going to need more hands."

"Okay," Dr. Lancaster says, nodding. "Omar can assist you. Yasmin too." She beckons her over.

It doesn't take long to find our rhythm. Yasmin holds a pair of cards while I run a seam of glue between them. Meanwhile, Omar preps the next apex, so that Yasmin doesn't have to let go of her upside-down V until it's dry enough to stand on its own. And then they switch.

"When we did this activity my year," Yasmin tells us, "I had to teach my partner how to line-dance, and he had to teach me how to ride a unicycle."

"A unicycle?" Omar asks. "What's that a metaphor for?"

"Balance, I suppose." Yasmin carefully lets go of the cards she's holding. They stay up. "I wasn't really thinking about it that way. I was more worried about looking like an idiot in front of my partner. He was this super-cute soccer player from Florida. I had the biggest crush on him."

I run a line of glue along Omar's cards. "Did you two keep in touch?"

"For a few months. I never said anything about the crush, though. Performing onstage wasn't the only thing I was afraid of in high school." She sets up the next pair of cards and waits for me to glue them into place.

When Dr. Lancaster calls for us to switch activities, Yasmin gets to her feet. "I'm on double-Dutch duty now," she says. "It was nice to chat with you, Sam. Maybe we can talk more this week?"

"Sure," I say, but I'm already distracted: Andrew's walking over.

"That looks like a solid metaphor," he says.

"Ha, ha."

"Want me to take it upstairs for you?"

"Maybe later." For now, I want to keep looking at it. I have to admit that I like seeing it standing there. Finished. Not falling.

"Just let me know when. In the meantime," Andrew says, holding up the jump rope, "you get to witness something no one has ever seen before."

"Speaking of things no one has ever seen before . . . ," Zoe says. She and Katie are looking at the VCR from all angles. "How old is this thing, Dr. Lancaster?"

"It's from 1989. Have fun with those instructions."

I turn to Omar. He's picked a piece of origami paper. It's teal, and it makes me think about my conversation with Andrew over breakfast. The sky at sunset.

"Good choice," I say. "That's my favorite color."

He smiles, but it's more like a grimace. His nerves are back. "Let's do this."

"Fold the page in half horizontally," I say.

He does.

Three folds in, I know we're in trouble. "I—I need to start over," Omar says. He crumples the sheet of paper and throws it aside. "I didn't fold it right."

"Okay." I hand him another sheet of teal paper.

He pushes it away. "Not teal. Maybe red will work."

"Okay." We start again. This time, we do five folds before he's backtracking.

"The creases have to be sharper," he says, almost to himself, as he does it again.

"What you're doing looks just like the picture on my instructions—" I start, trying to encourage him, but he makes a frustrated noise and wads the paper up.

"Green," he says, sounding a little frantic. "We'll try green."

"Okay." I hand him a sheet that's like fresh-cut grass.

He folds and folds, tongue sticking out of his mouth. He starts humming.

The jump ropes make a repetitive *slap-slap-slap* on the carpet. The double Dutch-ers laugh when Jenna gets tangled and has to hop in a circle. Katie says, loudly, to Zoe, "No, not *that* button! The one with the square on it!"

And Omar whimpers. "I can't do it," he says, ripping off a green petal.

"You're doing fine. The whole point of this is to try something we've never done before and to figure it out as we go along."

It's like he doesn't hear me at all. "I can't do it. I can't do it!" His face twists, and I know he's going to cry.

I lean in close. Put my hand on his hand, where he's tapping the table. "Hey. It's okay. It doesn't have to be perfect."

"I can't do it," he repeats, looking miserable.

I pull two sheets of yellow paper from the stack. I set the instructions flat on the table where we can both see them. "We'll do it together, okay?"

"You're not supposed to help me."

"I'm not." I sneak a glance at Dr. Lancaster. "I'm making my own flower. It just happens to be next to yours."

Maybe this is his version of Elmer's glue. Or maybe his moment of panic was just that—a moment. But side by side, folding slowly, checking our work again and again, we end up with matching golden daffodils.

He holds his up, giving me a watery smile.

"Gorgeous," I tell him.

"I feel really dumb right now."

"You're saying that to the girl who almost cried when her house of cards fell down." I look around the room. Dr. Lancaster is crouched with Katie and Zoe by the VCR, and the jump-rope squad is in their own world. Focused. Keeping time. "Do you want to talk to someone?" I ask Omar. "I mean, someone who isn't me?"

"No. I'm okay now. Thanks." He furrows his brow. "I hate when I freak out over things that don't matter."

"Me too." I set my paper flower down next to his.

"But in the moment, when it's happening, they feel like they matter. So much."

"I know." I think about stepping in that hole on Monday. How I wasn't hurt—not even a little—but it felt like the end of the world. "It'll get better."

For him, maybe. Not for you.

I shake my head, wanting my inner voice gone. And I say it again, hoping this time I'll believe it: "It'll get better."

sixteen

THAT AFTERNOON, WHILE DR. LANCASTER HAS A meeting with Andrew and Yasmin, Jenna and I set up our chair-barres in the Dogwood Room. Katie starts doing crunches and push-ups nearby. Dominic joins Katie on the floor, matching her move for move. Omar gets his graphic novel and sits with Zoe on the sofa, where she's watching a horror movie at low volume.

We're together. At the end of week one, that feels important.

When we're stretching out on the floor after finishing our barre exercises, Jenna scoots closer to me. "You said on Thursday you think you and I have some stuff in common," she says, keeping her voice low.

"Yeah."

"Do you find yourself comparing your body to everyone else's all the time?"

Yes. Always. And you always lose.

"Um. Sort of. Why?" I open my legs into a straddle split and lean forward, resting my stomach on the floor.

"Because that's what I do. I look at pictures and videos of myself on the ice, and I look at other skaters doing the same move, and I can't stop comparing us. Down to the littlest things. Like, how my fingers look. I'm never satisfied. *Never.*"

I turn my head to rest my left cheek on the carpet. There's a frayed area on my right ballet slipper where my big toe is about to poke through. It makes me think about how frayed I feel. Every day the threads holding me together are fewer and farther between.

"That's kind of it for me," I say quietly. "But kind of not. I know where my technique is. I know what I'm good at and what I'm still working on. I believe in my dancing. So when I compare my body to other people's bodies, it's not like they're doing something I wish I was doing. Something I could work on, or fix. They're just luckier."

"That makes sense." Jenna nods. "It sucks, but it makes sense."

"My body used to be perfect for ballet, and then—it wasn't. But that's not about anyone else. It's about me."

"Are you jealous?"

I think about Bianca. How I've been keeping her at a slight distance for the past few months—maybe even since *Nutcracker*. In a way, she represents everything I've lost.

On Monday, she starts her summer ballet intensive.

She'll be at The Washington School of Ballet in DC for the next five weeks. We both auditioned for that program, back in February. She got in; I didn't. She offered to wait to accept her place until we found out where I'd be going, but I told her not to be silly. TWSB was her top choice. She had to go.

We did all our auditions together this year. I think back to the one I thought I'd danced best at—the one where the teacher and the intensive director stared at me in the hallway afterward. I don't think Bianca ever feels those prickles at the back of her neck. I don't think she has any idea what it's like to be looked at as if you don't deserve to even walk down those hallways.

"Yeah," I whisper to Jenna. "I'm jealous."

I don't like thinking about Bianca like this. I don't like realizing that I'm the kind of person who is jealous of—even a little bit angry at—my best friend for something she can't control. Especially when, as Dr. Lancaster pointed out, Bianca's been nothing but supportive. It makes me feel like a terrible person. A terrible friend.

I need to change the subject. Lighten the mood.

"But as far as jealousy," I say to Jenna, "you don't have to worry about me, like, whacking you on the kneecap or anything."

Jenna blinks at me. "I'm sorry, did you just make a Nancy Kerrigan joke?"

"Too soon?"

"Yeah, you know, 1994 called. . . ." She gives me a tight

smile. "What's the equivalent for ballet? Don't you all, like, put glass in your rivals' pointe shoes?"

"Oh, all the time. I see a mirror or a window and I'm like, *Must break and sprinkle fragments in pointe shoes.*"

Katie overhears this last part. "What are you two talking about?" Her voice comes out strained; she and Dominic are in matching push-up positions, staring each other down.

"Sabotage," Jenna says.

"Speaking of which, would you two mind sitting on Dominic's back right now?"

"I'd still win," Dominic says through gritted teeth.

"Keep . . . telling . . . yourself . . . that. . . ." Katie shifts from one arm to the other.

"I'll give you this," Dominic says. "You're pretty tough for someone so small."

"Thanks."

"My money's on the kid," Zoe calls from the couch.

In the end, it's a draw. They have us count to three so they can drop at the same time. And then Katie looks at Dominic and says fiercely, "Rematch?"

He laughs. "Another time." They shake on it, and then we all join Zoe and Omar on the couches. "So what's this movie about?" Dominic asks.

"There's this ghost—she died, like, fifty years ago," Zoe says. "And this family moves into her house without knowing it. . . ." On-screen, a hot twenty-something playing a teenage boy waves a baseball bat at sharp objects that are flying through the room toward him. "You know what? Just watch it," Zoe says.

So we do.

DINNER'S A COOKOUT. Andrew's at the grill, wearing a "Kiss the Cook" apron. Omar and I sit nearby with our notebooks. I'm trying to work on the body part lists Dr. Lancaster assigned me yesterday, but it's hard to concentrate. It's Andrew's presence—and the smell of the hamburgers on the grill.

Maybe it won't kill me to have a burger. I could ask Andrew to make me a miniature one. Like, four bites. It would be so worth it.

Slippery slope, Sam, my inner voice chides.

I put pen to paper. What I dislike about myself: *Wide hips.* What I like about myself: *High arches—feet look great in pointe shoes.* What I dislike: *Stomach—how it pooches out even when I hold it in.* What I like: *My hair. I have good hair.* What I dislike: *Thick thighs.* What I like: . . .

"How's it going?" Andrew drops into the rocking chair next to me. He pinches his tongs in my direction.

"It's going okay," I say, frowning at my list. How can I have already run out of things I like about my body? What about my eyes? I write that down.

"Do you want me to leave you alone?"

"You can stay. I don't mind." I look up at him. He's backlit; there's a halo of early-evening light surrounding his sandy hair and the red-brown polo he's wearing. "Honestly, I think I—I think I'm better with you." I say the last part fast and soft, so Omar won't hear.

"I'm glad," Andrew says, just as soft.

I return my focus to my notebook. I try to let all the distractions fade away. The smell of cooking meat. Katie and Yasmin laughing in the kitchen. Omar humming to himself as he writes. Dominic jogging laps around the house, passing us again and again. The buzzing of insects and the calling of owls, getting louder as we drift toward sundown. The fireflies flickering on the lawn.

And Andrew. Next to me.

HE'S NEXT TO me again the next day, as I'm standing in front of the largest dining table I've ever seen. It has to seat at least fifty people. The place settings are immaculate. The wax fruit centerpieces look good enough to eat. There are more plush velvet chairs around the sides of the room, underneath enormous tapestries. A huge pipe organ covers one of the side walls, and two circular chandeliers hang from the high arched ceiling.

This room makes me think of fancy dinner parties where the women wear gloves and the men wear tuxes with tails. If I were invited to a party like that, I don't think I'd have any problem eating. I'd finish every bite and ask for more.

Of course, I'd probably also be wearing a corset, which would limit the bites I could fit in. I'd have to be smart. One taste of each delicacy—

"Sam? Andrew? We're moving on," Dr. Lancaster calls. I leave the Banquet Hall reluctantly, looking back over my shoulder before I turn the corner.

We continue on the self-guided tour, winding through room after extravagant room. The Biltmore House was built in the late 1800s by George Vanderbilt, the heir to the Vanderbilt shipping and railroad fortune. It's the largest privately owned home in the United States, with 250 rooms. Basically, it's like someone plopped a European castle in the middle of North Carolina.

Apparently I'm not the only one visualizing myself living here, because when we reach George Vanderbilt's bedroom, Omar announces, "I'll be sleeping here tonight." He turns to Andrew, his voice taking on a posh British tone. "I don't want to be awakened before ten a.m., my good man. I'll have breakfast in my dressing gown."

Andrew laughs and bows to Omar. "Very good, sir."

After that, it's a free-for-all. Jenna calls Edith Vanderbilt's room, which is decorated in bright gold and deep purple. Dominic takes a room that's kind of a rusty brown, because, in his words, "at least it looks like a dude's room." Katie squeals when we enter an oval room with printed peach fabric on the walls, cushions, and bed. Yasmin claims one that's equipped with two twin beds. "It's not like I have anyone to share a bed with right now, anyway," she laughs. Dr. Lancaster shoots her a look.

"Zoe, Sam, and Andrew—you still have to pick," Katie says.

"I need one that speaks to me," I joke. "This is really important, you know."

"I know which one I want," Zoe says. "I've been here before."

"Well, you won't beat my room," Jenna says firmly.

"Wait," Katie cuts in. "If Omar is George Vanderbilt and Jenna, you're Edith, does that mean you two are *married*?"

Omar links his arm through Jenna's. "Shall we continue touring the house, my dear?" Jenna shakes her head, looking amused.

Eventually we enter a room that I want. Red damask walls. Gold curtains. Lots of space and light. There's a tea service set up on a table by the windows. "This one's mine," I say. "Definitely worth the wait."

"And I'll take this one," Andrew says as we step into an adjoining room with blue walls and dark wood furniture. It's pretty much the definition of "handsome." I can picture a man—Andrew—in period hunting gear, complete with tall boots and a top hat, standing by the window. His faithful golden retriever lies at his feet.

As everyone else moves on, I peek back into "my" room. I imagine waking up there every morning. Having tea—or black coffee—by the window, looking out over the grounds. Then I return to the blue room. Real-world Andrew is waiting for me. "Hey, neighbor," he says.

Our bedrooms adjoin. Does that mean they were meant for a married couple? I look down at the Biltmore House brochure to hide how flustered I suddenly feel.

Andrew. And me. Married.

Now the picture in my head is of hunting-gear-wearing

Andrew kissing corseted, kid-gloved Sam. Which is nuts.

And nice. Really nice.

What are you thinking?

It doesn't matter if you like him. There's no way he's into you—

But what if he is? Why can't I stop feeling like he is?

Ahead of us, Zoe is crowing about her choice—the Louis XV, one of the most luxurious bedrooms in the whole house. I hear laughter. I hear a shush from one of the uniformed guards who stand in every other room, making sure no one touches the priceless furniture and fixtures.

I need to say something. Anything. Before Andrew walks away.

I blurt, "I got dumped two weeks ago." And then I want to go crawl in a hole. Not because of body image or anxiety or whatever, but because that is the most pathetic thing I could have said.

"I'm, um—I'm sorry," Andrew says. "That sucks."

"Yeah."

"Was it mutual? Did you see it coming?"

"Nope and nope."

I didn't cry when it happened—I was too good at not crying in front of people by then. But I couldn't help asking Marcus why. We'd been together for nine months. We'd had fun. He was my first kiss. I'm pretty sure I was his, too. And the only thing he could come up with to tell me was "You've changed. You're different than when we started going out."

Different. Code for fatter, softer, uglier.

I'd been right, that day at the ballet studio. He wasn't attracted to me anymore.

"I think I'm better off without him," I say to Andrew, not because I believe it as much as because it seems like what I should say.

"That may be true, but that doesn't make it suck any less." He runs his hand through his hair, that gesture he does whenever he's thinking about the best way to say something. All of a sudden, I want my fingers in his hair, too.

What is wrong with you?

"I probably shouldn't tell you this, but"—he hesitates, looking around the blue room at everything except me— "it's just that we're not supposed to give y'all too much personal information about ourselves. Dr. Lancaster's rules."

Now I *have* to know. "I won't tell."

"It's not even this big scandalous secret. All my friends at school know. My girlfriend, Caroline, and I—we're going through a rough patch. I keep wondering if we should . . ." He fades off. "Anyway, I kind of know how you feel."

"Oh."

See? He has a girlfriend. Too bad for you.

But . . . they're about to break up? Is that what he's telling me?

"Did your guy give you a reason when he dumped you?"

"Yeah." *You've changed*—I hear it over and over and over and over.

"Have you talked to him since?"

189

"No. It was only a week before I came here. And then Dr. Lancaster took our cell phones. . . . Why—do you think I should talk to him again?"

"I guess I think it's important to get closure when a relationship ends, so you can move on." Andrew finally looks at me. "Bigger and better things on the horizon, right?"

Could he mean him and me? "I hope so."

"I know so." He bumps my arm. "We should catch up to the group."

OUR TOUR OF the house finishes with the servants' quarters, the gymnasium, and the swimming pool in the basement. Then we wander around the lush, well-manicured gardens until we can't stand the oppressive summer humidity one more minute. Finally we pile back into our Perform at Your Peak van.

I sit between Katie and Omar. I listen to them come up with our Biltmore alter egos. Apparently I'm Lady Samantha, a debutante on holiday from the English countryside. Lord Andrew is a distant Scottish cousin, in the States on business. I want to tell them about the adjoining bedrooms—how that must mean Andrew and I are husband and wife—but I can't figure out how to say it in a way that doesn't sound gross. Or like I have a crush on him.

And my inner voice is going at full throttle:

He's your camp counselor. He's too old for you. He has a girlfriend.

But he's kind and funny and strong and smart and *cute*.

He gets me. He makes me smile. He puts me at ease. He's the last thing I expected to find at therapy camp, for so many reasons.

You're not pretty enough. Not thin enough. Not stable enough.

Zoe's kicking the back of my seat, like a four-year-old in an airplane. My inner voice syncs up with her feet: *No. No. No. No.*

When we reach our house, it's dinnertime. Dr. Lancaster has ordered pizza. Cheese and veggie and meat lover's and Hawaiian. I grab a slice of veggie. The one that seems to have the least amount of cheese on it. I take it out to the back porch, breathe in deep, and eat it in twelve bites.

Andrew is sitting on the other side of the porch. With Zoe. They're deep in conversation. He's wearing the same attentive, sympathetic face he puts on when he and I talk about serious stuff. He's listening to her. Nodding. He leans toward her and says something, too low for me to hear. Not that I want to eavesdrop; this looks private. But . . . I want to know.

Is he like this with everyone? Am I stupid to think it's just me?

Yes. Stop being so stupid.

He's allowed to talk to other campers. In fact, it's his job as a peer adviser.

"Sam," Jenna says, snapping me out of it. I look over at her. She's giving me a funny look. "Want to do a ballet barre?"

"Yes," I say quickly. I need to get off this porch, away

191

from Andrew and Zoe, before I drive myself crazy. Crazier. I'm starting to think Zoe might be right, calling this place Crazy Camp.

Inside, I dance *hard*. Not because of my upcoming ballet intensive. Not because I have to burn away the slice of delicious pizza. Because of Andrew. I have to stop thinking about him.

I close my eyes for développés, imagining myself not in the Dogwood Room, not in a dance studio, but onstage. The lights are warm on my face, but the cavernous auditorium is empty. There's no one in the wings, no other dancers onstage with me, no orchestra in the pit, no audience out in the house staring back. I'm doing these développés for me. For only me.

I open my eyes when the exercise is done, facing the window as I stretch out my calves. It's twilight, and I can see my reflection in the glass. Ghostly, like on my first night here.

Over my shoulder, another ghost: Andrew.

He's standing in the doorway, leaning against the frame. Our eyes meet in the window, and I spin to face him, feeling my cheeks flush. My first instinct, like it so often is, is to run from the room. But his eyes hold me where I am.

The seconds we look at each other feel longer. They slow and warp and stretch. And then he gives me a thumbs-up and continues down the hall.

I feel like a tiny piece of me trails after him.

seventeen

YASMIN FINDS ME IN THE BATHROOM THE NEXT morning. "Sam?"

I startle at her voice. I've gotten used to being by myself in the mornings. Getting up early so nobody will see me shower or change clothes. It's weird to have to interact with someone before I make the choice to go downstairs.

"You have a phone call. It's your mom."

I meet her eyes in the mirror. "My mom? At seven thirty?"

"Yeah. She says it's important."

I put my makeup in my shower caddy and follow her to Dr. Lancaster's office.

"Andrew and I are in the kitchen, if you need us," Yasmin says. And if I wasn't nervous before, her gentle tone of voice does it.

I pick up the receiver. "Hello?"

"Samantha. You've been ignoring my phone calls."

"Mom, I—"

"I shouldn't have to catch you by surprise first thing in the morning in order to have the privilege of speaking with my daughter."

"I know. It's just been so busy here, and—"

"I miss you, Samantha," she says, softening. "It's nice to hear your voice."

"It's nice to hear your voice too." I have to force the words out. My chest is tight.

"Tell me what you've been up to."

"Well, yesterday we went to the Biltmore Estate—"

"That sounds like fun. But I meant, what kind of discussions are you and Dr. Lancaster having? Have you been given any strategies to deal with your panic? Your summer intensive starts in two weeks, you know. You need to be ready, especially since you'll be joining a week late. All of the other girls will have a leg up."

"I know."

"Have you been exercising every day? And have you been improving your eating habits? I don't want to hear any more about spaghetti and meatballs. . . ." She says that last bit in a joking way, but I know she's completely serious.

I answer her questions. But I don't tell her everything.

I don't tell Mom that Dr. Lancaster and I talked about *her*. Or how much I've been thinking about the things she says to me. Or how anxious this call is making me.

I also don't mention Andrew. Not even in the context

of a random guy I might like. Mom wouldn't approve. She didn't like me dating Marcus, either. It may have had something to do with him asking me out while she was finalizing her divorce from Dad, but that wasn't the only reason. She likes to remind me that boys are a distraction from what really matters. She says I'll have plenty of time to date once I've joined a ballet company—which is probably not even true. I think she was a little relieved when Marcus broke up with me.

And that hurt. A lot.

When Mom starts in on ballet gossip—which of my classmates start their summer intensives today, which choreographers Miss Elise is planning to bring to our studio in the coming year, how many students my intensive accepts into the school's year-round program annually—I can't listen anymore.

"Mom," I say, stopping her midsentence, "I have to go."

"Your first session doesn't start until eight thirty. We still have seven minutes. And I'm already at work."

"Dr. Lancaster is calling me," I lie.

"Oh. Well, we'll talk tonight then."

"No, we won't." I surprise myself by saying it. And I immediately start backtracking. "We have a weird schedule today. I'm not sure what time I'll be available—actually it's that way all week, and I'd hate for you to keep calling and missing me—so, um. Why don't we just talk on Saturday?"

"Saturday." Mom sounds so disappointed.

"I'm eating well, I'm working out every day, and I think

I just"—I gulp and come out with it—"I need a little space. While I'm here."

"Space."

"Yeah. So I can figure everything out."

There's a long silence on the other end of the line. I want to fill it, but I force myself to hold out. I've said what I need to say, and I absolutely don't want to make things worse.

"All right," Mom finally says. "If that's what you need. But I'm trusting you to stay on track. And to be honest with me."

"I will. And thanks."

"Have a good day, Samantha. I love you."

"I love you too." I hang up and sit there for a few seconds, feeling exhilarated and relieved. And antsy. I've never stood up to Mom like that. I've never felt like I needed to. I meant what I told Dr. Lancaster: Mom and I are a team. But maybe it's okay to need to take a break from your teammate. To have some time apart. To get some air.

I close my eyes and do some of the breathing exercises Yasmin taught us on Friday. I don't know what the day is going to bring, but I don't want to start it feeling wound up like this. In fact, I want to set a goal for myself. "I will not have a panic attack this week," I whisper. "No panic attacks." Inhale. "No panic attacks." Exhale.

I'm interrupted a couple minutes later by a knock at the door. I jump to my feet, brushing myself off and straightening my tank top. I swing the door open.

It's Andrew. "Hey. You okay?"

I nod, trying not to look like my entire body has lit up because he's standing in front of me. Even though it has.

"I'm glad." He holds out a mug of black coffee. "Thought you might need this."

I take it, giving him a grateful smile. "Thank you."

"Missed you this morning." He bumps my shoulder, and I grip the coffee so it doesn't slosh.

He missed me. I feel my smile widening, and I bring the mug up to my lips to hide it. "Yeah, I had to talk to my mom. . . ."

"I know. Yasmin said she sounded upset. Everything all right?"

I think about the six days of freedom I have in front of me. "It will be."

"Awesome. Well, we better get in there." He nudges me again, and we head into the Dogwood Room.

"Good morning, Sam," Dr. Lancaster says as I sit between Dominic and Zoe.

"Morning. Sorry I'm late."

Dr. Lancaster looks at my coffee. "Did you get a chance to eat?"

"No, but I'm okay—"

"Yasmin will get you something." Dr. Lancaster nods at Yasmin, who leaves the room and returns with a plate of food. A waffle topped with fresh strawberries, blueberries, and honey. I stare at it. *No panic attacks this week*, I remind myself.

I look up to see Dr. Lancaster looking at me. She pushes me with her eyes. So I cut a square of waffle, stab a strawberry, and shove it in my mouth. It's good. Crispy on the outside and buttery in the middle. The strawberry is fresh and tart and the honey glides down my throat. I cut another square, this time with a blueberry on top. I wonder how many squares Dr. Lancaster will make me eat.

"Now that you know a little bit about each other and your respective struggles, we're going to spend the coming week doing what I call challenges," Dr. Lancaster says. "These are activities that focus in on or simulate an issue one or more of you is battling. For instance, the ropes course we did on Thursday became a specific challenge for Katie, even though you all participated—and, I hope, benefited from it."

I'm chewing on waffle square number three. Now it tastes dry. The honey is too sticky. The blueberry bursts in my mouth like a sour bomb.

"We'll be using resources around campus, and my colleagues in the psychology department will step in when we need additional people involved," Dr. Lancaster goes on. "They're all trained mental health professionals, bound by confidentiality, so you can breathe easy knowing you're in good hands." She consults her notepad. "Tomorrow morning we'll head to the football field for Dominic's challenge. Then we'll go to the film department's screening room for Jenna's challenge. Wednesday we'll do Zoe's tennis challenge first, followed by a cooking challenge for Sam. Thursday we'll walk over to the college's theater for Omar's challenge. And on Sunday, we'll return to the ropes course so that Katie can cross the suspended beams again."

"Cooking?" I ask. "What does that have to do with—"

"You'll see," Dr. Lancaster says. "Now, did you all bring your notebooks?"

Everyone holds theirs up. When I raise my hand to say that I don't have mine, Zoe thrusts it into my face. "Here. I swear, I didn't read it."

I don't know whether to believe her. But I smile, out of habit, and say, "Thanks!"

"I want you all to spend a few minutes brainstorming about what motivates you. Then we'll discuss as a group."

I put my partially eaten waffle on the floor by my chair and flip to a blank page. I start jotting down ideas. And I find myself thinking in images instead of words. Like I want to make another collage, instead of just a written list.

An empty dance studio, waiting to be filled with life and movement.

A pair of perfectly broken in pointe shoes.

The view from the stage, past the bright stage lights, into the blackness of the auditorium.

Me at six, in my favorite pink leotard with the ruffly skirt.

Me last December, in my Dewdrop Fairy costume.

A piano, to represent the music that moves me: Tchaikovsky's *Swan Lake*. Prokofiev's *Romeo and Juliet*. Arvo Pärt's *Spiegel im Spiegel*, the haunting score to the pas de deux from Christopher Wheeldon's *After the Rain*.

But how do I show the exhilaration of finally mastering a challenging step or phrase or variation? How do I show the triumph of pushing yourself beyond what you ever thought you could do? How do I show the feeling of being someone else—some*thing* else—onstage? Something better than yourself, something stronger, and richer, and fuller, and more beautiful?

THAT AFTERNOON, DR. Lancaster has me pull out the body-part lists I made—what I like and dislike about myself. She doesn't miss the fact that I was grasping at straws when it came to things I like. I wrote that I have nice fingernails. And that it's great that my leg hair grows slowly, because I don't have to shave too often.

"I'm going to ask you some questions," she says. "Let's see if we can't reframe some of these negatives as positives."

"Sure," I say, humoring her. "Why not."

"Thick thighs," she reads. "What about *powerful* thighs? Do they help you jump?"

"I guess. But there are people with thinner legs who can jump just as high."

"Big breasts and wide hips. Isn't it normal for someone your age to start developing a more womanly figure?"

I shudder at the words "womanly figure." "Not for a serious ballet dancer."

"Does your strong core support you during difficult balances and partnering?"

"My strong core—" I grab the notebook from her, wanting

to make sure my list didn't change while I wasn't looking. Nope, it still says *Stomach—how it pooches out even when I hold it in.* "Now you're just making stuff up."

"So you don't think you have a strong core?"

"No, I do. I wouldn't be able to do half of what I can do without it. It's just all this"—I pinch at my layer of chub for emphasis, and then drop it, horrified at myself—"that I hate."

"What's more important: what your body looks like, or what it can do?"

Her question feels like a trap. "They're both important."

"But do you value one more than the other?"

"Ballet is a visual art. It's about shapes in space. The transitions between shapes. But it's also about the bodies that are creating those shapes. What they look like."

"So you feel like only thin bodies belong onstage."

"That's not what I said." She's twisting my words. "And it's not about what I think belongs onstage. It's about what ballet company directors want. What audiences expect to see."

In a nutshell: not you.

"When did you start seeing yourself the way you think everyone else sees you?"

It takes me a second to figure out what she's asking. Which came first: my hatred of myself and the changes my body was going through, or my realization that other people didn't like how I looked? Chicken or egg?

I remember a specific ballet class this past winter. After barre, I took my usual place in the front right corner of the studio for center exercises. Not the middle of the room, generally reserved for juniors and seniors, but still in the first row. I danced where I could see myself in the mirror. Where I could be seen. Back then, I *liked* being seen.

We started our adagio exercise, filled with one-legged balances and high extensions. As I développéd my leg up toward the ceiling, I noticed something. A small roll at my waist, like my thigh was pushing against excess flesh. I frowned at it, and then carried my leg to arabesque a count late.

Miss Elise called out, "Watch your timing, Sam!"

But I couldn't stop watching my waist. Every movement wrinkled it in a new way. A forward port de bras gave me a pinch in the front, while an arching cambré gave me a lump of back fat. It felt like I was staring at a creature in a zoo. Or an alien. Not at the reflection I'd watched in daily ballet classes for almost ten years.

I finished the combination and stood in fifth position, breathing hard. My eyes darted around the room. In a matter of seconds, my body had become something unfamiliar and unwelcome. But had anyone else noticed?

A few weeks later, without telling me beforehand, my mom scheduled an appointment with the nutritionist who gave annual talks at our studio. He reminded me that the body is a dancer's instrument and that eating well is like rolling out tight muscles and bathing in Epsom salts—a way to be your healthiest, best-performing self.

I heard: *You're getting fat.*

My mom sat in the corner, nodding along. She stuck the charts and lists he gave me on our fridge at home, in the same place of honor where she used to put my crayon drawings of flowers and dinosaurs. Looking at the food pyramid later that night, I had my first panic attack.

Dr. Lancaster is still waiting for me to answer her. "I don't know," I whisper.

"Tell me what you do know."

I think for a second. "I know that I love ballet."

"Good—"

"I just don't know if ballet loves me back."

We sit in silence for another long second.

"Is it okay for me to love ballet, if ballet doesn't love me back?" My voice is still hushed. I feel like I'm getting at the crux of something big.

"I can't answer that for you, Sam. I wish I could, but there are some things you have to figure out for yourself."

"It would be easier if I didn't care so much."

"That may be true."

"But I don't want to care less. I wouldn't be me if I cared less."

Dr. Lancaster leans forward in her chair. "So how do you hold on to your love for your art, while also finding a way to love your body? Can those two loves coexist?"

With that million-dollar question, she sends me on my way.

eighteen

I'M STILL THINKING ABOUT HER QUESTION ON Tuesday morning, as we walk across campus to the football field for Dominic's challenge. Why do I continue to love something that gives me panic attacks? That makes me despise almost every inch of myself? And if I *can* start to accept my current body and how it will change my future, like Dr. Lancaster wants me to—a huge "if"—will I still love ballet just as much? Or will it become *this thing I used to do*?

I don't want that. But I don't want the panic or the self-hatred, either.

"What are you thinking about?" It's Katie. She's fallen into step with me.

"Something Dr. Lancaster and I talked about yesterday."

"Ah. Say no more." A beat. "Unless you want to? But no pressure."

"How do you . . . ?" I wish it was Andrew beside me and not Katie. Not only because of my crush on him, but also because this is something I know he'll understand. "How do you know when it's time to quit?"

"Like, quit ballet?" Katie says. "That escalated quickly."

"I'm not exactly planning on it. But what would make you quit gymnastics?"

She doesn't hesitate. "If I didn't enjoy it anymore, I'd stop."

"But how do you know when you're at that point?"

"I think I'd . . . know. Maybe I wouldn't want to practice. I'd resent having to get up early to go to the gym. I wouldn't feel like trying my best at meets."

"That makes sense."

"Do you still enjoy dancing?"

"Yeah. But it's hard with all this other stuff in my head. . . ."

"Totally."

We walk the rest of the way in silence.

And then we're on the field. It's not a huge stadium, but in the bright morning sunshine, surrounded by empty seats, it makes me feel small.

It doesn't have the same effect on Dominic. He puffs out his chest and starts strutting around like he owns the place. "My high school stadium is bigger than this," he says. Then he yells into the air, "Please welcome . . . Your! State! Champions!" He imitates the roar of the crowd and jogs to the fifty-yard line, waving.

Dr. Lancaster walks out from under the home-side stands. There are three men with her, each holding a clipboard and wearing a polo shirt for an SEC school: Alabama, Georgia, Tennessee. After what Dr. Lancaster said yesterday, I know they're not real recruiters; they're psychology professors. Still, they look pretty official. Their presence changes the energy in the air.

"Uh, hi," Dominic says to the men. Dr. Lancaster gives him a look, and he sticks out his hand. "Nice to meet you guys."

"Nice to meet you, son," the man in the Alabama shirt says. "Why don't you run some drills? Show us what you've got."

"Yes, sir," Dominic says. He jogs in place, rolling his shoulders and his head around. "But, uh, who am I supposed to play with?"

Tennessee-shirt points at the rest of us. "Looks like your team's right there."

I jump, and Omar blurts, "What?"

Dominic looks from us to the fake scouts and back again at us, frowning. "They don't know anything about football."

"So teach 'em," Georgia-shirt says. "Give us something to watch."

"Great. Uh, huddle up," Dominic says, drawing us into a tight circle. "Katie, Zoe, we've thrown the ball around, so, uh, I know you don't suck at catching it. You'll be my receivers. Sam, Jenna, Omar, you'll be the other team. Your job is to, um, stop Katie and Zoe from catching the ball. And stop

206

me from throwing it." He makes a frustrated noise, looking over at Andrew, who's standing off to the side with Yasmin. "This is nuts."

Andrew grins. "Just go with it."

So Dominic does. He sets us up in formation on the field. Gives us instructions. Yells, "Hike!" We run. Omar goes toward Dominic, but stops short and ducks as Dominic rears back to throw. Jenna's chasing Katie and I'm chasing Zoe. She's faster than me. And yet not fast enough—the ball sails past her and hits the ground.

I see Dominic glance at the clipboards on the sidelines and wince. He calls out, "Bring it back in! We're running that play again."

We do. Again and again and again.

And all of a sudden, Dominic snaps.

"I told you to go *long*, Zoe. Do you even freakin' know what that means? It means to run far and fast. And then to catch the stupid ball!"

Zoe's eyes are narrowing. "Excuse me?"

"You're not even listening to me. When the quarterback tells you to do something, you freakin' do it!" He throws the ball at her, hard. "Catch this!"

It drops into her arms and she makes a surprised *oof* noise.

"Okay, so you *can* catch it," Dominic sneers. "Good to know." He turns to the rest of us. I take an involuntary step back. This is not the Dominic we've seen over the past week. I don't know who this person is. "Huddle up. We're starting over—"

Zoe slams into him. "You total—" She calls him a few choice names, shoving him with each one. "You know what? This doesn't matter! Football doesn't matter! Your whole life is *so* not important. When are you gonna get that through your thick head—"

"It matters to me!" he shouts. I can tell he wants to shove her back, but he's restraining himself. Andrew steps in between them, but they keep yelling around him.

"This"—Zoe gestures at the stadium, the field, Dominic—"it's just a stupid game, and you need to get over yourself—"

"It's not just a game!" Dominic's mouth is twisted and his face is red and he's breathing hard. "It's—it's—"

"It's *what?*"

Dominic sits down on the ground. Puts his head in his hands. He doesn't speak for a long moment. Then I realize that he's crying. He curses, and says, wiping angrily at his face, "It's my future. Okay?" He drops his head in his hands again.

Andrew gives Zoe a look. "Don't move." He crouches next to Dominic, talking quietly.

"Are you okay?" Yasmin asks Omar, who looks like he's about to cry too. He nods fast, gulping. "Katie?" She nods. Yasmin looks to me. "Sam?" I nod.

Zoe lets out a guttural roar. She stomps over to Dr. Lancaster and yells, "I did not start that. You saw him! It wasn't me! And he shouldn't have started something he didn't want to finish, anyway—"

Dr. Lancaster steers Zoe off to the sidelines, talking to her in a low, firm voice.

I notice that the men with the clipboards have disappeared.

"Let's go sit down," Yasmin says, putting one arm around my shoulders and the other around Jenna's. We walk with her to the bleachers. Katie and Omar follow. We sit.

"Wow," Jenna says after a few minutes, her voice tight.

"Wow," I agree. Of all of us, Dominic seemed the most chill, the most . . . normal. But he told us last week he needed to be here. We just hadn't seen why.

Andrew helps Dominic to his feet. He picks up the football and holds it in front of Dominic, and Dominic nods. They jog away from each other, and Andrew fires off a pass. The ball soars high and long. Dominic runs until he's underneath it, and it drops into his hands. He sends it flying back.

Next to me, Jenna is uncharacteristically fidgety. She smooths back her ponytail, then adjusts her tank top, then dabs at her face with a tissue, then fixes her hair again. And I remember: her challenge is next.

"How are you doing?" I ask her.

She blinks at me. "Fine."

I hesitate. "Are you sure?"

"Mm-hmm." She squints at me, shading her eyes. "You're getting sunburned."

I move the strap of my tank top to check. She's right. "Good thing we're going inside soon."

"Good thing," she echoes, running her fingers over her ponytail another time.

Dr. Lancaster comes over to us a few minutes later,

Zoe trailing behind her. "Everyone okay? We're due at the screening room in fifteen minutes."

"We're still going through with Jenna's challenge?" Omar says. "After . . . that?" His voice rises to a squeak, and he clears his throat.

"Jenna, are you all right to proceed?" Dr. Lancaster asks.

"Mm-hmm." Her throat sounds even tighter than before, but she gets to her feet.

IN THE FILM department's screening room, Dr. Lancaster sets Jenna up at a podium in front of the giant video screen. Jenna grips the sides of the podium like it's the only thing keeping her on her feet. Her eyes are wide and her lips are pressed into a thin line.

"Do you think she's going to freak out like Dominic did?" Katie whispers from the seat next to me.

"I hope not." For her sake and for ours. I feel so on edge right now, and I know I'm not the only one. Katie, Omar, and I are all in the second row together, and our nerves jangle in the air around us. Dominic and Andrew are behind us, and Yasmin and Zoe are five rows farther back, in the corner. I imagine I can feel Zoe seething and sulking from all the way back there.

The AC is blasting. I'm shivering, despite my sunburned shoulders, as I watch Dr. Lancaster fuss with the wires connecting the laptop to the projector. Finally she gets the screen to flicker to life. As it comes into focus, I see that it's an online video site. The thumbnail image is of a skater in a royal-blue dress, bent almost in half as she spins.

Dr. Lancaster steps up to the microphone. "I'm excited to introduce today's very special guest commentator," she says, and Katie looks at me with raised eyebrows. "Jenna Lai is here to dissect a few skating videos for us. She'll be telling us each and every *good* and *correct* thing the skater does, so we know what to look for when we're watching skating in the future."

The lights dim. The video begins. The skater takes her opening pose at center ice. Her routine is to Gershwin's *Rhapsody in Blue*, and she starts by skating in a slow, luxurious circle, arms floating down to her sides. Then she travels backward, building up speed.

Jenna takes in a shaky breath. The microphone picks it up. "Jackie's known for having really solid short programs," she says. "Her energy grows in a nice way. She has a tough jump combination coming up here. I think it's a triple lutz, double loop. . . ."

On-screen, Jackie launches herself into the air, spins three times, lands, jumps again, spins twice, and lands in an arabesque, a triumphant look on her face.

"That was a strong landing," Jenna tells us as Jackie does a footwork pass across the ice. "Here comes another jump combination. . . ." We all watch. "And she sticks it again. She's skating so cleanly. And look at the fluidity in her arm movements. . . ."

Jenna talks us through the rest of the video, and then three more routines, sounding more and more at ease as she goes. She's almost clinical, the way she breaks down what's successful about each program. For one skater, it's all about flexibility. "Look at how straight her knee is in that arabesque!" Jenna says. For another, it's the passion she displays. "She wobbled there," Jenna points out, "but you feel her fire."

And then a video cues up that makes Jenna grab onto the podium again. "Um," she says, a crack in her voice. "That's me."

I sit forward in my chair.

"It is you," Dr. Lancaster agrees. "And I'd like you to dissect the video for us, just like you did with the others."

"But—" Jenna breaks off, looking lost.

On-screen, Jenna takes her opening pose. And in front of us, Jenna stumbles through an introduction. "This is my—it's Jenna's first time skating this routine on competitive ice. I got a—*she* has a new choreographer, with an increased focus on ballet technique. You can tell because of the . . . because of . . ." She watches herself start to skate. "Her arm movements are much more fluid than they used to be."

Skater-Jenna steps into a spin, her deep pink skirt fluttering behind her. She arches back, one leg lifted behind her, arms reaching for the sky. The effect is like a water lily swirling in a stream.

"Her arms—" Jenna says. "Her hands, they're—she—" The spin is done. Skater-Jenna starts picking up speed for a jump. "Okay, she's going to do a triple loop, double loop. She's going to try, anyway. Her preparation is strong, and . . ."

I feel like we all hold our breath as skater-Jenna launches herself into the air.

It looks good to me, but Jenna frowns. "She under-rotated the triple, so her preparation for the double was off—"

Dr. Lancaster clears her throat and Jenna blanches.

"But she saved it," she says quickly. "She won't necessarily lose component points. Um, there's a footwork sequence coming up. Jenna's been working on speed and clarity in her footwork. . . ." She keeps talking, through gritted teeth, until her on-screen self falls on a jump near the end of the program. Then she full-body winces and clamps her mouth shut.

Dr. Lancaster pauses the video with skater-Jenna scrambling up from the ice. "Tell us what's happening, Jenna," she says.

Jenna shakes her head, staring at the screen. Horror and disgust flicker across her features. "There is absolutely nothing good I can say about that."

"Take a moment. Think."

Jenna shifts from foot to foot. She closes her eyes. And she chokes out, "That's a new jump combination for Jenna. A lot of senior ladies don't have that one in their repertoire yet."

"Good."

The video continues. Skater-Jenna does a final sit-spin, jumps up, and glides to a stop. The crowd applauds, but when the camera goes to close-up on her face, she's wearing the same guarded expression she had when she first got here.

And she's wearing it now. "Are we done?"

"I'd like to go through a few more," Dr. Lancaster says, cueing up the next video.

While we're watching, the AC cycles on. I shiver again, rubbing my hands up and down my arms. And then a sweatshirt appears over my shoulder. I turn in my chair, squinting in the dark but knowing already who I'll see.

"Want this?" Andrew whispers, leaning forward.

I take it. I put it on and zip it up fast. It smells like him. I didn't realize until this exact moment that I knew what Andrew smells like.

"Don't know how much longer we'll be in here," he says, his mouth close to my ear. "Lucky I brought that, huh."

"Yeah."

I hear the squeak of him sitting back in his chair. I feel Katie's eyes on me. But I keep my eyes on Jenna. She's telling us about the nuances of various spin positions, and I can tell she's itching to point out what's wrong with what she's doing on-screen, but she stops herself. I shiver again, and this time it's not from the cold.

My challenge is tomorrow. I hope I'm up for it.

I breathe in deep and settle in to Andrew's hoodie's embrace.

nineteen

WHEN WE GET BACK TO THE PERFORM AT YOUR PEAK
house, Dr. Lancaster has us gather in the Dogwood Room.
Dominic and Zoe sit on opposite sides of the circle, but it
doesn't feel like it's far enough apart. The air is thick with
tension.

"Who wants to go first?" Dr. Lancaster asks.

After a few beats of silence, Dominic mutters, "Sorry I
lost my cool."

Dr. Lancaster touches Zoe's shoulder. "Zoe?"

"Whatever."

"That's not what we talked about—"

"Why should I have to apologize?" She crosses her arms
and juts her chin out.

"You're here to support one another, not belittle one
another's feelings."

"Why should I care about your feelings?" She talks right

at Dominic. "And I thought you didn't *do* feelings, anyway."

Dominic is slouching in his seat. His eyes are hooded. Now it's his turn to say, "Whatever."

"Dominic, do you want to talk about how the challenge felt for you?"

"Nope. Pass."

"Okay. Maybe we'll dive in later. Jenna, how about you? How did you feel about your challenge?"

"Fine." It's an automatic answer. No emotion behind it.

"Why do you think it was so difficult for you to compliment your own performance?"

"It was fine. Can we move on?" She sits up taller, her spine an iron rod.

"If you want to open up, it might help your peers prepare for their challenges—"

"I'd prefer to talk to you about it in private."

Dr. Lancaster nods. "All right." She looks at each of us in turn. "Remember, while your anxiety is internal, it's often a response to external stimuli. It doesn't exist in a vacuum."

Well, obviously.

I don't think I'd hate my body nearly as much if it weren't for how people look at me. If it weren't for what they say to me and about me. If I couldn't see myself next to skinnier dancers. If I weren't part of a ballet culture that cares so much about body type.

But there's still part of my anxiety that's *me*, specifically. I don't think every person in my situation would respond the way I have. Not everyone has this inner voice repeating,

You're fat, you're ugly, you're awful, you'll never get what you want, give up, give up on a constant loop. Not every dancer would turn into a shuddering blob of sweat and tears and sequins at the sight of her own body in the mirror.

I can't change the ballet world. And I can't change my body—at least, not as much as I want to. I'm stuck with these fourteen extra pounds weighing me down.

Unless you do something. There are ways. You know that. You're just too weak—

I don't want to think about that. I won't.

DR. LANCASTER AND I spend our forty-five minutes together talking more about body parts. Specifically, whose would I trade for mine? At first, it feels weird to be talking about Jenna's slim silhouette, Zoe's legs, Yasmin's abs, Katie's shoulders and upper arms, but I can see the picture coming together in my head. It's a collage—apparently that's my thing, now—of a dancer in arabesque, made up of so many perfect pieces. Frankenstein's Ballerina.

I know what Dr. Lancaster wants me to say: that I'm more than the sum of my parts. But I don't believe that, and I don't feel like lying to her. I'm too anxious about my cooking challenge tomorrow. Andrew's sweatshirt is the only thing keeping me together.

And Andrew himself.

As Jenna and I are stretching out on the floor after a punishing ballet barre, Andrew walks in. He crouches between us. I sit up straighter, sucking my stomach in. I grab his hoodie and wrap it around my shoulders so he won't take it with him.

"Just wanted to give you a heads-up," he says. His eyes have a mischievous gleam. "Yasmin and I have something fun planned for tonight."

"What?" I whisper.

"If," he says slowly, "we were to sneak out of the house later and go for a late-night swim at the lake, would you come?"

I gape, feeling his words like a punch to the gut.

A swim. At the lake. After what happened last week—

He touches my arm. "Sam. I get it. But I think you should come."

I still can't find words.

"I want you to come." He's looking at me like Jenna isn't even there. Like we're the only two people in the room, in the house, on the planet. "It's a Perform at Your Peak tradition. Our peer advisers did it for us, and we're doing it for you. We want you there."

"I, um . . . okay." I gulp. Nod. "Okay."

"Midnight. Meet at the back door." Now he looks at Jenna. She nods too. "Great," Andrew says. He gets to his feet, using my shoulder to push himself to standing. When he walks away, it feels like he leaves an imprint of his hand behind.

I rub the place where his hand sat.

"How's that sunburn?" Jenna has a small, knowing smile on her face.

"Sore," I say, sliding into my right-side split so I don't have to look at her.

She doesn't say anything else. Doesn't ask me any questions I can't answer.

THAT NIGHT, AFTER washing my face and brushing my teeth and changing into my pajamas—swimsuit underneath, wrapped around me like a bandage, squeezing me like a vise—I'm under the covers watching the clock tick toward midnight. Zoe, meanwhile, is sitting on her bed in her pink bikini top, shorts, and swim cap, like nothing about this needs to be sneaky.

"Are you *trying* to get caught?" I ask her.

"By who? Dr. Lancaster's in bed. Andrew and Yasmin planned this whole thing."

"But what if—"

"You worry too much, Barbs."

I scowl at her, sending all of my swimsuit anxiety her way. "Why is Andrew even letting you come along?"

"Because I made him. I said I'd wait until you all left and then wake Dr. Lancaster up."

"For real?"

"No. Although I could. Might actually get on her good side, for once." She pulls her knees to her chest. "I don't know why Andrew's letting me come along. Maybe because he's a nice guy. Why don't you ask him? You two seem tight."

I don't rise to her bait. We sit in a tense silence until the clock on the desk says 11:59. Then Zoe jumps to her feet, grabbing her towel. "C'mon."

She opens the door soundlessly and peeks out. There's no one in the hallway, but we can see Dominic and Omar disappearing around the corner at the bottom of the stairs. Zoe and I follow, and when we get to the kitchen, Andrew and Yasmin are there with Katie, Jenna, and the guys. Andrew opens the back door and, putting a finger to his lips, ushers us outside.

I make my way to his side as we jog across the dark lawn. "Are you sure we won't get in trouble?" I ask. Like that's the only thing on my mind.

"Yeah. This is totally safe. And y'all need to do something normal. Teenager-y."

The way he says "teenager-y" makes me deflate a little bit. He's in college—practically an adult. And I'm sixteen. But then he looks down at me and I see the white flash of his teeth as he smiles.

"I'm glad you're here."

If he's glad, I'm glad. "Me too."

But when we reach the lake, the anxiety I've been ignoring settles in. I pause where I crumpled to the ground a week ago. I take a step backward. Then another.

"Everything okay?" Andrew shines his flashlight at me. "Are you about to—"

"No." And yet, while I'm definitely not having a panic attack, I can't move another inch toward the water. I sit down on a log that's close to where the trail from the woods meets the dock and watch everyone else strip down, jump in, paddle around.

Andrew sits next to me. Bare arm to bare arm. "Sam, talk to me."

"I can't do it," I say softly. "I have to go back. You can say I forgot something."

"Because you don't want to wear your swimsuit in front of us?"

I don't respond, but he takes it as the yes it is.

He exhales in frustration. "Sam, you can't let how you feel about your body ruin your life. You can't let it keep you from doing things. Do you want to go swimming?"

I nod.

"Then swim."

"I can't."

He's quiet for a moment. "When I was thinking about quitting football, I almost took the chicken way out."

"You almost didn't quit?"

"No, I almost—I thought about—" A pause. "If I got injured, I could stop playing without having to tell my dad and my coach I was done with football. It would have been so easy: get in the way of the wrong linebacker, not catch myself when I fell, whatever. I could've had an out, and never had to say anything. Never had to let anyone down. But that wouldn't have been honest. I needed to be honest. Dr. Lancaster taught me that, even if when I was here, I didn't know I'd eventually want to quit."

I'm not sure where he's going with this, but I'm willing to let him make his way there. Besides, it feels like it's just the two of us. With Andrew's voice in my ear, his arm touching mine, I feel like we couldn't be more alone.

"I know it's not the same thing at all," Andrew says, "and I absolutely don't want you to take this as a suggestion. But why haven't you tried to starve yourself until you're as thin as you want to be?"

There it is. The question I hoped he'd never ask.

I stare at the ground. "I've thought about it. A lot." I don't tell him about the things I *did* try. I can't. "I'm not that brave."

"But that's my point. I don't think hurting yourself to get what you want is brave. I think it's braver *not* to take that route."

I sigh. "I guess you're right. Anyway, what if starving myself didn't help? What if I kept wanting to be skinnier and skinnier? What if I'm destined to always feel . . . wrong?"

He cringes. "I wish you could stop thinking of yourself as being 'wrong.'"

"You and me both."

"So . . . take the first step. Walk to the end of the dock, in your swimsuit—that I bet you look great in, by the way—and jump in. In front of everyone. Act confident, and maybe you'll see that there's nothing to be afraid of after all."

I look at him. "Fake it till you make it?"

"One way to put it."

There are only a few inches separating our faces. We're close enough to kiss. Such a small movement would bring us together. And he's looking at me with his eyes wide and his lips barely parted. . . .

"Are you two coming in or not?" Zoe calls from the water.

Andrew pulls away. He stands and tugs his T-shirt over his head, and I lose my breath. He looks down at me. "Come in. Please."

"I—" I inhale. It's shaky. And not just from the anxiety butterflies. I feel his nearness, our almost-kiss—if that's truly what it was—all over my body. "Okay."

He holds out his hand and pulls me to my feet.

"Can you turn around?" As much as I want him to like what he sees—to like *me*—I'm not ready to get undressed in front of him. Or anyone.

"Of course." He turns his back.

I slide my pj pants down and pull my tank top over my head. And then I'm standing there in my black one-piece, and the roar in my ears drowns out the water lapping and the June bugs humming. I take another deep breath.

And I run. Past Andrew. Along the length of the dock. I'm in the air, floating for a fraction of a second, and then I hit the water with a loud splash.

Andrew splashes next to me a moment later. He comes up out of the water smiling at me. I smile back. The water is cold and dark, but the moon and the stars are reflected on the surface and only my head and shoulders are visible, so I feel safe.

"What took you so long?" Zoe is swimming a backstroke circle around the others.

"I just—I had to—"

"We just had to talk about something," Andrew cuts in. "My fault." He swims closer to me. "Do you want to tell them about it?"

"I want to *not* talk about it. I want to enjoy this, now." Still feeling the rush I got from jumping in, I add, "With you." Then, because I can't believe I just said that, I quickly add, "With all of you." And then I feel stupid, so I shut up and paddle toward the rest of the group.

The water slips over my skin. I'm here. I'm swimming. It's scary, and not actually that scary at all. I flip onto my back, looking up at the dark sky and the bright moon. I let the water cradle me. I feel weightless.

twenty

WE SNEAK BACK INTO THE HOUSE AROUND TWO a.m. It's dark and silent and still. I'm afraid to make a single creak, for fear of waking Dr. Lancaster, and I don't take a full breath until Zoe and I are back in our bedroom. But no sooner do I change out of my wet swimsuit and climb into bed than she's standing by the door.

"BRB," she says, a wicked smile on her face.

"Where are you going?"

"Nowhere. Downstairs."

"Why?"

"Forgot something."

"What?" As far as I can tell, she has everything we left with. Bikini, shorts, swim cap, shoes, towel—not much to forget.

Zoe gives a dramatic sigh. "Oh, fine. You caught me. You can come with."

"Come with you *where*?"

"Come on, Barbs. Live a little." She holds the door open and beckons me closer.

I don't know exactly why I follow her, but I do. We sneak down the stairs and down the hall, our footsteps muffled by the plush carpet. Zoe stops in front of Dr. Lancaster's office. She turns the doorknob. The door swings open, and Zoe pushes me inside fast.

"What are we—"

"Shh!" She claps her hand over my mouth.

We wait to hear whether anyone followed us. I decide that the moment she lets me go, I am running—*running*—back upstairs. This was a horrible idea. I can't get caught in here with her. I should never have listened. There's only so far "live a little" should take you.

But when Zoe releases my mouth, she doesn't release my wrist. She pulls me over to Dr. Lancaster's desk and slides open the top right drawer. "Which one's yours?"

There are six cell phones in the drawer. I point at mine. Zoe hands it to me, then picks up the one that must be hers.

"How did you know—"

"I've been in here before."

"When?"

"The other night. I wanted to snoop around. It's a win-win—I either find out more stuff about all of you, or I get caught and sent home. Or I find out more stuff about all of you *and* I get caught and sent home. Guess that's a win-win-*win*."

"You read our files? Those are private!"

"Not anymore," she says with a smirk. Then she laughs. "You should see your face right now. No, I did not read anyone's private file. They're in a locked cabinet, and I couldn't find the key. Maybe Dr. Lancaster sleeps with it around her neck."

My hands are trembling. I wring them, trying to make the trembling stop. "Okay."

"I swear. Scout's honor. Your secrets are still safe."

"Okay."

She powers her phone on and starts texting.

"What am I supposed to do with this?" I hold my phone up, still uncertain.

Zoe flashes me a bright grin. "Whatever you want."

Whatever I want.

What do I want?

All at once, I know. On Sunday, in the blue room at the Biltmore, Andrew said I should talk to Marcus. To get closure. To move on. I don't give it any more thought. I turn on my phone, find Marcus in my contacts, and call him.

He answers on the third ring, sleep-groggy and yawning. "Hello?"

"Hey. It's me."

A long pause. "Sam?"

"Yeah."

"Is everything okay? What time is it?"

"Late. Early. Sorry."

"Aren't you at that therapy camp?"

"I am."

"Are you supposed to be calling me?"

"Nope."

"Oh." He yawns again. "Well, how are you?"

"I'm fine. I'm okay. It's hard here, you know? But I think I'm—" I stop. Marcus doesn't get to have a window into my thoughts anymore. It's his turn to talk to me. "I'm calling because . . ." I glance at Zoe and then decide that hearing what Marcus has to say is more important than hiding from her. "Why did you break up with me?"

"Wow, straight to the point. That's, um . . . new." He groans, like he's pushing himself to sitting. "I told you. You were . . . different. And I didn't know how to—"

A flash of righteous anger. "So you dumped me because I'm not as—because I— How shallow *are* you?"

"Wait, what? What are you even talking about? It's the middle of the night, Sam. Be straight with me."

I force myself to say it. "I got fat."

There's a bark of laughter on the other end of the line. It makes me want to throw the phone across the room. But I keep my grip. I wait.

"Hold on—were you being serious?"

"Yes," I say in a small voice.

"Sam. We didn't break up because you got . . . fat. Which you aren't, by the way. Not unless you've changed an awful lot in two weeks. If we're being honest here, I liked the curves." Now I can hear the smile in the corner of his mouth.

"Why, then?"

"You were so down all the time. Like anything was gonna make you cry. Nothing I did cheered you up. And when I'd ask you about it, you'd bite my head off. So then I didn't want to ask you at all. And whenever we'd go out, you were, like, so self-conscious. . . ." He pauses.

"Keep going. Please."

"I didn't know how to make you feel better. It didn't seem like you *wanted* to feel better. And I—I've had a lot on my plate, with baseball and science club and—being with you—it wasn't fun anymore. It was stressful. Frustrating. And I didn't need that."

"Oh."

"Ugh, I'm sorry, this is coming out all wrong."

"It's okay. I asked you. I needed to know."

What he's saying—it changes so much. He didn't dump me because of how I look. We broke up because I've been such a mess emotionally. And now I'm working on that. I'm getting better. I can be ready to be with . . . whoever's next.

Marcus yawns again. I can picture it, widemouthed like a lion. He always had yawns that looked so satisfying. "So are we cool?" he asks when he's done.

"Yeah."

"For what it's worth, I'm glad you're getting some help."

"Me too."

"All right, Sam. I gotta get up early."

"Good night, Marcus." It feels more like good-bye, but I don't mind as much as I thought I would.

229

"Night." He hangs up.

My phone goes dark.

"That was . . . interesting," Zoe stage-whispers from the couch. "Did you really think a guy dumped you because you were fat?"

"Yeah. I really did."

Zoe snorts. "Well, I guess now you know." She checks the time on her phone. "Anyone else you want to wake up and grill?"

I think about calling Bianca. But she's at her ballet intensive, and I don't want her to be too exhausted to dance well tomorrow. And anyway, I don't know what I need to say to her. I think I need to apologize . . . but for what? And how?

I log in to my email, scrolling past the spam until I find a message from Bianca, from Sunday night:

> Hey, Sam-a-lam-a!
>
> Just wanted to say hi, and let you know I'm thinking about you. I miss you. Wish you were here.
>
> I just got settled in my room in TWSB's dorms. My roommate is from San Francisco. She spent last year at San Francisco Ballet School! So I'm getting all the West Coast gossip. I'll fill you in next time we talk.
>
> Can you call? Or text? Or email? Do they have you on total lockdown? What's it like there? Inquiring minds want to know!
>
> Seriously, though, I hope it's helping. I'm here if you want to talk. Whatever, whenever.
>
> Love, B

Like always, Bianca ends her message with a ton of random emoji. This time, it's the sunglasses smiley, a cat with heart eyes, the dancing woman in the red dress, a flower, a duckling, and the Easter Island statue. I smile at the screen, hitting "reply."

Zoe clears her throat. "Time to wrap it up. Sorry."

"Okay." I type in:

> **Miss you too! So much. Lots to fill you in on, but no time now. Not supposed to be online. Xoxo, Sam.**

I wait for it to send, then turn off my phone and drop it into the drawer Zoe's holding open.

"Glad you came with me?"

"Yes. Have you brought anyone else down here?"

"Just you."

"Why me?"

"No real reason." She pauses. Shrugs. "Thanks for the key chain. Sorry for talking about your butt in front of everyone."

"How did you know I'd need to make a phone call?"

"Everyone needs to call someone," she says, and walks out the door.

WE START THE next morning on the college's tennis court. Zoe's supposed to be teaching us the rules of the game so that we can play a friendly match. Her challenge is about remembering that tennis isn't just parent-mandated work.

It's also a game—one she happens to be really good at.

She does seem to be having fun, judging by the insults she's sending our way. "Afraid of the ball, Ice Princess?" she shouts at Jenna, who's just ducked away from a hard serve.

I watch as Andrew jogs over to Zoe. He puts his hands on her shoulders. Says something, staring her down. She nods, hands on hips. Says something back.

"He's so good with her," Yasmin says to Dr. Lancaster. They're standing a few feet away. My back is to them. I keep scooping up tennis balls into a bucket. I keep listening. "She responds to Andrew," Yasmin goes on. "I can't get her to say two civil words to me."

"Different campers need different types of interactions from authority figures," Dr. Lancaster says. "Zoe needs what Andrew offers. But you and Omar seem to have hit it off."

"He's a great kid. And we have performing in common."

"You told me Katie confides in you too."

"Yeah. She reminds me of my little sister."

I've been lingering near them too long. I'm out of tennis balls to pick up. I should move away. But I want to hear more. I want to hear whether they'll say anything about Andrew and me. Have they noticed the time he spends with me?

"Ballerina Barbie! Get over here!" Zoe yells. Reluctantly I jog in her direction. "Show 'em how it's done," she says, tossing me a racket. I fumble in catching it. I take one of the balls from my bucket. I throw it in the air and, almost entirely by luck, serve it over the net. "Yes!" Zoe crows. "Let's all do it like that, okay?"

She lines us up, each with a few balls, and has us practice serving. I throw, swing, hit. Throw, swing, hit. Throw, swing, hit. Some serves go into the net. A few sail over, like the first one.

I woke up this morning feeling lighter. Like jumping in the lake and then talking to Marcus helped me shed a thick, heavy layer of myself.

My challenge is next. I was anxious about it yesterday, and I should be even more anxious about it today. But I'm not. I'm the calmest I've been since arriving here. I'm actually optimistic. I haven't felt optimistic about anything in months.

And a lot of it's because of Andrew. Pushing me to push myself, last night. Meeting me as I came down the stairs today, black coffee in hand. Telling me I can get through anything. When he says it, I feel it. He makes me stronger. Better.

He lifts his hand, shading his eyes from the sun. The way he's lit right now, it's like he's glowing. Radiating. And when he smiles in my direction, it's hard to see anything else.

twenty-one

THE FIRST THING WE HAVE TO DO WHEN WE ENTER
the campus café's kitchen is put on aprons and chef hats.
Like, the tall white puffy hats you see in the movies. Then
we have to wash our hands. A lot. When I'm done scrub-
bing, Dr. Lancaster takes me into the pantry to speak in
private.

"Do you know why you're here, Sam?"

I look around at the shelves of cooking supplies. I felt
fine as we were walking here, but now the first tendrils of
anxiety are slithering in. "Because I have some, um, food
issues. But I don't see how——"

"Andrew tells me you've been helping him with breakfast in the mornings."

"Yeah. I'm usually up early, so I thought, why not pitch in?"

I don't mention that I'm up early because I don't want to

shower or get dressed with anyone else around. Or that I'm actually helping with breakfast to be with Andrew.

"But as we've discussed, you have a hard time eating a lot of what we serve."

I nod, wary. "This challenge is about cooking, right? Not . . . eating?"

"Do you feel better eating when you know all the components of your dish? When you can assemble it yourself? For instance, at a salad bar?"

"I guess so. Maybe."

"Do you tend to think of some foods as 'good' and others as 'bad'?"

That one's easy. "Yes."

"What if you knew what ingredients were in the 'bad' food? What if you knew how the same portion sizes of different foods compared, in terms of nutrition? Eating healthily doesn't have to mean stress and deprivation. Learning to cook can help you take back some of the power food has over you."

"Okay. . . ." Now I'm really feeling anxious. I want to get on with the challenge. Or skip it entirely. Dr. Lancaster leads me back into the kitchen. Everyone's waiting. So is a pan of lasagna.

How did she know?

Lasagna is one of my mom's biggest no-way foods. And I used to love it.

Make good choices, Samantha.

"Sam?" Dr. Lancaster puts her hand on my shoulder.

I find my words: "Do I have to eat that?"

"Not yet. First, you're going to learn how to prepare it." Dr. Lancaster introduces the middle-aged woman who will be leading the session. "This is Lisa. In addition to being one of my associate psychology professors, she teaches cooking classes as an elective in the health department."

"Thanks, Debra," Lisa says, stepping forward. "So, we're all going to make lasagna today. We'll eat some for lunch, and we'll donate the rest to the science department's all-faculty meeting tomorrow."

They can have it. I don't want it.

Yes, you do. You crave it. You want every last calorie.

Lisa sets each of us up at a station on the counter, complete with a cutting board, a knife, a lasagna pan, and a basket of vegetables and other ingredients. I'm right next to her. Andrew takes the spot on my other side. I try to focus on his calming presence, not how shaken up I feel.

"Rule number one!" Lisa booms. "No playing with knives. A knife is not a toy." She points at Zoe, who was already brandishing her chef's knife. Zoe smirks at her but puts the knife down. "Rule number two!" Lisa goes on. "Follow my instructions. I'm really not in the mood to get food poisoning today."

Dominic snorts. Katie laughs too, but when we make eye contact across the shiny metal counter, she mouths, *You okay?*

I nod.

"We'll begin by chopping our vegetables. We have carrots, eggplant, zucchini, and spinach. Everything but the spinach gets cut up." Lisa pulls out a carrot and begins slicing. Her cuts are fast and even.

"You're like an Iron Chef!" Omar says, sounding delighted.

Lisa beams. "I'll tell Bobby Flay you said so."

"I love the Food Network," Omar tells Dominic. "Do you ever watch *Chopped*?"

He shakes his head.

"It's this show where four chefs have to compete, but they don't find out the ingredients until the moment the challenge starts. . . ."

I tune him out. I tune all of it out. I select a zucchini. I begin cutting it slowly, methodically, into slices. I find myself counting as I go, under my breath. Twenty-three zucchini circles. The carrots are next. The first one makes seventeen slices, and the second makes twenty-six. The repetitive motion is nice. *Chop, chop, chop, chop.* I can almost forget that this is food.

But when we start layering noodles and sauce and cheese and veggies, it starts to look like the thing I'm dreading. I'm trying to follow instructions, but it's hard for me to put on as much cheese as Lisa wants. Even though it says "light" on the package, I keep trying to skimp. But Lisa catches me.

"Math problem!" she calls out. "How many servings are in this lasagna pan?"

I stare at it. "Um. Eight?"

"Wrong! Twelve." She indicates with her knife where the cuts will be. "How many calories are in this package of ricotta?"

I read the label and gulp. "Seven hundred." That's, like, an entire meal. I have to put the container down fast. I feel gross just touching it.

You are *gross. So disgusting*—

"What is seven hundred divided by twelve?"

"Uh." I flounder until Dominic rescues me:

"Fifty-eight and a third."

Katie gapes at him.

"What?" he says. "I'm good at math."

Lisa takes my chin with two fingers and tips my face up toward hers. "If we use one container of this ricotta on each layer of lasagna, that's just over a hundred and sixteen calories' worth of ricotta in a single serving. How do you feel about that?"

Mortified. I feel mortified. "Better, I guess."

"And what are these?" She shakes the pasta box at me.

"Whole-wheat noodles . . ."

"Right."

"So basically, this lasagna is going to taste like cardboard," Zoe cracks.

"I'm sorry, what was that?" Lisa asks Zoe, widening her eyes in mock horror.

"I said, this is going to taste like—"

"I *thought* you said you wanted to help me clean the

kitchen when we're done!"

"What? No!" Zoe steps away from the counter. "No way."

"It'll be good for you. Cleaning builds character."

When Lisa walks across the kitchen to check the oven temperature, Zoe flings a piece of carrot in her direction. It misses and lands between me and Andrew. I'm so keyed up that I don't stop to think about what I'm doing. I pick the bit of carrot up and throw it back at her.

Zoe looks from the carrot to me, a smile breaking across her face. "Oh, it's *on*."

"Zoe . . . ," Andrew starts, his tone a warning. Then he gets hit in the head with a piece of uncooked pasta.

"Twenty points to Slytherin!" Zoe spins and launches a slimy slice of eggplant at Jenna. It hits her bare arm and drops to the floor with a splat.

"Ew." Jenna wrinkles her nose. She lobs a slice of zuc-chini at Zoe in return.

"Guys, stop!" Yasmin shouts, but it's too late.

Omar throws a handful of spinach across the counter at Dominic, and Dominic tosses a globe of mozzarella at Katie, and Katie sends a lump of ricotta toward Jenna, and Zoe unscrews the lid to her jar of marinara and—

"Hey!" Dr. Lancaster shouts. Hearing her raise her voice is almost as surprising as the fact that we just had a food fight. A short food fight, sure. But it happened. And it was enough to release the tension inside me. For now.

I glance at Andrew. His mouth is twitching.

"It's all right," Lisa says dryly from her spot over by the ovens, where she watched the whole twenty-second drama unfold. "They've *all* just earned themselves kitchen cleaning jobs."

Everyone groans, but no one seems too upset.

We finish assembling our lasagnas and get them into the oven. Then Lisa doles out the chores. I'm put in charge of rinsing dirty dishes, Dominic gets handed a mop, Omar has to put away ingredients, Katie wipes down the countertops, Jenna sets the table for lunch, and Zoe has to take out the trash. Not just the trash we created over the past hour— yesterday's garbage, too. Zoe struggles past me, holding a giant bag at arm's length. It smells *terrible*.

Andrew stays next to me, loading items I've rinsed into the industrial-sized dishwasher. "How are you feeling?" he asks.

I spray down a bowl. "Weird."

"What do you mean?"

"I didn't love that—but I didn't have a panic attack. That's progress, right?"

"How do you think you would have done if this was your first day here?"

"A lot worse." I shudder and hand him the bowl.

"Then yes, I'd say today was progress."

"What was your individual challenge, when you were a camper?"

"Dr. Lancaster had me write down all the things my

coach and my dad and everyone else said to me, about football. Positive and negative. And then everyone read them at me while I ran passing drills."

"Wow. That sounds intense."

"It was. But after a few minutes of hearing it all together like that, it just became . . . noise." He takes a handful of wet silverware from me and drops it into the dishwasher. "I found a way to stop listening to the voices and get done what I needed to get done."

"Did you get upset?" No matter how much better I'm starting to feel, I'm pretty sure that I would have imploded in Andrew's situation.

"I got frustrated, sure. But it made me focus harder."

I rinse the last few dishes and then ask, "So do you think learning to cook is a good idea for me?" I know Dr. Lancaster's opinion on the matter, but now I want his.

"Well, you did buy that apron on Friday at the general store. Maybe it's fate."

I let out a puff of laughter. "Right, fate. But seriously. Will it make it easier for me to eat in front of people? You're a psych major—what do you think?"

"I don't know. So far, most of my coursework has been about history and theory—like, Freud's thoughts on human development versus Jung's versus Erikson's. I did take Abnormal Psychology last semester, but it was an overview of all the mental and emotional disorders out there. We didn't talk so much about treatment."

"Oh."

"I guess my question to you, as your peer adviser, would be: how do you feel, knowing we're about to eat that lasagna?"

I peel off my rubber gloves. I think of the look on my mom's face if she caught me with a plate of pasta. "Anxious. But maybe not as anxious as I should be."

"The whole point is that eating *shouldn't* make you anxious, Sam. Neither should looking at yourself in the mirror, or having other people look at you."

"But it does. All of it."

"I know." He smiles at me. And despite my nerves, his smile makes me feel warm inside. Whatever I think of myself, there's nothing wrong with me in his eyes.

He has a girlfriend.

He said they're having issues. He practically told me they're breaking up.

He's too old for you.

Four years isn't that big a deal, really.

You're a camper. He's a counselor.

I don't care.

When the lasagna comes out of the oven, sizzling and steaming, Lisa gives me the first plate. I cut a small sliver and blow on it to cool it. Everyone is watching me, waiting for the verdict. "Can you all, um, turn around?" I'll never get this bite down with their eyes on me.

Everyone turns except Zoe. She stares at me a few seconds too long before saying, "Oh, you mean right now?" Then she turns.

I open my mouth and I put the lasagna in and I chew. I suppress a moan of satisfaction. It is *so good*. The cheese is creamy and the veggies are tender and the sauce is bright and tart.

"Delicious," I say to the group. "And hot." I exhale steam.

"All right, folks—dig in!" Lisa says, slicing more squares.

I eat my entire serving in eleven bites. I use my fork to scoop up the sauce and spinach that remain on my plate. Then I push back from the table. I'm perfectly full. And I'm happy, too. I completed the challenge. I was anxious, and I still saw it through. When I look over at Andrew and see him smiling at me, I feel even better.

AS WE WALK back to the Perform at Your Peak house, Andrew stays beside me. I wish we were holding hands. I wish he had his arm around my waist.

Once I start thinking about his hands, his arms, I get this picture in my head of us dancing together. I bet he'd be a great dance partner. Strong, attentive, gentle.

I love partnering.

Or at least I used to. Before I gained fourteen pounds.

It isn't necessarily my fault I didn't get to do any pas de deux this year. After Bryce graduated, Theo was the only guy left in our senior company. He's really talented—but he's also shorter and skinnier than me. No way could he lift me more than a few inches off the ground.

But Andrew . . . I bet he could make me fly.

His voice cuts into my thoughts: "What's up? You're making a funny face."

"Nothing," I say, rearranging my features.

"Do you want to talk about it?"

"No, it's okay."

"Come on. I thought we were past that." He bumps my shoulder, and the tornado swirls up inside me, but instead of anxiety, it's all anticipation.

"I was thinking about partnering."

"Partnering?"

"Yeah, you know, when a guy and a girl dance together, and the guy lifts the girl—of course, it doesn't have to be a guy and a girl, it could be two guys or two girls, or a whole group—" I'm getting off track. "The point is, I miss it."

Floating through the air. Leaping farther than I could ever have leaped on my own. Turning faster, balancing longer. Feeling two bodies become one, shaping the space.

"Why do you miss it? What's stopping you from partnering?"

I gesture at my body.

Andrew looks me up and down. I try not to squirm.

"Okay," he says, his voice neutral. "You're gonna have to clue me in."

"There's no one at my studio who can lift me."

"You're kidding. What kind of scrawny guys do you have at that ballet school?"

That makes me laugh. "One. Not exactly a body builder."

"Huh. Well, I bet I could do one of your fancy ballet lifts

with you. And I barely do any weight training anymore."

I catch my breath. Move over, daydream. "Are you serious?"

He looks thoughtful. "I wasn't . . . but why not? I'll let you teach me some ballet lifts. I bet you ten dollars I can get you above my head." He glances at the rest of the group. "We should probably do it tonight. After curfew."

The two of us. Alone together. Dancing.

I can't wait.

twenty-two

DIY GRILLED-CHEESE SANDWICHES. THAT'S WHAT greets me when I step into the kitchen at dinnertime. The buffet is filled with fixings. The scent of butter and melted cheese and bacon and onions drifts through the air. I stop in the doorway, and Zoe runs right into my back.

"What's the matter, Ballerina Barbie? Can't handle the cheesy goodness?"

"Shut up," I say. But I don't move forward into the kitchen.

Zoe goes around me. "Good comeback."

I'm not in the mood to think of a better one. Not when my stomach is doing pirouettes from my chat with Andrew earlier—and from the food in front of me.

Yasmin is at the stove. "Pick your bread, cheese, and whatever else you want," she says. "I'll do the rest."

"Actually, can I make mine myself?" I ask.

"I'm having sourdough and low-fat cheddar with turkey bacon." Jenna comes into the kitchen from the dining room. "If you need some inspiration."

Her words startle me. Why did she say that? Did she notice I've been copying her meals?

"Sounds good," I say quickly.

It does sound good. But I decide to test my new skills and build my own sandwich. I get multigrain bread and top it with a single slice of low-fat cheddar. I add fresh tomatoes and onions and spinach. When I count up the calories, it's not bad at all, so I decide I can have a swipe of butter on each side to help toast the bread. I stand at the grill, spatula in hand, until my sandwich is browned to perfection.

And when I sit down at the table, I'm able to eat it.

Sure, it will probably be harder in a dance environment. Or with my mom. But right now, I'm eating something I made myself, and it tastes great.

"So, Sam . . ." I look up from my last bite to see Katie giving me a mischievous smile. "What's up with you and Andrew?"

I blush as red as the tomatoes on my sandwich. "Nothing. Why?"

"I don't know, it seems like you two spend a lot of time *talking*. . . ." Katie puts extra emphasis on that last word.

"He's helping me work some stuff out."

"Work stuff out?" Jenna asks, looking skeptical.

"Anxiety stuff."

"Right."

"He's definitely cute," Katie says, sneaking a glance over her shoulder at Andrew, who's in the kitchen with Yasmin. "And he's funny, and nice, and—"

"And a lot older than you," Jenna cuts in.

"He's in college, not a nursing home," I say. "Not that it matters."

"You like him," Jenna says. It's a statement, not a question. "Does he like you?"

I open my mouth and shut it again.

"Well, I think it's awesome," Katie declares. "A summer romance." She crosses her hands over her heart. "I've never had a boyfriend. Have you?"

"Yeah. We broke up before I came here."

"So you're on the rebound," Jenna says, cocking her head to one side.

"Not exactly." I don't know how to explain the connection I feel with Andrew, so I try to deflect attention away from myself. "Are you dating anyone, Jenna?"

"No. I am currently single."

"Sam and Andrew, together—it's so exciting!" Katie squeals.

"It's really not anything . . . ," I say. But I know my face has given me away.

Jenna shakes her head. "Fine. Enjoy your flirtation. Just—" She stops, checking herself. "Never mind. Don't listen to me. Have fun."

Zoe plops down next to me. "Have fun with what?"

"Sam was thinking about taking a walk after dinner." The lie flows seamlessly out of Jenna's mouth. "But I told her it was going to rain."

"Oh. Yeah, you should probably skip the wet T-shirt contest," Zoe says, taking a big bite of her sandwich.

I mouth *Thanks* at Jenna. After the way Zoe teased me about our private therapy files last night, she's the last person I want to know about me and Andrew.

He enters the dining room and I let myself stare at him for a second. I take in his broad shoulders and the way his sandy hair is complemented by the color of his polo shirt—burnt orange today, the color of a summer sunrise.

We have a date tonight.

No. You don't.

My inner voice doesn't sound convinced.

He walks over to our table. "Sam, your mom left a message while we were out."

"She did?" I should have known she couldn't make it a week without calling.

"She wanted us to let you know she left a message with your ballet intensive to make sure you're officially registered to start a week late. She or your ballet teacher will call here when they have confirmation that you're good to go."

"Oh. Great." I pause. "Did Mom want me to call her back?"

"No. She said she'll speak to you on Saturday—unless

she hears something sooner."

I'm so relieved. Nothing can spoil my night.

ANDREW AND I are supposed to meet at the back door at twelve thirty. I wait until I'm pretty sure Zoe is asleep to toss back the covers and swing my legs over the side of the bed. I went to bed wearing black yoga pants and a black tank top. Now I pull on a black long-sleeved shirt in case it's chilly outside.

I'm opening the door when Zoe sits up in bed. "Where are you going?"

"Bathroom," I whisper.

"Why are you wearing a different shirt than before?"

"I got cold. Why do you care what I'm wearing?"

"It's, like, a hundred degrees in here." She flops back down onto her pillow.

I wait to see whether she's going to say anything else, and then I leave.

I do go to the bathroom—partly because I have a little time to kill and partly because if Zoe follows me, I want her to find me in here. I run my fingers through my hair and pull it into a loose ponytail. I put cover-up on the two zits that have appeared in the middle of my chin, and I apply a little mascara. I stare at my reflection. I look . . . I look okay. Pretty good, even.

When it's 12:32, I head downstairs, carrying my sneakers and walking silently on the carpet. I round the corner at the bottom of the staircase and tiptoe to the kitchen.

When Andrew sees me, he smiles. "You look like a cat burglar."

Is that a good thing? Does he think my all-black outfit is sexy, or ridiculous?

"Thanks."

"Ready?"

I nod.

He slips a key into the lock. "Yasmin's giving us an hour. She's reading in the Dogwood Room. She'll text me if anything happens here."

"You told Yasmin?"

"I needed backup. Don't worry. She knows nothing's really going on."

For a moment, I'm crushed. But then I realize: of course he has to tell her that.

"Any problems with Zoe?"

"She's asleep." I hope she stays that way.

"Good. Then let's do this."

We go out to the gazebo—not far from the house, in case we need to get back fast, but mostly out of view of the bedroom windows. We should be safe. Still, as we jog through the grass, wet from the evening's rain shower, I keep looking behind me. I can't shake the feeling that all the lights in the building are going to turn on at the same time, the windows bright and blazing, to catch us in the act. But it doesn't happen. We walk up the painted wood stairs and set our flashlights on the benches so the beams point in toward us.

"So. How do we do this?" Andrew asks.

"I need to warm up a little first."

"Go for it."

I squat down in a wide second position, feeling my hamstrings lengthen. I shift from side to side, stretching out first one leg and then the other. Then I drop down into a straddle split and lean forward until my stomach touches the wooden floor.

"You're really flexible." Andrew says.

"Not really. This one girl at my studio, Becca, could moonlight as a contortionist."

"Come on. I can barely touch my toes," Andrew says. "See?"

I push up onto my elbows. Andrew is bending over, knees nowhere near straight, fingertips brushing the floor. When he sees me looking, he twists his face like the stretch is killing him. Then he sits and pulls his legs into the worst butterfly stretch I've ever seen. His knees point toward the ceiling and his back is hunched, like he's Quasimodo.

"How long did it take you to be able to do that?" he asks.

I move into a butterfly stretch that's like his in name only; when I press the soles of my feet together, my knees rest on the floor. "I've always been pretty flexible. And I've danced for ten years. Every day after school, and for a few weeks every summer."

"You're pretty hard-core."

That makes me smile. I *am* hard-core. Ballet dancers are super hard-core. But it's not often that football players—or anyone else who runs and jumps and throws and catches a ball—recognize how hard dancers work. "Thanks."

"You're welcome. Though maybe being too hard-core is part of the problem?"

My smile drops away. "We're moving right into 'therapy' mode, then?"

"I just meant, maybe taking some time off to be here, and giving yourself a break now and then the rest of the year, might not be such a bad thing. That's it."

"Being hard-core is the only way I'll make it as a dancer, with my body. If I try any less, I'll keep getting fatter and fatter, and then I'll be nowhere."

"You're not fat," Andrew says.

"I am."

"No, Sam, you're not."

It's a Wild West standoff. High noon instead of the middle of the night. I can practically see the tumbleweeds blowing between us.

He's the first to break. "If I can't change your mind, let's get to this partnering thing. Turn me into a *dancer*." He exaggerates the word—*don-suh*—and gets to his feet.

I stand too. "First, we should just see if you can even lift me. Trying anything more advanced won't work if I'm too heavy—"

Before I even finish my sentence, he's scooped me up, one arm behind my back and the other behind my knees. "Done." He bounces me up and down in his arms a few times. "You're about to owe me ten bucks. I take cash or credit."

I relax into his arms. And then I feel incredibly awkward, so I wriggle free and drop to the ground, stumbling to stay on my feet. Not my most graceful moment.

"Okay, Baryshnikov," I say. "Why don't we start with a basic assisted sauté."

"What's a so-tay?"

I step toward him. Stand in front of him, facing away. Try to quiet the pounding in my chest. "Put your hands here." I pat my sides, and then I feel his hands resting lightly in the same spots. "I'm going to jump, and you'll lift me."

"Sounds easy enough." His breath tickles my neck. It reminds me of the blindfold exercise last week, when he helped me knot the bandanna at the back of my head.

"So I'll go one, two, three—and bend my knees—and then jump on four."

"Okay."

I count us off. I jump, lifting my arms into fifth position, pointing my feet, squeezing my thighs together, holding my core muscles strong. My fingers almost touch the gazebo ceiling. Andrew puts me down a little hard, but otherwise—it worked. And it felt *great*.

"Again?" I say. "Try to help me not crash down to the floor, okay?"

"Got it."

I count, and jump, and float. This time I'm able to roll through my feet and bend my knees to cushion the landing. No thud. "Good!" I'm getting excited—and it isn't just Andrew's touch. I haven't been lifted like this in *so long*.

"Want to try a leap and carry?"

"Sure. Whatever that is."

"I'll prepare like this—" I take two small running steps toward him. "And then I'll leap and you'll use the momentum to carry me forward. As far as you can; it's not like we have a lot of room here."

"So I just stand here and catch you?"

"No, you take those two steps behind me. This is me being you." I demonstrate his part, even miming lifting myself and putting me down.

He's nodding. "Okay."

We try it. The first one isn't great, but the second one is better, and the one after that is even better. Andrew isn't graceful, but he's strong. And he listens. When I tell him he's squeezing me too tight, and not to grip me with his fingertips, he lets go really fast and waits for me to show him how much pressure to use. When he doesn't count off the timing properly, he wants to do it again right away to fix it. Maybe it's the sports discipline, or maybe it's just Andrew's personality, but even in his first and probably last ballet lesson, he's taking it seriously.

It only makes me like him more.

I don't have any idea what we look like—we might look horrible, probably *do* look horrible—but I'm walking on air. I've missed this so much. Touching the sky. Hovering above the ground for a second before I land. It's amazing.

"Let's try a fish dive."

"A fish dive?" Andrew cracks up. "Is that, like, a seafood

restaurant that makes you puke?"

I laugh louder than I mean to. "No, um, I'll go into arabesque in front of you. Like this." I lift my left leg behind me and extend my right arm forward. It's a position that feels as natural as breathing. And yet I'm having trouble breathing with him standing there. "You'll put one arm under my leg and the other around my waist, okay?"

He does, being careful about where he grabs me. It's not just that he's trying not to hold me too tight. He's staying far, *far* away from any . . . delicate areas.

"Like this?"

"Yeah. But you're going to have to, um, pull my body against yours. So the weight isn't all in your arms. Ready?"

His grip tightens around me. "Ready."

I pick up my standing leg and point my right toe toward my left knee. "Okay. Now dip me."

"Do what?"

"Dip me."

"Fish, dip—you're making me hungry."

"Just . . . bend me forward so my leg goes up and my body goes down, and— You know what? Put me down."

He does.

I mimic the guy's position in the lift, holding my own imaginary ballerina, and show him the dip. "Once you have me in the pose, you bend your knee like this and lean this way."

"Got it." He repeats the move a few times. "Wanna try again?"

"Yeah." I get into position. He lifts me. And then, as if he's been training for years, he dips me and brings me back up.

"I think I'm pretty good at this partnering thing."

"You're a natural." I drop my bottom foot to stand on it again. When he lets go, I miss being in his arms. I miss having my back pressed against his chest.

"Having fun?" he asks.

"Yes," I say fervently. "Thank you."

"Then let's do another one."

I wonder whether he's having fun too. Whether he wants to hold me again, like I want to be held.

When his phone alarm goes off to signal the end of our hour, he has me in a shoulder-sit lift. I jump down and we rest, side by side, on one of the wooden benches. We're so close, I can feel the sweat soaking through his T-shirt. I don't move away. Neither does he. We're still and silent for a second, staring toward the house. That second feels like an eternity. I don't want this eternity to end.

He stands up, and it's like he's being ripped away from me. He extends his hand to help me to my feet, and I take it like I'm drowning and he's my life preserver. When he lets go, I can't stop feeling the absence of his touch.

I sneak back into my room and pick up the dark chocolate Hershey's Kiss he gave me a week ago. I've kept it in the drawer in my nightstand this whole time. I peel away the delicate aluminum foil. I run my fingers over the chocolate's smooth surface. I breathe in the sweet scent. And then, before I can think too much about calories or what time it is or anything else, I pop it in my mouth. I let it melt. Slowly.

I fall asleep with the forbidden taste of chocolate on my tongue.

twenty-three

THE NEXT MORNING, I CAN'T STOP THINKING ABOUT Andrew. His eyes catching the moonlight. His bright smile turned intimate, like it was designed especially for me. His hands on my waist, our bodies pressed together. Did he feel the sparks I felt? Is he thinking about me the way I'm thinking about him?

And where do we go from here? What happens next?

Physically, I'm in the college's theater, watching Omar stammer through a monologue onstage. Mentally—and emotionally—I'm still in that gazebo.

"Are we supposed to heckle him or something?" Katie asks from my left.

"There's no way," Jenna answers from my right.

"So how are we supposed to be involved in the challenge?" Katie whispers. "With everyone else's, we all did stuff."

"Not with mine," Jenna answers. "You just watched me."

"Oh yeah."

They're talking around me. Through me. Normally I'd hate it, but right now, I'm grateful. Andrew is a few rows in front of us, sitting with Dominic, and I'm enjoying admiring the back of his head.

"'To be, or not to be—'" Omar intones from center stage.

"No, no, no!" One of the fake scouts from Dominic's challenge is now playing a theater director, calling instructions at Omar from the audience. "More introspective."

Omar repeats the line once. Twice. Three times. He starts pacing. Rubbing his head like it hurts. "I don't know what you want. What am I supposed to do here? What do I do? I don't know what to do!"

"Try taking a deep breath," Dr. Lancaster coaches from the front row.

He gasps and then yelps, "'To be, or not to be!' Was that better?"

"It's not about the quality of your acting," Dr. Lancaster says. "It's about how you feel in this moment."

"Agh!" Omar moans, pacing faster. "I feel anxious! And this isn't even real! Why am I anxious when this isn't even real?"

Andrew turns to say something to Dominic. I trace his profile with my eyes.

I want to dance with him again. I want to do more than that.

Back in the Dogwood Room an hour later, Dr. Lancaster asks us what we're most nervous about, when it comes to leaving here. My first thought: not seeing Andrew every day. And yeah, I know I have bigger concerns than that. But after last night . . .

Jenna starts talking about her upcoming competitions. "Regionals and Sectionals are in just a few months," she says. "I didn't break the top five at Nationals last year, so I have to make top four at Sectionals to qualify this year, and the competition—it's a tough field." She shakes her head. "I'm seventeen. There are girls Katie's age who are hitting their routines more consistently than I am."

"You made it to Nationals last year," Katie says.

"And then I fell on three jumps in my long program, in front of a bunch of TV cameras," Jenna says, her voice turning bitter. "You saw the footage."

"So this season, you'll take things one event at a time," Dr. Lancaster says patiently. "You won't make Nationals into a dark specter that's looming in the distance. You'll focus on yourself and not your competitors. You'll remember to trust your training. And you'll breathe."

"Of course I will," Jenna says. She reaches up and yanks her ponytail tighter.

"Why don't we spend some time before lunch crafting power statements?" Dr. Lancaster looks around at the group. "Power statements are mantras you can tell yourself when you're having a rough time." She starts writing ideas on the whiteboard.

"I have what it takes!"

"I've worked hard to get here!"

"I always do my best!"

"The most important thing is to try!"

When she sends us away with our notebooks, I chase after Andrew. "Want to take a walk? Help me brainstorm?"

"Sure."

We start across the lawn. We pass the gazebo and head down the path into the woods until we reach the lake. In the late-morning light, the water is a clear, vivid blue. There are ducks and geese calling, and in the distance, I can see people canoeing.

Andrew walks to the end of the dock and sits, feet hanging toward the water. "We should sneak back out here tonight," he says. "It's supposed to rain every night next week, so this might be our last chance."

"I'd love to." I sit next to him. "Same time and everything?"

"Yeah. Can you rally the troops?"

I nod.

"So let's brainstorm. Do you want your power statement to be something about your performance? Or how you look?"

"Ugh, I guess it should be about my body. Right?"

"If your body is what causes you to panic, then probably." He pauses. "And you need to stop thinking about your body as 'ugh.'"

I let out a nervous laugh. "Sorry, I didn't even realize I said that."

"Don't beat yourself up about it. It's hard to change your mental patterns. And I think you're saying stuff like that less than you were even a week ago, so that's good."

"Yeah, I'm trying—"

"Because you're *not* fat, or ugly, or whatever you think about yourself."

"I—"

He takes me by both shoulders. "Really. You're not."

Another nervous laugh escapes. "Well, I'm certainly not beautiful."

"Yes, you are." He looks thoughtful. "You're beautiful. That could be part of your power statement."

As if this moment is just about a power statement. I can't move, I can't breathe, I can't think. All I can do is stare into Andrew's eyes.

"Try this: 'My body is flexible, and strong, and beautiful.'"

"My body is flexible, and strong, and . . . and beautiful." I choke on that last part.

Liar.

"My body is flexible, and strong, and beautiful," Andrew repeats.

"My body is flexible, and strong, and beautiful." I'm able to say it more firmly, and this time there's no answer in my head.

"That's not so hard, is it?"

"It's easier to say than to believe."

"Believe it." He lets go of my shoulders and faces the lake again. I stare at him, unable to pick out one emotion from the storm inside me.

Marcus never told me I was beautiful. Pretty or cute or hot, depending on his mood and what I was wearing, but not *beautiful*. Having heard it from Andrew, I don't think I can ever go back.

I have no idea how to respond.

Luckily, Andrew doesn't ask me to say anything. He lies down on the dock, tucking his hands behind his head and closing his eyes.

I look down at him. His handsome face. The sliver of skin I can see where his polo has come untucked from his khakis. He kicks his feet as they dangle off the edge of the dock, like a little kid. I lie down next to him. I put my hands behind my head too. Our elbows touch, but he doesn't move his, so I don't move mine.

I feel like I'm in this perfect space. It's only the width of a soap bubble—strongly bonded, but liable to burst at any moment. I don't want it to burst. So I stay inside it, letting the sun's rays warm my skin and Andrew's words warm my heart.

DR. LANCASTER CAN tell something is different about me. "You seem happy today," she says. "Anything special going on that you want to share?"

Yes.

"Nothing in particular."

"Are you looking forward to going to your ballet intensive?"

"Yeah, I'm really excited." Only ten days until I'm there. No phone call from my mom or Miss Elise yet, confirming my spot, but I'm not worried.

"Do you feel like you've picked up some skills over the past week and a half that you can put into practice in the dance studio?"

I nod. "I can try some of Yasmin's breathing exercises when I start feeling anxious. I've tried them once already, after . . . after the last time I talked to my mom. I was feeling wound up, and breathing actually helped me calm down."

Dr. Lancaster doesn't ask what my mom had me wound up about, but I know she's filing that bit of info away for later. "Good. What else?"

"Um. I think I want to do more cooking when I get home. That's not something for the ballet studio, but I guess for life."

"Wonderful."

"And maybe I'll take art in school next year?" I add, thinking about my photo collages. My mom might not like it, since art isn't in my career plan, but maybe if I say it's for therapy, she'll back down.

"All of this is excellent. How about when you're in a situation where you need to push past any anxious or panicky feelings and perform? Did you come up with a power statement that might help you?"

I take a deep breath and spit out the mantra Andrew created for me: "My body is flexible, and strong, and beautiful."

Dr. Lancaster looks impressed. She lets my words dance in the silence for a few seconds before speaking. "Wow, Sam. Do you think you could have said that when you came here?"

I answer honestly. "No. And I'm not sure I really believe it yet. But . . . maybe I could. One day. I mean, I believe the first two parts, but not . . ."

"'Beautiful' is a powerful word," she says.

"Yeah."

I can't tell Dr. Lancaster about Andrew. Not yet—when I don't know for certain that he feels about me the way I feel about him. Maybe not ever, since he's a peer adviser here. I don't want him to get in trouble.

I can't tell her about the way he held me in the moonlight.

I can't tell her that the word "beautiful" came from him, not me.

But I do wish I could tell her how he listens to me and hears me and understands. How he *sees* me, maybe even better than I see myself. He's good for me, I'm certain of it, and if I hadn't come to Perform at Your Peak, I never would've met him.

"I'm glad I came here," I say instead. It's a surprise to me, and I think it's a surprise to Dr. Lancaster, too. She looks thrilled.

"I'm glad you're glad, Sam." She makes a note on her ever-present legal pad. "Next week, we'll be focusing a lot on the future. In fact, our end-of-camp ritual has everything to do with your hopes for your future. I ask each camper to write down something positive about his or her experience here, tie it to a helium balloon, and set it free over the lake."

I can picture it, the six of us watching our balloons float higher and higher. I want to write *My body is flexible, and strong, and beautiful* a hundred times and send up a hundred balloons.

"Since you'll be going straight from here to your ballet intensive," Dr. Lancaster continues, "I hope you'll give your full attention to everything we discuss about moving forward. You'll get to put it into practice almost immediately."

"Okay," I say, still imagining my flock of balloons vanishing into the clouds.

"You're talented and ambitious, and there's no reason to let poor body image hold you back from achieving your full potential."

"Right." Almost exactly what Andrew said two nights ago, at the lake: *You can't let how you feel about your body ruin your life.*

"There are opportunities out there for you in the dance world. You have to be willing to chase them. You have to be willing to take the leap."

"Take the leap," I repeat. "How?"

"When you want something, and you believe in yourself and in it, but there's a gulf you have to cross to get there—in this case, how you've been feeling about the changes to your body—sometimes you have to just decide to leap across that gulf."

"Take the leap. I like it." I know she's talking about ballet, but I'm still thinking about Andrew. Maybe it's time for me to take the leap into what I think could be a really wonderful thing. Not just for me. For both of us.

I keep repeating Dr. Lancaster's words to myself for the rest of the day. I think them as Jenna and I do an afternoon ballet barre together, as my spine bends and stretches and my toes reach toward the sky. I murmur them as all six of us Crazy Campers relax on the couches after dinner. I tell them to my reflection as I wash my face and brush my teeth before bed. I write them in my notebook, over and over, while Zoe and I wait for midnight to arrive so we can sneak back out to the lake.

"Do you want to go down to Dr. Lancaster's office again tonight?" I ask Zoe, closing my notebook and setting it on my nightstand.

"Got another important phone call to make?"

"I need to send an email." I've decided I have to tell Bianca what's going on. There has to be someone in my life who knows the whole story. And if I start by telling Bianca about Andrew—about how he makes me feel—then I can work my way back and tell her about everything else. The reasons I've been so . . . not myself. I can apologize for shutting her out. For taking her friendship and support for granted.

"Sure," Zoe says. "Sounds good."

"Thanks." Knowing I'm about to come clean with my best friend—it makes me even more excited. And anxious, but the *good* kind of anxious.

I feel like I've been on a roller coaster since I got here, and now I'm racing toward the final loop. It's up to me to keep the momentum going. And I want to keep circling. I want to go up and up and up.

twenty-four

I'M FLOATING ON MY BACK, WATCHING THE CLOUDS blow across the sky. They hide the moon and the stars. Change the night's deep blue to a deep gray. It's darker tonight than it was on Tuesday, and I'm glad for the flashlights Andrew and Yasmin brought. They're positioned on the dock like spotlights, pointing out over the water. They light up the area where we're swimming, but the rest of the lake is a dark void.

Yasmin is singing, accompanying herself on the guitar. It's a soulful ballad I don't recognize, and I wonder whether she wrote it herself. Her voice ebbs and flows like the water lapping around my head. A lyric jumps out at me: "our fingers intertwined like vines, yours and mine, catching the sunshine." I like that image. I picture myself walking with Andrew, holding hands. It makes me smile.

When I'm tired of floating, I paddle over to the dock and

climb up. I wrap my towel around my body fast. I'm still not ready to sit there in only my swimsuit.

Baby steps.

Jenna swims over to join me. As she hoists her body up onto the deck, her tankini shifts, revealing a wider swath of midriff. And something else, on her hip bone, peeking out over the top of her swimsuit bottoms. A row of thin, raised scars. Spaced so uniformly apart, it's like they were drawn in with a ruler. Jenna moves the flashlight as she comes to sit next to me, and without the light hitting them, I can't see the scars anymore. But I know what I saw. I can guess what it means.

Jenna looks at my face, then down at her swimsuit bottoms, and immediately puts her hand across her hip.

"Oh," she says.

"I'm sorry. I didn't mean to . . ."

"It's fine."

I can tell by her voice and her expression that it's not fine. She sounds like cold, brittle Jenna from day one. Not the girl who's finally begun to thaw toward me, toward this place.

"I'm sorry," I say again.

"I don't want to talk about it."

"Okay."

Katie shrieks as Dominic picks her up and throws her into the lake, over Omar's head. Zoe swims so far away from the dock that Andrew calls for her to come back. Behind us, Yasmin switches to a happier-sounding tune, something about falling in love on a rainy summer afternoon. Jenna and I sit side by side in silence.

Seeing those scars has me thinking about my secrets. The things I don't want to talk about. The things I wish I could erase from my own memory.

But then Andrew swims over, climbs onto the deck, and starts toweling himself off, and it's hard to think about anything other than him. The T-shirt he pulls on, damp and clinging to his skin. His wet hair sticking out in all directions. His smile. He sits next to me. He claps when Yasmin finishes her song. I clap too.

One by one, the others join us on the dock. We chat as we dry out in the warm air. Soon the conversation turns to horror stories. Not like the movies Zoe watches—our own, real-life horrors. It's Omar's fault. He tells us about the time he fell flat on his face playing Gavroche in a local production of *Les Mis*. He was climbing the barricades, missed his footing, and tumbled down. "They had to stop the whole play because my nose was pouring blood." Omar laughs. "It was *everywhere*."

"Dude, that's gross," Dominic says, giving him a high five. "But I've got you beat. I puked my guts out on the fifty-yard line in front of a college scout."

"Ew!" Katie squeals.

"What happened?" Zoe asks, leaning forward.

Dominic frowns. "Like you care."

"I care, okay?"

Dominic sighs. "Whatever. It's a short story. My coach

invited the recruiter from Florida State—my top choice—
and I pushed so hard to impress the guy that I guess I got
dehydrated. I booted all over the field."

"That is gross," Jenna says, "but I can top it."

"Oh yeah?" Dominic says.

"I once got so anxious before a competition that I threw
up during the practice skate," she tells us. "Two words: frozen vomit."

We all groan.

"It had to be scraped off the ice. They had to postpone
the start to clean it up." Her face falls. "That was probably
one of my lowest points." She meets my eyes, then looks
away, and I think again about what I just saw. The scars on
her hip.

I shift a half centimeter closer to Andrew, for courage, and speak. "I've never gotten a bloody nose or puked
onstage, but I can tell you an embarrassing story."

"Bring it, Ballerina Barbie," Zoe says.

"There was this older girl at my studio, Eliana Diaz.
She's with The Washington Ballet now. When I was a freshman and she was a senior, she kind of took me under her
wing. She called me her protégé. Gave me private coaching.
I was the only freshman she did that for, and it made me feel
so special." Everyone knew Eliana Diaz was going places, so
if she thought I was going places too, then clearly I was.

"Fast forward to this past spring. The Washington Ballet's tour was passing through Tennessee. My mom bought
tickets, and I emailed Eliana to tell her I'd be in the audience.

She wrote right back and said she'd meet me by the stage door afterward. She'd introduce me to her friends in the company."

Bianca had a family reunion that weekend, so even though she'd already gotten into The Washington School of Ballet's summer intensive, she wasn't able to go with me to see the company. That turned out to be a good thing.

"After the show, I waited outside for half an hour. And then there she was. But it was like Eliana didn't recognize me. She saw me, and she clearly knew it was me, but she wasn't seeing the person she thought she'd be seeing—if that makes sense."

I remember her eyes widening, her long lashes blinking a few times, her lips drawing together. And then a pasted-on stage smile.

"She walked over and said, 'Hi . . . Samantha, right? Do you want me to sign your program?' I was too mortified to do anything but hand it to her. While she was signing it, her friends from the company showed up. One of them was like 'Oh, is this the girl you were telling us about? Your Mini-Me?' Eliana said, 'No, that's someone else. But Samantha also dances at the school where I trained growing up.' And she handed me back my program and said, 'Thanks for coming!' and walked off."

"That is messed up," Dominic says emphatically.

"Yeah, beats my bloody nose," Omar admits.

"It's awful," Yasmin agrees, "but you know she was being a snob—right?"

"I guess."

I never told Bianca what Eliana did. It occurs to me that since they're both in DC right now, I probably should. I make a mental note to add it to tonight's email.

"So beat *that*," I finish, looking around at the group.

"I can top it," Zoe says right away. But then she goes quiet. Her silence feels charged. It's the calm before the lightning strike. The buzz before the bug zapper takes another victim. Zoe looks in my direction. I wait to be zapped. But all she says is, "I don't really think your problems are stupid. I get that you're having issues. I just get so mad. At all of you."

"Mad at us?" Katie says softly. "Why?"

"You're so freaking lucky, and you don't even know it."

"Lucky?" I echo. "You want to feel the way I feel? You can have it. I'm built completely wrong to do the thing that I love most in the world, and every day"—I let out a long breath—"every day it breaks my heart."

"At least you know what you love," Zoe shoots back. "Hearing you talk makes me so jealous. I practice and work out so I can get better at the thing I hate. My parents are only happy with me when I do well at this thing I hate. I'm bored, and I'm exhausted, and when I go home, they're gonna expect me to jump in like nothing's changed, and—"

She wipes at her eyes.

"I'm not like you guys. You love what you do. You love it so much, it makes you crazy, and that's a problem, but it's also incredible. I want to love something that much."

"Why do you hate tennis?" Katie asks.

"God, so many reasons. I've done it since I was five. I'm not saying I know everything, but . . . I kind of feel like I know everything. I want to learn something new. And I don't know what that is yet, so I want to try lots of things. I want to find something I love doing, not just something I'm good at. And tennis takes up so much freaking time! I leave school early so I can get in extra tennis practice. I've missed every school dance for tennis, either for practice or because I had to get up early for a match the next day, and my parents didn't want me to be too tired. I don't have any friends who don't play tennis. I have friends at school, kind of, but we don't hang out. Everyone hangs out without me. And my parents—"

She breaks off, and I remember her face when she tried to get sent home and they'd refused to come get her. The catch in her voice: *They said no.*

"I hate being their little trophy winner. They make me feel like without tennis, I'm worthless." She turns to Andrew. "But I have to be worth *something* more than this thing I don't even like doing—right?"

"Of course you're worth something," Andrew says. "You'll find the thing you love. If your parents truly care about you, they'll support you on that journey."

Zoe doesn't look convinced. "Just because your dad eventually came around doesn't mean my parents ever will. They genuinely think I'm going to be the next Serena Williams."

"Remember what we talked about," Andrew says, and they share a look I can't decipher. I move even closer to him, feeling territorial.

"So what would you want to do, if you didn't play tennis?" Yasmin asks.

"I don't know. Professional poker? Astrology? Or curling—that sport where they sweep the ice with brooms?"

"You could take up pizza tossing," Katie says.

"I could." Zoe nods. "Or I could sing opera."

"Can you sing?" Jenna asks.

"Nope. But why should I let that stop me?"

"Dream big," Dominic says.

Andrew checks his watch. "I hate to break this up, but we should head back."

And then we're all a shuffle of movement, finding cover-ups and shoes, squeezing water out of shorts and T-shirts, bumping into one another on the narrow dock.

I don't want the night to end. And when I look at Andrew and he smiles at me, I think maybe he doesn't want it to end, either. The group starts walking away, and I chant Dr. Lancaster's advice to myself: Take the leap. Take the leap. Take the leap.

I gather every bit of courage I have and touch Andrew's arm. "Hey."

"Hey, yourself."

"Can we hold back a second?"

He looks after the others. "Sure, Sam. What's up?"

I wait until the last member of our group disappears down the path. I can still hear their voices, but I can't see anyone. Which means they can't see us.

I'm so, so nervous. Do I just . . . ask him? How? *So,*

Andrew, do you like me as much as I like you? Should we do something about that?

"Um," I say, stalling. The moon breaks from behind the clouds, and the light catches his face just right. I see the scar on his chin. "How'd you get that scar? Football?"

He laughs at the question. "Sledding crash."

"Sledding?"

"Yeah. I was nine. It was the first good snowstorm we'd had my entire life—like six inches—and so me and my buddies decided to go sledding. But we didn't have sleds. Why would we? We'd never seen real snow."

"Never seen real snow?" I tease. "You're from Georgia, not the Sahara."

"I'd seen snow. Just not, you know, accumulation. You gonna let me finish?"

"Sorry. Go on."

"We took the lids off some trash cans and went to the top of the hill at the end of my neighborhood. Got in and pushed off. Turns out trash can lids are hard to steer. Mine went sideways, out of control, and I hit a bump and flipped. Cut my chin on the curb."

"Ow!"

"No kidding. I cried like a baby. My friends never let me live it down." He grins. "Is that really what you wanted to ask me?"

"Oh. No. I just, um." I take a step closer. I feel his body tense up, even though we aren't touching. He suddenly looks as nervous as I feel.

I want him to kiss me. I want that *so much*.

But he doesn't move. He stands completely still.

"Sam," he says softly. "I don't think—"

Take the leap.

I rise up onto my tiptoes and touch my lips to his. It's everything I'd imagined—until I realize he isn't kissing me back. In fact, he's pushing me away from him. Backing up. Hands lifted to ward me off. Face pleading.

"Sam, I don't—I'm not sure—why—I didn't mean to give you the wrong idea—"

I blink at him, trying to process what he's saying.

"I told you, I have a girlfriend. And I'm your peer adviser—your counselor. And—we can forget this ever happened, right?"

Forget. Right.

I want to melt into a puddle and seep into the ground. I want to jump in the lake and stay underwater. For once in my life, I want to be so, so heavy.

"Sam? Please say something."

There are no words. I run.

I HIDE BEHIND the gazebo, gasping for air. I'm crying and panting and I have my hand clapped over my mouth like that will keep the sounds inside me.

Stupid, stupid, stupid—

I don't understand.

He rejected you. What else is there to understand?

But I thought—

You thought wrong.

Andrew runs by, calling my name. I duck farther into the shadows. I watch him slow to cross the lawn. His shoulders are slumped. His feet scuff at the ground. He looks broken and sad, and I want to hug him and make it better except that clearly he doesn't want that, not from me, anyway, and how could I have been so—

Stupid.

Naive.

Delusional.

Weak.

Ugly.

Fat.

Disgusting.

And on and on. Eventually, when he's long gone, I go inside. I close the back door behind me and walk through the kitchen and up the stairs and down the hall and into my bedroom.

"There you are!" Zoe is sitting up in bed.

I don't answer.

"I noticed you and Andrew stayed behind. . . ."

I don't answer.

"Are you two hooking up? I wouldn't have pegged you as the hook-up-with-a-counselor type, but . . ."

I don't answer. I change into my pajamas, not even caring whether Zoe sees my body.

"C'mon—you kiss, you tell. That's what roommates do."

I don't answer. I throw back my covers and get into bed.

I feel like I'm sleepwalking. I wish I were—then tonight would only be a bad dream.

"Okay, seriously? I thought we had a breakthrough back at the lake. You and I should be all kumbaya now, right?"

I don't answer. I stare at the wall.

"Sam? Do you still want to go down to Dr. Lancaster's office?"

I don't answer.

"Are you okay?"

I don't answer.

twenty-five

I GET DRESSED THE NEXT MORNING IN THAT SAME sleepwalking fog. I hear Zoe talking to me, but it's like it's through heavy earmuffs. And I'm on delayed reaction. She taps me on the shoulder, and it takes me a few seconds to realize I'm supposed to turn around. Or ignore her. Whatever. Make a decision. By the time I do, she's left the room.

I sit on the floor in front of my suitcase, staring at it without seeing it.

I still don't understand what happened last night.

I think back to that perfect moment, right before everything imploded. The moonlight reflecting on the water. The breeze kicking up tiny waves against the dock. The hum of the June bugs. The blinking of fireflies. Staring up at the guy who *knows* me—the real me—and who tells me I'm beautiful.

Lies. And you believed him.

A knock. I scramble to my feet. What if it's Andrew? What if he's come to explain what went wrong between us? But then the door swings open. It's Katie.

"Sam?"

I take a breath before I answer, hoping my voice won't sound as foggy, as thick, as broken as I feel. "Hey. I'll be down in a bit." More lies. I might not come downstairs at all. I might stay up here forever.

"I know you're upset. Zoe came to get me. She thought you might talk to me, since you won't talk to her." She hesitates. "Can I come in?"

"Sure." I return to the floor and shuffle outfits around in my suitcase like I'm trying to choose. Like it matters what I look like.

Katie sits on my unmade bed. "What's going on?"

"I don't want to talk about it."

"Is it about Andrew?"

I don't respond.

"Whatever it is, I'm sure it's going to be okay. . . ."

A flash of anger. At her optimism. At her as-yet-unbroken heart. "What part of 'I don't want to talk about it' wasn't clear to you?" I snap.

Katie jerks back.

The anger drains out of me. "I'm sorry." I go back to poking through my suitcase.

And then Dr. Lancaster is in the doorway. "Sam? Can I speak with you?"

She knows. I know she knows. And she knows that I

know that she knows. The whole story is written on her face.

I swallow past the painful lump in my throat. "Can I get dressed first?"

"Of course. Come to my office when you're ready." She looks at Katie. "Yasmin is waiting for you in the Dogwood Room, Katie."

"Okay. Sam, I'm here if you need me."

She leaves, and Dr. Lancaster leaves, and I'm alone.

WHEN I SWING the door open, Dr. Lancaster is seated behind her desk, hands clasped on the dark wood surface. Andrew is leaning against the wall.

I want to leave. Go out the front door and down the gravel driveway and off into the sunset. But Dr. Lancaster says, "Come on in, Sam," so I sit down in the chair across from her.

I feel Andrew looming over my shoulder.

"Andrew told me what happened," Dr. Lancaster says. "He came to me this morning—and I'm glad he did. We need to talk about it. And Andrew has some things he has to say to you. But first, I need to hear it from you: were you alone with Andrew last night, after lights-out?"

I don't want to talk.

I don't want to hear anything Andrew has to say.

Or maybe I do. Maybe I need to know the truth. Even if it means accepting that everything between us was a figment of my overactive imagination.

I want to keep myself from getting hurt again. Block out the pain and the noise. Hide inside this sleepwalking feeling.

I also want to make myself hurt *more*, for being so stupid. For daring to believe and to feel and to hope.

"Sam." Dr. Lancaster's voice is kind, but firm. "You're not in trouble. I need to make sure you're safe. Just tell me what happened. Did the two of you kiss?"

After a second, I nod.

"Did he kiss you, or did you kiss him?"

It's a simple question, but it makes all the difference in the world.

I can barely get the words out. "I kissed him."

"Why?"

"I thought—" I finally let myself look directly at Andrew. And I see that he's a wreck. His eyes are dark-circled. His hair isn't brushed. He's wearing yesterday's rumpled clothes. "I thought you liked me," I tell him.

"Andrew?" Dr. Lancaster's tone is different than when she spoke to me. I got her calm, gentle therapist voice. With him, her voice is sharper, harder. No-nonsense.

"I did—I *do* like you, Sam. As a friend. Not as anything more than that." He cringes as he says it, like he knows exactly how his words are slicing through me.

"But last night, when we were at the lake—"

Dr. Lancaster cuts in: "The lake?"

Andrew looks like he wants to shrink even farther back into the wall. "I took the kids last night," he says quietly, leaving Yasmin out of it. "It happened after that."

"Andrew, you know that is *completely*—" Dr. Lancaster stops. "Sam, go on."

I don't want to go on. He referred to me and the other campers as "the kids." That stings almost as much as the word "friend." But despite the ache inside me, I find a way to keep talking.

"We spent so much time together. You paid extra attention to me. You cared about me. Or you acted like you did."

"I do care about you. As a friend," he repeats. "I was trying to help you. I only ever wanted to help you. And I didn't give you any more one-on-one attention than I gave Dominic or Zoe." He looks at Dr. Lancaster, pleading his case. "I swear."

"But the partnering—"

"Was really fun."

"It was romantic. You felt the sparks too. And you'd been flirting with me—"

"I guess I flirted a little, yeah." Andrew presses the heels of his hands into his eye sockets. "I thought it might make you feel good about yourself, especially after you told me about getting dumped. But I was up front with you. I told you I have a girlfriend. And I'm here as your peer adviser. I thought you knew where the line was."

Dr. Lancaster starts, "Andrew—"

"I didn't mean to lead you on, Sam. I didn't mean for any of this to happen."

"You were lying to me." I feel like I'm cracking in two. "I trusted you."

286

"I wasn't lying. You have to understand—"

"You told me—" My voice comes out strangled. "You told me I was beautiful."

"I wanted you to be able to tell *yourself* you were beautiful," Andrew says in a low voice. "There's a difference."

"But . . . *why?*" I mean all of it, from the beginning.

"The first night we were here, I almost gave you a panic attack. The next day, I actually did give you a panic attack. I felt bad, and I wanted to make it up to you. And then, the more we talked, the better I got to know you—" He shrugs, looking helpless.

"I think I've heard enough," Dr. Lancaster says. "Andrew, you didn't intend to strike up a romantic relationship with a camper?"

"Of course I didn't." The look on his face now: desperation. "I thought I could help her, like you helped me. And I had some ideas—how to step outside the box with her therapy. I took a risk, and I thought it was paying off. She was doing so much better." He turns to me, insistent. "You were. I know you were."

"To be blunt, Andrew," Dr. Lancaster says, anger simmering in her voice, "you're an undergraduate. You've taken two semesters of psychology. You don't have the training or the experience to make those kinds of decisions. It doesn't matter how good your intentions are. Taking campers' treatment into your own hands puts them at risk. It puts everything I do here at risk."

She turns to me, her voice softening once more. "Sam,

is there anything else you need to tell me?"

I shake my head, not trusting myself to speak.

"Okay. Sit tight here for a second. I'll be right back." She stands. "Andrew, you can go pack your things."

"He's leaving?" I hear my voice from far away. "You're leaving?"

Of course he's leaving.

And it's your fault.

"I can't allow him to stay here, Sam," Dr. Lancaster says gently.

I look at Andrew, lingering in the doorway. "But . . . your college credit . . ."

Andrew winces, and it hits me, hard, how much my stupid kiss has cost him. The guilt, on top of everything else I'm feeling, threatens to capsize me.

"I'm sorry, I didn't think. . . ."

"No, I'm the one who's sorry," Andrew says. "I promise, I didn't mean to—I would never have wanted—this isn't what I thought—"

"Enough." Dr. Lancaster holds the door open for him to exit. When he's gone, she turns to me. "I'll be right back. I promise."

I SIT THERE, staring at nothing, until the phone on her desk rings.

I look from the phone to the door, expecting Dr. Lancaster to burst through it. Instead, the ringing stops.

It starts again a minute later. I glance at the digital

display. It's my local area code. But it's not my mom's number, and it's not the ballet studio. Maybe it's Miss Elise's cell phone?

I hesitate, my hand hovering over the receiver, and then I pick it up. "Hello?"

"Hi, can I speak to Samantha Wagner?" It is Miss Elise. Her soft, Southern-accented voice is unmistakable.

"Hi, Miss Elise. It's me."

"Oh, I'm so glad I reached you," she says, and despite how horrible the morning has been, my spirits rise. The intensive. I still have that to look forward to. Until: "I don't know how to tell you this. . . ."

I sink back in my chair.

"I spoke to the director of your intensive this morning. She called me first thing."

I manage to whisper, "And?"

"I'm so sorry, Sam. The program's full, so they can't take anyone from the waiting list."

This isn't happening. It can't be.

It can. It is.

You knew it would.

"They wanted to hold off until the last minute to make sure to give us accurate information, and since the program starts on Monday, the last minute is basically . . . today."

I'm shaking. I squeeze the phone with one hand and my knee with the other.

"I want you to know how disappointed I am for you. You deserved this opportunity. But I'm so glad you're where you are. Getting you healthy and happy is the most important thing."

My throat is closing up. The room is swimming. And spinning.

It's over. It's all over. Your plans, your dreams, they're—

"Do you want to call your mom, or do you want me to do it?"

My mom. She's going to be so—

I take in a hitched breath. And then I'm gasping. Gulping. Drowning.

I drop the phone.

If you weren't so fat—

So weak—

So useless—

"Sam! Look at me." Dr. Lancaster lifts up my chin. I blink away the tears to see her crouching in front of me. "We're going to breathe together now. In . . . and out. . . . In . . . and out. . . ."

With her coaching, I'm able to fill my lungs with air. I'm still crying—deep, shuddering sobs—but soon that eases too. Then all that's left is emptiness. Numbness.

The phone rings again, and Dr. Lancaster leans over me to answer it. "Yes," she says, looking at me. "She's okay. Listen, we'll have to call you back. Mm-hmm. Thanks." She hangs up.

"That was your teacher again. She was worried. She heard you crying, and then the phone went dead."

"Oh."

"Do you want to fill me in?"

I shake my head.

"You shouldn't keep those feelings locked inside."

"I'd like to lie down." My voice sounds like it belongs to someone else.

"I understand." She helps me stand up. "I'll come get you for lunch."

I don't plan on eating lunch, but I nod anyway. It's easier to agree. To give in.

I head upstairs but stop cold in the hallway when I see Andrew coming out of his bedroom, duffel bag in hand. We make eye contact. It's like he's giving me a wordless apology. But that's not what I want. I want him to make it so that last night, the past two weeks, all of it never happened.

He takes a step toward me, reaching out. "Sam—"

I pull away so fast, I hit my wrist on the banister. It hurts. I cradle my arm, eyes stinging. Then I push past him into my and Zoe's room and shut the door.

You ruined everything, my inner voice growls. *For yourself. And for Andrew.*

Your weight gain. Your neediness. Your inability to cope. It all led to this moment.

The ballerina collage I created last week is hanging on the wall. The dancer made of clouds and dandelion puffs and sunshine. I reach up and pull the picture loose. I take a corner in each hand and rip it in half.

It's not as satisfying as I thought it would be.

I let the pieces drop to the floor.

twenty-six

A KNOCK AT THE DOOR. I DON'T GET UP. I ROLL OVER onto my side to face the wall.

Next, I hear the door swing open. Footsteps coming toward me.

"Sam? It's time for lunch." It's Yasmin. She pats me on the shoulder.

"I'm not hungry."

"You need to eat. Dr. Lancaster said—"

"I'm not hungry." In the hours I've been lying here, thinking about the spectacular way in which my life has fallen apart, I realized that Dr. Lancaster doesn't matter. This place doesn't matter. I came here for a single purpose: to make sure I didn't have a panic attack at my ballet intensive. Now there's no ballet intensive. Which means I have no further reason to try. To care.

Yasmin leaves. I get about five minutes of peace and

quiet. Five minutes of staring at the wall, thinking about nothing.

You have nothing.

You are nothing.

Then Dr. Lancaster shows up. "Sam. It's lunchtime. I'm sorry you're hurting, but I can't take no for an answer." She sits on the bed by my feet.

"I'm not hungry."

"I allowed you to skip breakfast. I can't allow you to skip lunch as well."

"I told you, I'm not hungry—" My stomach growls. I let out a bark of laughter. Betrayed by my own body, yet again.

"Up," Dr. Lancaster says.

I roll over. Stand. Follow her out of the safety of my bedroom and down the stairs and around the corner to the kitchen.

"I made you a plate." Dr. Lancaster hands me a Caesar salad with five strips of grilled chicken on top. It's lightly drizzled with dressing and sprinkled with flakes of Parmesan.

"I don't want this."

"Do you want to make your own salad? That's fine too."

I shake my head. "I don't want any of this." To my own ears, I sound amazingly calm. Inside, I'm a tsunami roaring toward the shore. I don't know when—or who—it will hit. But it's coming.

"What *do* you want, Sam?"

"I want to be left alone."

"I'm afraid I can't do that. I need you to sit down and eat some of this salad."

I stare at the plate in my hand. "What happens if I say no?"

"Please don't say no."

"Are you going to force-feed me? Andrew——" I choke on his name. On the pang of rejection and on my own guilt and self-loathing. "He could've held me down, but you and Yasmin can't. Or will you make Dominic do it?"

"No one is going to hold you down, Sam."

"Then here." I shove the plate back into Dr. Lancaster's hands so hard that most of the salad ends up on her blue button-down. I glare at her. "I. Don't. Want. This."

"Dr. Lancaster . . . ?" Yasmin, behind me.

I spin around. They're all there.

Katie's the first to speak. "We heard about what happened——"

"It's fine. I'm fine. Everything's fine. I'm just *not hungry.*"

Dr. Lancaster sets my plate down on the kitchen island. She grabs a paper towel to dab at the Caesar dressing on her shirt. "Sam, I know how hard this morning has been for you. After you eat, we'll talk more about it——"

I interrupt her, and suddenly I'm shouting. "I don't want to *talk* about how hard everything is! I want it to *stop being so hard!*" The wave inside me crashes into the shore. "You want me to eat? Fine. I'll eat." I pick up a chicken strip with my fingers and shove it in my mouth. "There! Satisfied?" I chew and swallow. "Look, I'll have another!"

My breath is coming fast. Not from panic, but from how incredibly unfair all this is. This summer was supposed to be the start of everything. The rest of my life. Now it feels like the beginning of the end.

I gorge myself on chicken strips, and then, without thinking about what I'm doing, I grab the bottle of Caesar dressing and squirt some directly into my mouth. It's gross, but I manage to keep it down.

"That's enough, Sam," Dr. Lancaster says, taking the dressing from me.

"Is it? Did I eat enough for you? I'm so glad." I fall back against the kitchen island, hands on my heaving stomach. The group is still staring at me. I plaster on my brightest, sparkliest smile and ask, "Enjoy the show?"

I'm outside my body, watching from above. The girl I see standing in the middle of the kitchen has a matted pony-tail and salad dressing in one corner of her mouth. Her smile is shattered. Her eyes are wild and sad. She's out of control.

I'm out of control. I have no control over anything in my life.

My parents didn't tell me they were separating until the day my dad moved out.

My mom didn't talk to me before she took her side job at my ballet studio, making it even harder for me to escape her watchful, critical eyes.

Marcus broke up with me out of the blue. And Andrew—

And, of course, my body changed on me. I couldn't do a thing to stop it.

I can't fix it. Any of it.

For every piece of myself I pick up, three more drop to the ground.

"Let's go, Sam." Dr. Lancaster guides me past my fellow campers. They part for me, like my misery might rub off on them. Omar's muttering again: "I don't like this. I don't like this. I don't like this." His words echo in my ears all the way down the hall.

In her office, Dr. Lancaster sits me down. "Talk to me." It's not a request.

"No." *This* I can control. If only this.

"Then I'll wait until you're ready." She drops into her chair and crosses her legs. Stares at me. I stare back, cradling my bruised wrist.

Time passes.

WHEN I'M DONE not talking, I'm supposed to find Yasmin. She's supposed to keep an eye on me. But I feel like being invisible.

I slip past the Dogwood Room and through the kitchen to the back door. Then I freeze, hand on the knob. On the counter by the sink: a glass canister filled with Hershey's Kisses. *Andrew.* I tuck the canister under my arm and take it outside.

It's drizzling, which matches my mood. In fact, I wish it were raining harder. I *should* be walking in the rain, my clothes growing damp and my hair frizzing. I deserve this. I deserve every bad thing that has ever happened to me.

I take out a Hershey's Kiss. I unwrap it. I let the chocolate melt on my tongue.

Because I'm feeling masochistic, I visit all the places where I thought something was happening between me and Andrew. Every spot where I misinterpreted what was going on. I eat a Hershey's Kiss on the porch steps where we sat together. Another one walking behind the gazebo, where he stood so close to me to tie my blindfold. Then I go inside the gazebo, remembering our partnering session. How alive I felt with his hands on me.

Two more Hershey's Kisses.

I leave the gazebo, where our ghosts are still dancing. I go through the woods to the lake. The rain picks up, and I listen to the drops patter on the leaves. I walk to the end of the dock and eat two more chocolates in honor of the two times Andrew coaxed me into the water. Then I return to the spot where our kiss happened last night. I can still feel our lips touching, like the moment left an afterimage in the air itself.

I sit down in the wet dirt, trying to sort through my feelings. I'm angry at Andrew for flirting when he didn't mean it, and I'm angry at myself for not seeing that he didn't mean it, and I feel terrible about getting him fired, and his rejection hurts like an open sore inside me, and I *miss him*. Even after everything, I want him here.

I finish the entire canister of Kisses, crumpling the shiny foil wrappings into tiny balls and scattering them around me.

That's where Yasmin finds me. "Sam!" she gasps, wrapping her arms around me. "I was so worried—I didn't know where you went!"

She didn't know where to look. Andrew would've known where to look.

As she leads me away from the lake, reassuring me that I can talk to her about anything, anytime, I feel like I'm saying good-bye. To Andrew. To what I thought we had. To the version of myself he helped me see.

I also start to feel sick. The chocolate and chicken and dressing slosh and swirl inside me. I don't know whether it's because dark chocolate and Caesar salad don't mix, or because the world has spun off its axis since yesterday, but I want to throw up.

I really, really, really want to throw up.

Yasmin guides me back inside. I change into dry clothes. I sit in the dining room cutting construction paper into thinner and thinner strips. I listen to everyone's conversations without actually hearing them.

At one point, Jenna and Katie come over. "What do you need?" Jenna asks crisply. "Distraction? A shoulder to cry on? Space?"

I stare at her.

What I really need is a whole new body.

A fresh start.

A blank slate.

But those aren't options. "Space," I finally say.

"Okay." Jenna pats me on the shoulder. Katie gives me a

careful hug, like she's worried I might lash out again. Then they let me be.

The pile of construction paper slivers in front of me grows. Green and blue and purple, like the bruise that's blossoming on my wrist.

My lunch threatens to come up, yet again.

I keep it down.

At dinner, I put more food on top of what's already there. Seven bites of shepherd's pie, eaten while Dr. Lancaster watches. I see her relief that I'm not fighting her this time. What she doesn't know is that I used up all my anger earlier. I'm empty again.

None of this matters, I tell myself as I swallow sawdust. *None of this matters.*

And then, later that night, Mom calls. I take the phone from Dr. Lancaster's outstretched hand. I wait for what I know is coming.

"Samantha, I've been trying to reach you all day."

"Okay."

"Elise called me after she spoke to you."

"Okay."

"Are you all right?"

"Yeah." My reply doesn't sound a bit genuine, but she moves on anyway.

"When we decided to send you to Perform at Your Peak, Elise assured me that it wouldn't impact your training plans. This summer is a vital one for your career. Without this intensive—I don't know what we're going to do. You'll start your junior year off at a deficit. You certainly won't be invited to a year-round ballet school. And—"

I hold the phone away from my ear for a few seconds. I glance at Dr. Lancaster, who's sitting on the couch in case I need rescuing again. Everything about this moment feels inevitable. I return to my mom.

"—certainly glad you've kept up with your practice while you're there. We won't have a moment to waste when you get home. You can do Elise's summer workshop, of course, and maybe I can hire a private coach to work with you as well. And—"

"Mom."

"Yes, Samantha?"

"Do you know what I did after I found out?"

A long pause. "What?"

"I ate about three dozen dark chocolate Hershey's Kisses." I hang up on her. Then I turn to Dr. Lancaster. "I'm going upstairs."

She nods. "I'll get Yasmin—"

"I'd like to be alone." I shove my trembling hands into my armpits and lie to Dr. Lancaster's face: "I'm fine. Just tired. You don't have to worry about me."

She gives me a searching look. "You'll come to me if you need anything at all."

Another lie: "Of course." I pair the words with a shaky smile that's as much a performance as any ballet I've ever danced. In order for her to leave me alone, I have to strike the right balance of vulnerability and strength. She has to

300

believe that I won't in a million years do what I'm about to do.

I can barely believe what I'm about to do.

But it's inevitable.

I go upstairs. Not to my room. To the bathroom. I lock myself inside the farthest stall. I sit on the floor in front of the toilet. I stare it down.

Throw up.

I don't move.

You want to. You'll feel better.

I don't. I won't.

Take control.

Bile rises up inside me. I swallow it back down. It burns my throat.

Do it.

I get on my knees and lean over the toilet.

Do it!

I stick my finger in my throat.

I gag, and I scoot back fast. I'm pressed against the stall door, crying now, and breathing hard. I wipe my snotty nose with the back of my hand and catch sight of the bruise on my wrist.

My stomach rumbles and roils.

You aren't strong enough—

You'll never have what it takes—

I hear Andrew's voice in my head, too. He wouldn't want me to be in here.

He lied to you. Everything he said to you was a lie.

Maybe not everything—

Everything.

I groan, holding my stomach. I want to throw up. I want to be empty.

Try again.

I do. And again, I gag, and I stop.

You can't even do that right. You're useless. You're nothing—

I curl into the corner of the stall, knees to chest, and rock.

This is the thing I never told anyone. The thing I'm constantly trying to forget.

Earlier this year, when I wanted to lose weight and nothing was working—when I started feeling so desperate, so helpless, so scared—I decided to try making myself throw up. I only did it a few times. I hated doing it. I hated *myself* for even considering it.

I lost a few pounds. It was just water weight. My body getting dehydrated. But people noticed. They told me I was looking good. I knew throwing up was a bad idea, and I knew I shouldn't keep doing it, but there was a part of me that wished—that still wishes—

"Sam?"

I open my eyes to see Jenna crawling under the divider from the next stall.

"I heard you crying in here and I thought maybe I'd given you enough space for today." She looks from me to the toilet. "Are you sick?"

I shake my head.

"Did you make yourself throw up?"

Another no.

"Are you going to?"

I want to, and I don't. I'm not sure which side is going to win.

Jenna gets the saddest look on her face. Then the sadness turns to resolve. She lifts up her shirt. Pulls down the waistband of her shorts. Shows me her scars.

"I used to cut myself," she says. "I did it when I made too many mistakes on the ice. But . . . I stopped."

I blink, trying to clear away the tears. And I say, out loud for the first time ever, in a voice like sandpaper, "I used to make myself throw up. But . . . I stopped."

"But you still think about it?"

I nod. "Do you?"

"All the time." She drops her shirt. "Do you want me to stay with you?"

The tears well up again. "Yes."

"All right." She takes my hand.

twenty-seven

SATURDAY.

I get up. I get dressed. I eat a few bites of tasteless breakfast. I sit in the Dogwood Room as Dr. Lancaster introduces Andrew's last-minute replacement, a thirty-something colleague of hers named Ron, and as she gives the day's lecture. Something about excellence versus perfection. Something about achieving our goals. Something about looking for opportunities.

I am neither excellent nor perfect. I am not achieving my goals. I have no opportunities.

I'm crawling through today, waiting for it to end so I can crawl through tomorrow.

I feel the others orbiting me. I don't give them anything. I have nothing to give.

Dr. Lancaster spends an hour with me on Saturday afternoon, and another hour on Sunday morning. I barely say a word either time. I stare at a spot on the floor between my toes. I run my fingers over the bruise on my wrist, which has gone from blue and purple to green, with yellow around the edges. I melt back into the couch cushions and want to keep melting.

But after lunch on Sunday, Katie approaches me while I'm sitting on the front porch, gazing out at nothing. "Hi," she says, sitting down next to me.

I nod to let her know I heard her.

"You know we're doing my challenge at the ropes course this afternoon, right?"

"Yeah." My voice feels creaky from disuse.

"I'd really like you to be there."

"Oh."

"I need you to hold my hand while I cross. Do you think you can do that?"

I can walk across a beam. I can hold her hand. I can be good for *something*.

You're not good for—

"Sure," I say, sighing and leaning back. "Are we leaving soon?"

"In, like, an hour?"

"Okay."

Katie puts her arm around my waist. "Thank you. This means a lot." She drops her head onto my shoulder. "By the way, Jenna said to tell you that you should tell Dr. Lancaster about the thing. She didn't tell me *what* thing, but she said you'd know what she meant."

I go rigid. I was wondering, somewhere behind the fog, when that was going to come up. My inner voice starts whispering, *You can't tell. There's no reason to tell. And anyway, you didn't do anything. At least, not here—*

"You know what she means, right?"

"Yeah," I say quietly. "I know what she means."

AN HOUR AND a half later, we're standing on the wooden platform in front of the suspended balance beams. "Katie," Dr. Lancaster says. "Tell me how you want this to go." Unlike last time, she's harnessed in next to us, wearing khaki shorts, a yellow T-shirt, and white Keds with yellow ankle socks.

"I want another pair to cross first, and then Sam and I will cross," Katie says, lips set in a line. She looks upset, but it's a different kind of upset from last week. Then she was pale and shaking, on the verge of tears. Now it's like she's staring at a mountain she has to climb. And she doesn't want to do it, but she knows she has to. She knows she *can*.

Looking at Katie—seeing her bravery firsthand—I realize that all of them have changed. I can see Jenna's gradual opening and letting go. Omar's moments of confidence and Dominic's moments of vulnerability. Even Zoe has changed for the better since getting here. I'm the only one who's gotten worse.

Dr. Lancaster stands next to Katie, asking her questions as Yasmin and Jenna cross the beam. I try not to listen in, but it's hard not to overhear, given that I'm harnessed two feet away.

"How are you feeling?"

"Anxious."

"How anxious, on a scale of one to ten?"

"Eight. No, seven."

"Are you breathing?"

"Yes." Katie gulps in air. "See?"

I look down at the ground, where Zoe, Dominic, Omar, and Ron are waiting. They look really far away. Or maybe it's how far away I still feel. I glance at Katie's determined face, then at her white-knuckle grip on my hand.

I should try to focus. This is important.

Dr. Lancaster extends her hand toward the beams. "Take your time, girls."

Katie steps right up to the edge. "No rituals today," she tells me, looking grim. "I just have to walk across, like it's no big deal. Like I've done it a thousand times."

"Tell me when you're ready."

"I'm ready."

We take a step. The beam sways under my foot and I check my balance. Out of the corner of my eye, I see Katie do the same thing. Her fingers dig into my hand, but she doesn't stop moving. We bobble again, then hit our stride. Right foot, left foot, right foot, left foot. My vision narrows to the beam in front of me. All I see is a camel-colored line in space. And all I feel is my feet and my right hand. Three points of contact that keep me from falling.

In what seems like seconds, we're at the other side. Katie steps up onto the platform and stands completely still, looking stunned. Then she lets out a loud whoop. She turns to me and wraps me in a bear hug. She lets go, gives another ear-piercing whoop, and starts jumping up and down and shaking her butt in the happiest happy dance I've ever seen.

Cheering from below. Dominic is pumping his fist in the air. Omar is shouting "Bravo! Bravo!" Zoe gets everyone to chant Katie's name. Next to us on the platform, Jenna, Yasmin, and even the ropes-course coordinator are applauding. And when I look back at the opposite platform, where Dr. Lancaster is still standing, I see her wearing her "proud parent" smile.

Katie hugs me again, and I want to cry. It's not that I'm not happy to see her conquer her fear. I am. If it's possible to be simultaneously thrilled for someone else and devastated for myself, that's what I am.

I don't want to keep moving backward. I want to be where Katie is right now. I want to be the one so full of relief and happiness that my body can't contain it.

She looks like she could fly off the platform. I've been there. I was there the first time I nailed a triple pirouette en pointe. I was there on *Nutcracker* opening night, performing Dewdrop Fairy in front of a packed house. I was there when I received my initial acceptance letter to this summer's ballet intensive.

I know how it feels to fly. I want that feeling back.

And just like that, I know what I have to do.

"YOU'VE GOT MORE balls than I gave you credit for," Zoe says after I tell her my plan and her crucial role in it. "I was gonna call another meeting of the Secret Society of Crazy Campers tomorrow, but this is *so much better*."

"Does that mean you'll help me?"

"Are you kidding? Never mind helping you—which is fine—this is like the ultimate 'eff you' to my parents, and to this place. I'm totally in."

"And you can get what we need?"

"Leave it to me." She heads up the stairs but pauses at the top to look down at me, chin in hand. "My little Ballerina Barbie's all grown up."

I roll my eyes at her, feeling more like myself. The fog is lifting. I'm putting myself back together, brick by brick. Filling in the cracks. And if this plan works . . .

It won't—

It will. It has to.

I find Katie and Jenna in the Dogwood Room. I tell them, keeping my voice low, what Zoe and I will be doing tomorrow. I also tell them why it has to be Zoe who helps me. "She's been trying to get sent home since we got here. She won't care if it backfires."

"Don't *you* care if it backfires?" Katie asks, eyes wide.

"Of course I do. But"—I gulp—"I have to do this. So,

um, don't tell anyone where we've gone. At least, not until it's too late to stop us."

"We won't," Jenna says. "Be careful, okay? Drive safe."

There's only one thing left to do after that. I knock on Dr. Lancaster's office door feeling anxious but resolute. When she says, "Come in!" I don't hesitate.

"Sam!" she says, clearly surprised that it's me. "Is everything okay?"

"Yeah. Can I talk to you for a few minutes?"

The words "can I talk" flip a switch inside her. She beams at me. "Of course. What's on your mind?"

I sit. I examine my fingernails. I poke at my bruised wrist. "There's, um, something I need to tell you. Tonight." In case tomorrow is a huge disaster.

"What is it?"

"I—"

Stop. Seriously.

I say it fast, before I can change my mind. "I wanted to make myself throw up on Friday. If Jenna hadn't found me and sat with me, I might've gone through with it."

I don't know what kind of a reaction I was expecting. Horror. Disgust. But Dr. Lancaster's face doesn't change. That's what gives me the courage to keep talking.

"I haven't done that in a long time. I tried it earlier this year, when dieting wasn't working, but—I didn't like doing it, so I stopped. And then on Friday, everything felt so out of control, and I was so overwhelmed. . . ."

Why are you doing this? my inner voice screeches.

Because this might be my last chance to really talk to her, I remind myself, *and this is the thing I still need to say.*

"Thank you for telling me, Sam. Have you told anyone else?"

"Just Jenna."

"Not . . . ?"

Andrew. I stare at the floor. "No. But he—he said something that I can't stop thinking about. He told me that when he wanted to quit football, he thought about letting himself get hurt, badly, so he wouldn't have to tell his dad he didn't want to play anymore." I look at Dr. Lancaster, wondering whether it's okay for me to be talking about Andrew in here. "He told me he realized hurting yourself to get what you want isn't brave. And I guess I—I've been beating myself up for wanting to make myself throw up, but I also beat myself up for not being strong enough to do whatever it takes to be thin, and I—"

I'm wringing my hands. My stomach is in knots. I keep talking, even though everything in me is screaming *Stop stop stop stop stop.*

"Why is it so hard for me? Why can't I be like him, and say, nope, I don't want to do something that hurts me, and be done with it?"

"Well, first of all, he was speaking to you with the benefit of hindsight. He quit football a year and a half ago. You're still very much in the dance world. You're grappling with your issues in real time."

"Right, but—"

"Secondly, the fact that you're grappling at all is commendable. You're stronger than you think. And tonight, you took an important step on your journey."

"I did?"

"You did."

"Oh. Thanks, Dr. Lancaster."

"You're quite welcome. Do you want to keep talking about this?"

I check the clock. I have to get to bed early. And I have so much to do before then. "Not tonight. Maybe another time?"

"Of course." She pauses, looking apologetic. "You know, though, that I'll need to continue to monitor you at mealtimes, given what you told me this evening."

"I understand." I'm not exactly surprised. And if tomorrow goes well, it won't matter. I stand up. "Thanks again. And, um, I'm sorry."

"For what?"

For what I'm planning to do.

"For the past couple days. For getting salad on you, for yelling at you, all that."

"Apology accepted. I'm glad you and I are on speaking terms again."

We probably won't be, the next time I see her. If there is a next time. But even that thought can't kill my relief. I said the hardest thing there was to say, and I'm still here. Not only that, I actually feel *lighter*.

I feel ready.

twenty-eight

WE TIPTOE ACROSS THE GRAVEL DRIVEWAY IN THE
predawn darkness. The world feels hushed, like even if we
weren't trying to be stealthy, we'd feel compelled to keep
it down. "What if someone hears you start the engine?" I
whisper to Zoe.

"Then we're screwed," she whispers back.

I freeze. "What?"

"I was joking. Mostly." She makes a face. "I don't know,
maybe Dr. Lancaster will think we're the garbage truck or
something."

I've already moved on to my next worry. "And what if
they send people looking for us?" We've reached the van
we're going to steal—I mean borrow—for the day. It has the
Perform at Your Peak logo—a football player in the Heis-
man pose in one *P*, a pirouetting ballerina in the other—in
bright blue on the side. "Our ride's not subtle."

"We don't need subtle," Zoe says. "We just need keys and a head start." She looks at me, twirling the keys she took from Dr. Lancaster's desk around her index finger. She's got them on her new North Carolina State Wolfpack key chain. "You chickening out?"

"No way." I'm going to my ballet intensive, and I'm going to convince them to let me audition again, and I'm going to get in. That's all there is to it. I am taking control of my destiny. I brought my suitcase and everything. If they want me to start today, instead of next Monday, after Perform at Your Peak is over, I won't even have to come back here for my things.

I stifle a yawn.

"Sooner we get on the road, sooner we can find a Starbucks," Zoe says, opening the driver's-side door.

The next few minutes are agonizing. We get into the van. Zoe adjusts the driver's seat and puts the key in the ignition. "Here goes nothing," she mumbles. She turns the key. The sound of the engine starting up is so loud against the morning silence. I brace myself for alarms. To see Dr. Lancaster or Yasmin or even campus security running toward us.

But no one comes.

Zoe inches down the gravel driveway. And again, it's *so loud*. The crunching of gravel beneath our tires is an avalanche. When we kick up a rock, it hits the underside of the van with a sound like a gunshot.

But no one comes.

We make it to the main road. I look back. I can no longer see the house.

"You have the directions?" Zoe asks.

I show her my phone as the automated voice says, "In a quarter mile, turn left."

Zoe grins. "Then away we go."

I DON'T TRULY relax until we've been gone for an hour. Until the sun has come up, and we've gotten some coffee, and no one has chased us down.

Zoe turns on the radio. She finds a pop station and starts singing along with the latest Taylor Swift song, pounding a drumbeat on the steering wheel. When the song ends, she crows, "We did it, Thelma!"

"Thelma?"

"You wanna be Louise?"

Oh. Like the movie. "I don't actually know which one is which. Never seen it."

"Me neither. But don't they go off on some big road trip?"

"I think so. I think they also drive off a cliff at the end. . . ."

"Well, let's hope it doesn't come to that."

I still feel strange having this rapport with Zoe. If someone had told me two weeks ago that we'd be partners in crime—that we'd be *bantering*—I'd have laughed in their face.

She echoes my thoughts. "Who would've guessed, Barbs: you and me."

I laugh. "Seriously."

"Thanks for giving me a reason to jailbreak."

"Are you kidding? Thank *you*. I couldn't do this without you."

"They're gonna kill us," Zoe says. But she doesn't sound worried. If anything, her smile only gets bigger.

We're quiet for a couple miles. Then, out of nowhere, she says, "Just tell me you're not doing this because of Andrew."

I take a sip of my coffee: black, the way he always made it for me. "I'm not doing this because of Andrew."

"Try again, and say it like you mean it." She gives me the side-eye.

"I'm not—" I sigh. "Okay, maybe it is a little because of him. But I'm not here because he, um—"

"Shot you down?" Zoe inserts helpfully.

Now it's my turn to give her the side-eye. I'm not surprised that she knows. It's only surprising that she waited this long to bring it up. "Yeah, that. But, um, before that happened, he made me feel—"

"Swoony?" There's a snicker in her voice.

I glare at her. "Confident. Like I actually had a chance at, you know, life. Despite how awful the past few months have been."

"I hear that. So what, exactly, happened between you two the other night?"

"I, uh. I kissed him."

"Whoa! Way to make the first move."

"Yeah, well, it didn't quite work out the way I wanted."

"I didn't say it was a *smart* move. No offense."

316

I take another sip of bitter black coffee. "But I really thought he liked me! He talked to me and he listened and he seemed like he cared about me. He was *there* for me."

"That was his job. He did the same thing for me."

Hearing her say that so casually—it's like someone's jabbing an icepick into my sternum. It makes me want to argue with her. "You don't understand——"

"Okay, tough-love time. Have you heard of this thing called transference?"

I shake my head.

"It's when you fall for your shrink. It can also be where you treat your shrink like a parent, if you have daddy issues or whatever. But basically, because the person is acting really invested in your life, helping you figure things out, you start to feel like there's a relationship there. But there's not. They're still your shrink."

I frown. "How do you know about this?"

"My mom had an affair with her therapist a few years ago." Zoe's grip on the steering wheel tightens. "If you tell anyone else that, I will murder you."

"Understood."

"Granted, the guy was a——" She calls him a few nasty names. "He basically set her up. But that's the reason my dad took her back after it was all said and done. She said it was transference—that she was getting something from the therapist she wasn't getting from my dad. One more thing to work out with her next shrink, right?"

I'm still trying to wrap my mind around the concept.

"It's a real thing? People falling for their therapists?"

"Yep."

"Wow." I pause. "But Andrew isn't a therapist."

"He wants to be. He couldn't stop talking about his psych classes. How interesting it all is, learning how people's minds work."

"Sounds like he talked to you a lot about school stuff. . . ." Once again, I'm a tiny bit jealous.

"I think he was trying to inspire me to find my own passion, once I quit tennis. Spoiler alert: it won't be psychology. Anyway, does that make you feel better?"

It does—and it doesn't. I still feel what I feel. I was still rejected by someone I really liked, only a couple weeks after being dumped by my previous boyfriend. I still have to look at every conversation Andrew and I had through a new lens. One that isn't quite so rose-colored.

"You probably shouldn't take my word for it. Having a messed-up mother doesn't make me an expert." She looks in my direction, changing lanes. "And I mean it: if you tell anyone about my parents, I will hunt you down."

My phone rings. Both of us jump. Zoe looks at the phone, where I've dropped it in the cup holder, like it's something alive. And vicious. I pick it up with two fingers and check the screen. It's my mom. I let the call go to voicemail, but it starts ringing again immediately.

"I think they know we're gone," I tell Zoe.

"Don't answer."

I let it go to voicemail again.

Maybe Zoe can tell I'm wavering, because she says, "So tell me about this ballet camp. Why is it so important?"

I fill her in about summer intensives and year-round programs and apprenticeships and company contracts. That takes some time. Then we sing along to the radio some more. We stop for a quick breakfast, a bathroom break, and more coffee. We talk about our schools and our home-towns. The people we dance and play tennis with. The best movies we saw recently. And we drive, and we drive, and we drive.

I STAND IN front of the building, looking up. It's all gray stone and mirrored glass, simultaneously imposing and sturdy and sparkling. The way the morning sunlight is hitting the windows, I can't see in. But I know that the upper floors are all dance studios, built to look out over the city.

Bianca and I auditioned here together back in January. We stood in this spot. We took class in one of those studios. We got consecutive audition numbers so that we'd always dance in the same group. We spurred each other on with our energy and excitement. We calmed each other's nerves.

Today I have to go it alone.

The anxiety rises up in my stomach. I gulp it back down.

I wish I had time to call Bianca right now. I wish I'd thought to call her from the road. With everything that's happened since Thursday, I never got a chance to write to her. I pull out my phone and shoot off a text:

Auditioning again in Nashville today. Long story—fill you in later. Wish me luck!

"Are you going in, or do I have to carry you?"

I tuck my phone back into my bag. "I'm going in."

Zoe nods. "Okay. I don't really want to sit and wait for you, so I'm gonna walk around. Sightsee, or whatever. Text me when you're done?"

"Will do."

She punches me in the shoulder. "Go get 'em, tiger."

I give her a weak smile in return.

I pull open the heavy front door. I'm hit with a blast of cold air that smells slightly funky. It's that perpetual dance-studio scent. No matter how often you clean, no matter how many air fresheners you use, there's always an underlying odor of sweat and feet.

I walk up to the front desk. There's no one there, so I look around. At the portraits of company dancers that line the walls. At the posters advertising performances from the past few decades. I can hear the tinkling of a piano down the hall. Also the strains of a piece of classical music I don't recognize, a cello's mournful tone paired with a violin, sharp and swooping. And I hear voices. Girls in black leotards and pink tights are heading for the stairs. They look about my age. Which means they must be my level. Or the level I'll be if I make it through today.

I will make it through today.

"Can I help you?"

I turn back to the desk. A gray-haired woman in a faded black pantsuit is standing there, bustling with some papers.

I clear my throat, which has gone dry. "Hi. I'd like to speak with Ms. Levanova?"

The woman looks me up and down, her gaze lingering in a way that makes me feel like my skin is on fire. "Dear, are you sure you're in the right place? The recreational and community classes are in our other building, across the street."

That's all it takes. My inner voice starts chanting *Fat fat fat fat*. But even though my stomach is doing entrechat quatres and my heart is beating faster and faster, I stand my ground.

"Is this where the summer intensive is?"

"Yes, but it's audition-only. Orientation was yesterday." The woman extends an arm back toward the door I came in. "Open classes are—"

"I auditioned. I was accepted. I was supposed to miss this first week, which meant I had to be on the wait list, and I found out on Friday you aren't taking anyone else from the wait list, but since I got in originally, I wanted to stop by and see if I can reaudition. . . ."

My voice is muffled through the roaring in my ears. Did I really come all this way only to get stopped by an overzealous receptionist?

"I'd really like the opportunity to show you what I can do—"

"What's going on?"

I can breathe again. The Russian accent is unmistakable. Ms. Levanova will remember me, because she's the one who auditioned me. After the audition class, she complimented my classical technique. Even if I look different, I don't look *that* different . . . right?

"Samantha? What are you doing here?" Ms. Levanova glides toward us on turned-out feet, like the hallway is a stage. "Did you not get our message? We're very sorry, but—"

"I got it. But I was—I was hoping I could convince you to change your mind."

She gives me a pitying look. "Is not how it works, my dear."

"Please. Just let me audition again. I belong here. I know it." I'm *this close* to dropping to my knees. "Please."

She stares me down. Unblinking. I try not to blink back. Not to shrink away. So much depends on this staring contest.

"I'll show her out—" the receptionist starts.

Ms. Levanova lifts a hand. "No, Dolores. Is okay." She appraises me, and I think about the pounds and inches I've gained since the last time she saw me. The curves that weren't there before. This is the moment of truth. The moment I find out how much they really matter.

"One class. No guarantee."

"Thank you!" I want to throw my arms around her. I want to jump up and down. I settle for squeezing my hands into fists and channeling everything I feel into them. "Thank you!" I say again, as my fists quake.

"Well, go!" Ms. Levanova says, fluttering her hand in a way that's both very Russian and very retired prima ballerina. "It will not do to be late!"

IN THE DRESSING room, I drop my dance bag next to an empty locker and pull out the two leotards I brought. Black with a pink piping detail, or all-black with a lace back? The one with the pink makes my chest look smaller, but the one with the lace back cinches me in more at the waist. I look from one to the other, unable to make a decision.

"Wear the one with the lace."

I spin to see a girl standing behind me, already dressed for class.

"They're serious about the all-black dress code," the girl says. "Plus that lace is really pretty." She sticks out her hand. "I'm Hannah."

"Thanks. I'm Sam." We shake.

"See you in there." Hannah slings her pointe shoe bag over her shoulder and heads out the door.

I watch her go. And I realize: she didn't say anything about my body. She didn't even look at me funny. I'd forgotten what that felt like.

I shake myself out of it and change clothes. I pull on my

pink tights and black leotard, grabbing a black wrap skirt in case we're allowed to wear them. I get my shoe bag, which has my newest pair of ballet slippers and my perfectly broken in pointe shoes, plus my toe pads and toe tape. I shove the rest of my stuff in the locker. On my way out, I stop and check my bun. There's not a wisp out of place.

I look good.

As good as you're ever going to look—

No, I tell my inner voice. Not now.

I check to make sure there's no one else in the dressing room, and say it out loud: "I look good." And then, even though thinking of anything related to Andrew makes my heart hurt, I add, "My body is flexible, and strong, and beautiful."

I almost believe it.

twenty-nine

ONE BALLET CLASS WAS ALL IT TOOK. I WAS HOOKED.
I loved everything about it: my pink leotard with the attached
ruffly skirt, my brand-new pink ballet slippers, getting my
hair slicked back into an elegant bun. I loved skipping around
the room to tinkly piano music. I loved standing with my
spine long and tall, like a princess wearing a sparkly tiara.
I loved the graceful curtsy Miss Johanna had us perform to
start and end the class. And I loved Miss Johanna herself. I'd
seen her perform in *The Nutcracker*, and I was in complete
awe that the Sugar Plum Fairy was my teacher.

I was six, and I'd found what I wanted to do with the
rest of my life.

Flash-forward to when things got more difficult. Less
magical; more real. Sore, shaky muscles. Bruised and
bloody toenails. Pointe-shoe blisters. Not to mention having
to compete for roles, and the agony of waiting for cast lists

to be posted. And yet I didn't waver. I never questioned my dreams—or my ability to reach them.

Until my body betrayed me.

I pause in the doorway to the studio, thinking about how ballet used to make me feel. I look around the room. This is home. I belong here. I have since my very first class.

And yet, right now, I feel a little sick. I'm going to be so out of shape. Everyone's going to stare at me. Laugh at me. And it will be worse than the front-desk woman, because these girls will see me dance, so they'll be judging that, too.

What if, in addition to all being skinnier than me, they're all better dancers? What if I really don't deserve to be here, no matter how much I want it?

I think about running away. It would be so easy. I could go back to the dressing room and spend the next two hours hiding in a bathroom stall, and then text Zoe that I'm finished, I didn't get in, too bad, let's go back to Crazy Camp and face the music.

But I've come this far. No more going backward.

There's an open spot on the other side of the room, at the barre closest to the piano. I walk over, forcing myself to move slowly, to look calm and casual, to ignore the eyes that I feel following me, to ignore the whispers.

And there are stares, and there are whispers. These girls met one another last night. They're probably all living in the same residence hall. They stayed up late comparing training styles and pointe-shoe makers and favorite ballerinas and dream dance partners. I'm new. I'm unknown.

And you look like an elephant—

I take my place at the barre. I note that everyone's wearing flat slippers, so I put mine on and tuck my pointe shoes beneath the barre for later. I start to warm up. I roll through my feet, feeling the familiar pops and cracks. I stretch my calves. I swing my legs back and forth, loosening my hips. And then I développé my right leg up onto the barre, stretching it out in front of me and massaging my right arch with my hand.

Facing the blank wall, I can focus on what it feels like to be inside my body, instead of thinking about what I look like. But when I turn to stretch my left leg on the barre, I can see myself in the mirror. I can see how big my thigh looks from this angle, and how bending forward over my leg turns my waistline into rolls despite how hard I'm sucking my stomach in. I can see the dancers spread through the rest of the studio, stretching and chatting. I can see—at least, I think I see—eyes aimed in my direction.

There are two girls across the room. A pale redhead and an African American. Looking my way. Smiling. I stare at them in the mirror, trying to decipher their expressions. Another friend joins them, and I wait for them to point me out. I wait for her to start laughing at me too. But the red-head just puts her hands on her hips and makes a mock-stern face at the newcomer, and then they hug, and . . . maybe whatever joke they're sharing isn't about me.

Maybe.

But I'm feeling so anxious right now, and it's getting worse by the second.

I haven't exactly enjoyed being around other dancers lately. The girls at my studio fall into two categories: short and thin, or tall and thin. I'm five feet six and a half—smack in the middle, heightwise—and . . . no longer thin.

Admit it. You're fat.

These girls are all—and I look so—

My breath is coming faster. I'm dizzy. My stomach spins and churns.

The clock on the wall says class starts in two minutes.

I drop to the floor and curl up in child's pose to do one of Yasmin's breathing exercises. I put both hands on my back, close my eyes, and inhale, feeling my rib cage expand. I exhale, feeling my hands drop down. I try to block out the room around me. I try to block out the noise in my head. Andrew told me, during my cooking challenge, that he found a way to stop listening to the voices and get done what he needed to get done.

I can too.

I murmur Dr. Lancaster's words to myself a few times: "Take the leap. Take the leap." Even though the phrase will be forever linked in my mind with kissing Andrew. Even though I feel like I might be leaping into catastrophe.

Ms. Levanova enters the room, clapping her hands together. "Good morning, ladies. Welcome to your first class of the intensive!"

And probably your last—

Stop.

Come on. You know—

No. Stop.

I scramble to my feet. Place my left hand on the barre.

"We'll begin with the pliés."

The pianist plays a slow, elegant waltz as we bend our knees and straighten them, warming up our joints. Tendus come next. We brush our feet along the floor to the front, side, and back, working through our toes. Then dégagés, then fondus, and on and on. As I move my body through each sequence, I feel more and more at ease. My head clears. My stomach settles. I relax, even as my muscles tremble with effort. I can pinpoint the exact moment when I start to sweat, the first beads of moisture that form on my forehead and on my lower back.

I feel good. And as I look around the room, my confidence grows. My extensions aren't the highest in the room, but they're also not the lowest. And they're properly placed. My feet arch dramatically, and my arms and head and upper body float and swoop through the port de bras. I'm in control of every movement. Nothing happens without intention. Without care.

For the center waltz combination, the pianist chooses a Philip Glass piece. As I wait for my turn to travel across the floor, I watch her play, rocking with the rhythm, eyes closed, experiencing each note as it passes through her fingers. I close my eyes too. Just for a moment. I feel the music flow through me.

When it's my turn to dance, I step forward. I breathe in. I take off.

I'm not doing steps. These aren't balancés and fouettés and pirouettes. They're everything I've felt over the past two weeks, and over the past seven months. I pour myself out. I tell my story. I get lost in it.

And when I reach the opposite side of the room, I'm breathless.

Hannah's waiting for me. "Wow," she says in a low voice. "That was . . . gorgeous."

I blush. "Really?"

"Really."

"Thanks."

"You have to show me how you land those attitude turns. I never put my heel down at the right time. . . ."

We shift into talking technique, but my adrenaline doesn't fade. I sail through the waltz combination on the left side, and I dart through petit allegro, attacking each jump and beat with clean precision, and by the time we get to grand allegro—big leaps—I'm flying. I'm lighter than the thick, humid air in the studio, soaring so far above the floor, not even gravity can hold me down.

thirty

AFTER CLASS MS. LEVANOVA TAKES ME TO HER OFFICE.
"Samantha," she says, sitting down and crossing one leg gracefully over the other. "How are you feeling?"

"Good." It's true. The question is, how long will I keep feeling good? My high is fading fast. What Ms. Levanova is about to say could change everything.

Because what I discovered just now, in class—what I remembered, what I didn't realize I'd lost—is that I *have* to dance. It's my oxygen.

"I will be brief, because I have much to do today, to launch the intensive—and because I received a call from"— Ms. Levanova glances at a note on her desk—"a Dr. Debra Lancaster asking about you. You told no one you were coming here?"

"Not exactly—" I cringe. "Did she sound mad?"

"*Da.* You must talk to her."

I nod. "Of course."

She looks at me with narrowed eyes. "And you would never do something like this while at our intensive? You would not simply drive off one day, without warning? This is not allowed, Samantha."

I gape at her. "No, I would never—"

Ms. Levanova waves her hand to cut me off. "Well then. Here is the situation. I cannot make a place for you this summer. I'm very sorry."

She's so matter-of-fact that her words take a second to sink in.

"You are a very talented dancer, Samantha. Your dancing is not the reason that we have to say no."

She's talking about your body. How fat you've become since she saw you last.

I clutch my shoe bag in front of my stomach. My eyes fill up.

"You know you will not find it easy to have a professional ballet career with your body type," she goes on, and I feel like I'm living my worst nightmare in real time. "I'm sorry to be so blunt, but you must know this."

She looks at me long enough that I realize she's expecting an answer.

And I can't deny the truth any longer. "I know." A tear slips out. Glides down my cheek. Drips off onto my bare collarbone. I brush it away. "And it's not worth training someone who looks like me—"

"What?" She looks genuinely astonished. "Samantha, this is not why we say no."

"What do you mean?"

"I fight for you," she says, shrugging eloquently. "How can I not fight for someone with such talent and passion? Who drives, in secret, from another state, simply to have the chance to be seen? Why should you not get the excellent training we provide? But administration says we cannot allow you to join when the program is full. My hands are tied." She touches her wrists together, extending them toward me to illustrate her words.

"Oh. Okay." I start to stand up, ready to slink back to the dressing room, but she holds up her hand: a silent but commanding *Stay put.*

"Your body, for classical ballet—maybe it will not work. But does that mean you must stop dancing entirely? No!" She pounds the desk for emphasis. "If you must dance, and you feel that in here"—now she pounds her chest—"you find a way."

As she talks, I see how she must have been as a performer, back in the day. Her power and her fire fill the small room.

"Ballet is not for everyone. This is the way it is. But *dance*—she is for everyone."

I think about the conversation Dr. Lancaster and I had a week ago, when I realized that as much as I love ballet, ballet might not love me back.

"Are you saying I should quit ballet?"

Ms. Levanova looks affronted. "Of course not! Ballet is the root. She is the tree from which so many other forms grow. She is the backbone. You must not stop. But perhaps . . ."

I wait with bated breath. Perhaps *what*?

"Perhaps you must broaden your horizons. See what else there is."

"But what if . . . what if I'm not good at anything else?"

"Nonsense. Good ballet training can go with you anywhere. Will you immediately become a contemporary dancer, or a modern dancer, or a jazz dancer? No, but that is why we study. That is why we practice. That is why we explore." Now she has a mischievous look in her eyes. "Many of my colleagues would not give you this advice. They would say, 'Ballet is all! To do anything else is to settle! To diminish yourself!'"

I can hear my mom saying those very things, minus the Russian accent. Mom is the main reason I've studied ballet and only ballet thus far. Maybe I'm not the only one who needs to broaden her horizons.

"I have been in the world of ballet a long time," Ms. Levanova says. "Much longer than you. So you must trust what I'm saying."

"Yes, ma'am."

"Are you certain to have a career in another style of dance? No. You have only a small amount of control over the future. You could become injured. You could lose your passion. You could discover something else that interests you more. But there is no reason not to try everything you can to reach a career, if it is your dream."

"Yes, ma'am."

"On that note, I would like for you to meet someone."

She gets up and goes out into the hallway. I hear voices, and then she returns with a younger African American woman.

"Samantha," Ms. Levanova says, "this is Nicole Paxton. She is a former dancer with us, and she now directs a contemporary dance company in Atlanta. She is here to choreograph a ballet for our students. I asked her to look in on the class."

I hold out my hand. "Nice to meet you."

"Hi, Samantha." Nicole perches on the edge of Ms. Levanova's desk, her long, muscular legs dangling down. "I'm gonna cut to the chase. I love the way you move. And I understand you're looking for summer training opportunities."

I nod.

"My company's pretty new, and this is our first year hosting a summer intensive. I'd like to invite you to take part. Unfortunately, I can't offer you any sort of scholarship—it starts in two weeks, and we've given out all the funds we have. But I think you'd be a good fit for the work I do and could learn a lot. So what do you say?"

"It's—is it a ballet intensive?" I stammer out.

"Yes and no. It won't be what you'd get here. Less focus

on pure classical technique. We'll push you to move in a different way. Have you done much contemporary work?"

"Not really. My studio's pretty classical."

"Well, you can't be a bunhead forever." Nicole glances at Ms. Levanova like this is an inside joke between the two of them, and Ms. Levanova lets out a soft laugh.

"How soon do I have to let you know? I'm totally interested, but——"

But this isn't what you want, my inner voice whispers.

Contemporary dance, instead of classical ballet.

A new company holding its first-ever intensive, instead of the established, prestigious program I've dreamed of attending for years.

But Ms. Levanova said it flat out, and I have to admit that she's right: classical ballet might not be the place for me anymore. I had plans. Goals. But things changed. I changed. So maybe all that's left to do now is to let go.

Is that what "take the leap" really means?

"Talk to your folks about it," Nicole says. "Can you let me know by Wednesday?" She stands, fishing around in her pocket. "Here's my card. Website, phone number—everything you need's on there."

I take the card, running my fingers around its crisp edges. "Thank you."

"Thank me by coming to the intensive and showing up ready to work." With a wave of her hand, Nicole's out the door.

Ms. Levanova inclines her head at me, looking pleased.

"I hope is not too much of a consolation prize?"

"It's—it's a wonderful opportunity. Thank you."

"You're quite welcome. Now I must make a few phone calls. And you—I understand you have a long drive ahead of you."

"Yes, ma'am." I stand and drop into a quick curtsy.

"I will see you at auditions for next summer." It's not a question.

"Yes, ma'am," I repeat, and she dismisses me with a wave.

Back in the dressing room, I don't change clothes right away. I sit on the thin wooden bench in front of the mirror, looking at myself. My carefully slicked-back hair is frizzing around my face. I have dark sweat patches on my leotard. And sitting down like this, my thighs are flat and wide and my stomach pooches out in that way I hate.

But I take a deep breath and try to see past my body parts, like Dr. Lancaster and I talked about. I try to see what got me into this intensive, the first time around. What made Ms. Levanova want to fight for me today. What made Nicole invite me to her intensive.

Nothing about this summer is working out how I wanted. But there's something new on the horizon. A new door opening. I just have to decide whether I want to leap through it.

ZOE'S WAITING FOR me outside. "Did you get in?"

"No."

She curses, turns on her heel, and storms off toward the parking garage where we left the van, muttering under her breath.

I race to catch up with her. "But," I say, "I got something else." I explain it to her, and she slows down to listen, and by the time we're inside the van, she's grinning again.

"You're gonna do it, right?"

"I don't know. . . ."

"Don't be an idiot. Go to the stupid intensive." When I don't reply right away, she adds, "What else are you going to do the rest of the summer?"

"I could take private lessons at my home studio—"

"This whole intensive business is about getting to the next level, right?"

"Yes."

"So the next level isn't exactly what you thought it'd be. So what?"

"You don't understand—"

"I understand that you're being ridiculous." She turns the key in the ignition. "Fine. Throw away an unexpected opportunity that got handed to you on a silver platter. See if I care."

I fasten my seat belt. "You really think I should go?"

"Look, I know nothing about ballet. Except what I saw in *Black Swan*, and you told me that doesn't count. But yeah, I think you should go. You'd be stupid not to."

"Well, I wouldn't even have the choice without your help today. So thank you."

"Don't thank me until we get back," Zoe says. "Dr. Lancaster is *not* happy."

"You talked to her?"

"She called my cell nine times in two hours. I decided to answer before she started checking hospitals and morgues."

"Oh."

"Yeah, she's . . . not happy."

"Well . . . how do we want to spend our last few hours of freedom?"

"Samantha Wagner, I do believe I'm rubbing off on you."

"Maybe that's not such a bad thing." I turn up the radio, and Zoe and I jam the whole way back to Crazy Camp. She drums on the steering wheel. I dance in my seat. We sing at the top of our lungs. And far too soon, we're turning onto the gravel driveway in front of the Perform at Your Peak house. Zoe slows to a crawl.

We pass two police cars. A campus security truck. And . . . my mom's car.

Then we can see the house. Everyone's waiting for us on the porch. Their heads spin in our direction.

"Good luck," Zoe says, putting the van in park.

"You too."

thirty-one

"WHOSE IDEA WAS THIS?" DR. LANCASTER LOOKS from me to Zoe and back to me again. Her expression is etched in stone.

"Mine," I say.

Zoe's quick to add, "But I'm the one who stole your keys and drove the van. I took our phones out of your desk, too." I don't know if she's trying to protect me from Dr. Lancaster's anger or if she wants to make sure she gets credit for the part she played. Maybe both.

Outside, in the hallway, I hear my mom yelling. "I am going in there to speak to my daughter!"

"Mrs. Wagner." Yasmin's voice. "I'm sorry, but you need to stay out here—"

"You're lucky I'm not suing you! I still might!" There's a sharp knock at the door. The handle jiggles. "I'm taking Samantha home now," my mom says through the thick wood.

"I'm leaving?" I say to Dr. Lancaster. "The camp isn't done."

"It is for you," she answers. "For both of you. Zoe, your parents are on their way. They were delayed by a luncheon your mom had to attend today."

"Of course they were," Zoe grumbles. But then she brightens. "We're getting kicked out! We did it! Third strike's the charm!"

I blanch. "I didn't exactly want to get sent home."

"Perhaps you should have thought of that," Dr. Lancaster says, "before you stole a van and drove off to God-knows-where without telling anyone."

"I know, but—I had to." I lean forward in my chair, toward Dr. Lancaster, needing her to understand. "I didn't do this to cause trouble, even though I know it did." The police cars outside are evidence of that, never mind my mom's shouts about lawsuits. "I did it because I had to go to that intensive. I had to try. I had to show them what I'm capable of. I had to show *myself* what I'm capable of. I had to"—what I'm about to say is a cheap shot, but it's the truth—"I had to *take the leap*, like you told me."

"Not quite what I meant, Sam." Dr. Lancaster's voice is tight.

"Maybe not, but it worked! I didn't get to stay at the intensive—obviously, I'm here now. But I got invited to another program, and I think I'm going to go."

I'm talking fast. If I'm about to get dragged out of this room and driven home in disgrace, at least I can tell Dr.

Lancaster how much I appreciate her first.

"I couldn't have gotten through today without you, and without this place. I did some of Yasmin's breathing when I got anxious, and I said my power statement in the dressing room before class, and I didn't run away even when I wanted to. Even when I was so intimidated by all of the other girls there. How perfect they looked. That's all really great progress, right?"

"Yes, but the fact remains that—"

"And I had . . . I guess you could call it an epiphany? I really don't like feeling like things are out of my control, and they have been for so long, and I was trying to make everything better, but I couldn't. But today, I took control. And the crazy thing is, it didn't work out the way I wanted it to, but maybe it worked out the way it was supposed to. Or maybe there is no 'supposed to,' because things just happen and you deal with them and keep moving forward—"

"Sam—"

"And maybe I have to figure out what I can control and what I can't, so I can focus on the right things." I'm out of breath. "Is that right?"

Dr. Lancaster presses her fingertips into her temples where her blond hair is graying. "Zoe, would you wait outside for a few minutes?"

"Sure." Zoe stands. "Thanks for the adventure, Ballerina Barbie. And keep in touch. Isn't that what you're supposed to say at the end of summer camp?"

I laugh. "I will. I promise."

Zoe nods at me, salutes Dr. Lancaster, and then leaves.

"Well," Dr. Lancaster says as the door clicks shut.

"I'm sorry, again. Not that I went, because like I said, I had to. But for all of this." I gesture at the door, at everything outside this office. I can't hear my mom yelling anymore, but that's not necessarily a good thing. She only yells when she's really, really mad—and the silence that comes next is the eye of the storm. "When do I have to leave?"

"As soon as we're done here."

"Oh." I wait for her to tell me to go, but she doesn't speak again right away.

Instead, my phone buzzes. I glance at the screen. It's a text from Bianca:

> **Just out of rehearsal. WHAT'S GOING ON?!?! Your mom left me four messages. Call me!**

"Something important?" Dr. Lancaster asks, in a voice that must be the closest to sarcasm she's able to get.

"Yes," I answer honestly. Bianca *is* important. More than I've let her know. "But I can answer it later."

"Is there anything else you'd like to discuss with me?"

We spend a few minutes talking about how I felt before ballet class, during class, and after. I finally tell her about my nasty inner voice. How it's still there, always there, and how sometimes it's louder and sometimes it's softer, and how this morning I was able to start telling it to stop. And we touch on my issues with control. My epic realization that maybe everything—my anxiety, my body image issues, all of it—comes from wanting to feel in control.

"So now that I figured that out, am I cured?" I joke.

"I'm going to recommend that you keep speaking to a therapist when you get home. I have a few contacts in your area. I'll send you their names and numbers." She makes a note on her legal pad. "If your anxiety persists, you might also benefit from medication to help you manage it."

"Oh."

"But overall, I'm pleased with your progress. The girl I met two weeks ago would never have done what you did today."

"No kidding."

She's quiet for a few moments. "You know, I studied dance for a number of years growing up. I truly do love ballet. It's such a wonderful art form."

My mouth drops open. "Why didn't you tell me sooner?"

"Because we weren't here to talk about me; we were here to talk about you." She raises her eyebrows at me. "Would knowing I used to dance have distracted you?"

I think about that. "Yeah, probably." I needed her to be impartial. Otherwise I never would've opened up.

"Regardless, my experience wasn't like yours. I wasn't going to be a professional dancer. I didn't have the talent. But my love for the art form eventually led me here."

This is game-changing information. But whereas with Andrew, I had to rethink every conversation we shared, I've just learned that Dr. Lancaster understood me better than I ever gave her credit for. "Thanks for telling me now," I say.

"You're welcome." She stands and shakes my hand. "Best of luck."

MOM WANTS TO get on the road immediately, but I can't leave without saying good-bye. I tell her I need to make sure I didn't forget anything upstairs in the bedroom or bathroom, and wave for Katie and Jenna to follow me.

"So?" Katie hisses the second we're out of sight. "How did it go?"

I give them the short version of the story, and when I'm done, Katie squeals and throws her arms around me.

"We knew you could do it!"

"Congratulations, Sam." Jenna smiles.

"It stinks that you have to leave, though," Katie says. "Also . . . your mom is scary."

I laugh out loud. "She kind of is. It's gonna be a long ride home."

We quickly exchange contact information. Then my mom starts calling me from downstairs. I can't stall any longer. On my way out the door, I wave at Zoe, who's sitting with Yasmin in the hall next to Dr. Lancaster's office. I hug Dominic and Omar and tell them to get my info from Katie and Jenna. I get one more hug from Katie and, to my surprise, a small squeeze from Jenna. And then the front door closes behind me, and my mom and I are walking down the front steps and across the gravel driveway to her sedan.

She's giving me the silent treatment. Never a good sign.

It's only a matter of time before she boils over.

It happens just after we cross the state line into Tennessee. "What were you *thinking*, Samantha? I did *not* raise you to behave like this. Running away? Stealing a van? And what's this I hear about you getting one of your counselors fired by hitting on him? Explain yourself."

The guilt over what happened with Andrew rushes back in. Will he have to change his major? Will Dr. Lancaster blacklist him from ever getting a job? I wasn't the only one who got hurt, and I can't even talk to him to apologize.

"That camp was supposed to help you," Mom goes on. "It was supposed to further your career aspirations. Not turn you into a juvenile delinquent." She says, louder, "You stole a van!"

"We brought it back—"

"Do you think this is funny?" She looks at me, and then back at the road, and then at me, and then back at the road. "Do you know how hard I worked to pay for your training this summer? Two jobs! I put in so many twelve-hour days! And you're willing to let it all slip away. No—you're *throwing* it away. You're—"

"That's why I did it, Mom! Because I'm *not* willing to let it slip away! You should be proud of me for going today. For making them give me another chance."

"I'd be prouder if you'd been accepted."

I sit back, gasping, like she slapped me. "What?"

Mom looks like she's been slapped too. She's gone white. "I—I'm sorry. I didn't mean that. I was angry, and it just . . . came out."

I stare at her, and I find the words I've been holding back for months. "You can't talk to me like that. Not anymore."

"Samantha, I—"

"It's not helping me. In fact, it really hurts me."

"You know I've never said anything like that before—"

"Not exactly like that, no. But . . ." There are so many examples I could give her. So many backhanded compliments. So many harsh critiques. "You keep telling me that I need thick skin to be a professional ballerina."

"And I believe that to be true—"

"Well, I'm probably not going to be a professional ballerina, Mom. You and I both have to accept that."

"But—"

"And I don't need you to thicken my skin. I need you to support me."

"What do you call working extra hours to pay for your training and your therapy? And giving you private coaching? I've done nothing *but* support and encourage you—"

"Not the way I needed it."

"Well, why didn't you tell me what you needed?" Mom sounds like she's on the verge of tears. She's strangling the steering wheel.

"I didn't know what I needed."

"And now you do?"

"I'm starting to, yeah." I'm choked up too. "The past couple months have been . . . really hard. And it would be great if you could, I don't know, acknowledge that. And maybe tell me I'm awesome from time to time, instead of always telling me I'm fat."

"I've never told you you're fat!"

"Yes, you have. Maybe you didn't use that word, but . . . yeah."

There's a long silence from the driver's side.

"Do you want to talk about what happens when we get home?" Mom finally asks, hesitant now. "I put in a few phone calls to private coaches after we spoke on Friday, and I have some leads. Or is that . . . not what you need?"

I take in a shaky breath. The air filling my lungs tastes sweet. Almost . . . hopeful.

"Actually, I know what I want to do." I tell her about Nicole's contemporary dance intensive. How she saw me in class and invited me personally. "It starts in two weeks. It's not classical ballet. But maybe it's time for me to see what it's like outside the ballet bubble."

Mom's blinking a lot. "Is this really what you want?"

"I think so, yeah. At least, I want to try it out. It's a great opportunity."

She's quiet for another long moment. Then, sounding defeated: "I want you to succeed. You know that, right?"

I nod. "But maybe I need to learn how to be happy first."

When she doesn't say anything more, I turn on the radio. It's playing one of the songs Zoe and I jammed out to this morning. I don't jam out this time. I just listen. I stare out the window. I watch the miles tick by toward home.

thirty-two

I FOCUS ON THE MOVEMENT. MY ARMS EXTENDING away from my shoulders. My back curving and arcing. My knees bending and straightening. My feet pressing into the floor.

It's the first day of Nicole's summer intensive, and yes, I'm anxious. I'm surrounded by the unfamiliar. Dancers I've just met. A new city. A daily schedule filled with dance styles I've barely studied. Even my wardrobe feels strange. Instead of my usual leotard, pink tights, and pointe shoes, I'm in a tank top, leggings, and ankle socks. My hair's in a ponytail instead of a bun.

But the movement, this first-thing-in-the-morning ballet barre—*that* I know. So I'm throwing myself into it. Body, mind, and heart.

My new therapist, Dr. Chen, has me thinking a lot about what I can control and what I can't. We had three sessions in the two weeks I was home, and I'll be talking to her on the phone twice a week while I'm here. The next time we chat, I'm supposed to report in: Did I latch onto something outside my control? Did I feel the downward spiral start? Was there an instance when I allowed myself to let go and move forward?

I'm not good at letting go and moving forward. Not yet.

I'm still so attached to *Before*. So anxious about *After*.

But I'm working on changing. I'm trying to focus on *Now*.

I watch Nicole demonstrate the next barre combination. I memorize the choreography and perform it to the best of my ability. I trust my years of training. I try to keep my mind open.

This is what I can control.

Someone in the room might be staring at me. Might be judging me.

That, I can't control.

The prickling at the back of my neck, the way my pulse speeds up, the sudden desire to run away, to hide . . . I know how to respond.

I face the barre while Nicole talks to the accompanist. I close my eyes and I breathe in deep, counting to five with each inhale and exhale. I murmur, "My body is flexible, and strong, and beautiful. I am taking the leap. And it's going to be *amazing*."

Dr. Chen suggested that last bit.

The music starts. I put my left hand on the barre. Stand in fifth position. And I begin to move.

I HAVE A few phone calls to make that night. Promises to keep—not only to the people I'm calling, but also to myself. If being open about what's going on inside my head is supposed to be the new normal, I have to start as soon as possible.

First, a brief check-in with my mom. We've been on eggshells around each other since that tense car ride home from Perform at Your Peak, but I can tell she's been trying. She brought up my diet only once in the past two weeks, and she let me cook dinner twice. She also let me rest at home for a few days instead of pushing me into a ton of extra ballet classes right away. When I said I was ready to go to the studio, she drove me—and then went to the grocery store instead of staying to watch me dance. She's even signed up for some therapy sessions of her own.

For the first time in years—definitely since Dad left, if not before—there's space between us. I know where she ends and I begin.

She answers on the first ring, like she was waiting by the phone. "Samantha?"

"Hi, Mom."

"Hi, sweetie! How was your first day?"

"Good. Hard."

There's a pause. "Anxiety-hard?"

"A little," I admit. "But also hard physically. I am going to be so sore tomorrow!"

She laughs. "That happens when you jump back into a full schedule after taking time off." A beat. "I didn't mean that in a negative way. I promise."

"I know, Mom. Thanks."

"Do you want to tell me about your teachers?"

I give her the short version. Who I'll be studying with, what they're each like in the classroom, how comfortable I felt with them today. And I tell her a bit about the other students here. Not what they look like. How they move. Some of them are ballet based, like me. Others come from contemporary or jazz backgrounds. A few know one another from the competition circuit. I know no one.

"But my roommate seems nice," I finish. Suzanne's a petite, muscular modern dancer from Chicago. She welcomed me with a hug and then told me to help myself to her bedside candy stash whenever I wanted. Right now, as Mom and I say our good-byes, I'm sucking on a cherry Life Saver. Turning my tongue crimson.

I call Bianca next. "Sam-a-lam-a!" she squeals into the phone.

"Hey, B."

"How's Hot-lanta?"

"Hot. How's DC?"

"Also hot. Ooh, but you know what's *so* cold?"

"What?"

"The look I gave Eliana when I passed her in the hall today and she said hi."

When I got home from Perform at Your Peak, I finally called Bianca. We were on the phone for more than an hour, and I think I was the only one who said anything. I told her about my panic attacks. About what was causing them. I told her why I'd thought Marcus had broken up with me, and why he actually did break up with me. I told her about Perform at Your Peak. What we did there. Everyone I met.

I told her about Andrew.

And I apologized for pushing her away. For being a lousy friend.

Then we both had a good cry and made plans to spend an entire weekend together when we get home from our intensives.

"I can't believe you never told me what Eliana did to you!" Bianca says now. "But don't worry. I already started telling the girls here not to trust her. She's going *down*."

I laugh. "Thanks."

"So what's new with you? I want to know everything."

I give her the same details I gave my mom, but Bianca-fied. That mostly means adding which of the guy choreographers and dancers are hot, so she can look them up online and judge for herself. I'm telling her about the Argentinian dancer who'll be teaching us flamenco when she interrupts me.

"We don't have to talk about guys if you don't want to. If it makes you anxious."

"It's okay."

"Obviously, we're not talking about what's-his-face—"

"Andrew."

"I know that," she says, sounding exasperated. "I didn't want to say his name because we're not talking about him."

I can't help but smile at her logic. "Oh. Right."

"And since Marcus turned out to be a—"

I cut her off. "I don't want to say anything bad about Marcus."

"He dumped you. It doesn't matter why. That makes him a loser in my book."

"Yeah, but . . ." I think again about our late-night phone conversation. "He's a good guy. And I wasn't in a good place for a lot of the time we were together."

"But you're in a better place now, right?"

"I'm working on it."

"Good. And you know you can talk to me?"

"Yeah. I'll try."

"Do or do not," she says solemnly. "There is no 'try.'"

"Are you quoting *Star Wars* at me?"

"Just dropping some Yoda wisdom on my BFF."

I check the time. I have one more phone call to make, and then Suzanne wants to introduce me to some girls she danced with at an intensive last summer. We're supposed to go out for frozen yogurt at a spot around the corner from the dorms, and I'm actually thinking about having a small cup. A kid-sized serving. Just to see what happens.

"Gotta go," I tell Bianca. "Talk soon?"

"Definitely. Love you, Sam-a-lam-a."

"Back atcha, B." It's the phone sign-off we've shared since middle school. It wouldn't feel right hanging up without it.

I plug my phone in to charge and then dial "Thelma."

"Barbs. 'Sup?" Zoe says when she answers. "You talk to Kwan or Bear yet?"

"Nope. Just you."

Zoe, Jenna, Katie, Dominic, Omar, and I have had an ongoing email chain since everyone got home from Perform at Your Peak. Somewhere in the middle of the thread, we came up with our Crazy Camp nicknames. Zoe named herself Thelma after our Thelma and Louise–style road trip. I'm Barbs, since I'm coming to grips with maybe not being a ballerina after all. Jenna is Kwan, since she got Zoe to admit that striving to be like one of the greatest female figure skaters of all time wasn't really a bad thing. Katie is Bear, after Mr. Bear, her good-luck charm—and because it's funny to give the toughest name to the tiniest, bubbliest person. Omar is Bruno, thanks to that Bruno Mars hat he bought at the general store, and Dominic is Chunks, not only because he once threw up on the fifty-yard line but also because he's the opposite of chunky.

"Status report?" I ask Zoe. She told her parents a few days ago, in no uncertain terms, that she was not playing tennis in the fall. They were angry. They threatened to ground her, to take away her phone, to send her to another therapist. But she didn't back down.

"All quiet on the Western Front," she says.

"Meaning?"

"I'm still getting the silent treatment. Like they think if they just wait me out, I'll change my mind. But Andrew said—" She stops. "Sorry."

"It's fine." I know she's been in touch with him. She emailed me about it a week ago. And it stung, for sure. I shut down my computer and cried a little. But then I stopped crying. I pulled myself together. Not in a bad, I'm-ignoring-my-emotions kind of way, but in a good way. A healthy way. I felt what I was feeling, and then I moved on.

I asked Dr. Chen about transference in our second session. I told her what Zoe told me about being in love with your therapist. Dr. Chen said it's not that simple, but that we can talk about my feelings for Andrew—why I fell so hard and so fast—if I want. When I'm ready.

I don't know when I'll be ready. I do know that I'm better off being single for now. Maybe for a while. I can't rely on someone else to make me feel good about myself. I have to learn to do that on my own.

"Sam?" Suzanne sticks her head in the door. "You almost done?"

"Yeah," I tell her. Then, to Zoe: "I have to go. My roommate wants to hang out."

"I hate her already."

"Well, she's no you. She hasn't even insulted me yet. Can you believe it?"

"Amateur," she scoffs. "Okay, before you hang up, I have to give you your top-secret mission."

We've all been challenging one another to do things that scare us. And to provide evidence, if possible. A few days ago, Katie sent us a blurry photo of herself, midflip, on the balance beam. She had one of her teammates take it. She captioned it "Bear Gets Back on the Horse." Meanwhile, Jenna's supposed to tape herself at practice and send us the raw footage—even if she screws up—and Dominic's supposed to send us a screenshot when he emails Florida State to schedule a campus visit.

"Is this new roommate of yours smaller than you?" Zoe asks.

"Yeah."

"We're going to need a picture of the two of you together. In your tightest dance clothes. No hiding. No slouching. Got it?"

I make a face, but I say, "Got it."

"You have forty-eight hours to complete your mission. This message will self-destruct, blah blah blah. Later, Barbs."

"Bye, Thelma." I hang up.

I let my phone charge for a few more minutes. I fold the dance clothes I went through this morning, trying to pick the right first-day-of-class outfit. I tidy my desk. Put away my new journal and pens. Then I glance at the bulletin board on the wall. I've tacked up my ballerina collage, the one I ripped in half. There's a tape line running down the center now. I almost like it better this way. Imperfect, like me. Uneven seams and raw edges and still reaching.

Next to the collage, there's a photo of a tiny red balloon, barely a pinprick in the vast blue sky. Since I missed the last day at Perform at Your Peak, I had to release it on my own. I tied a piece of paper with the words "Take the leap" to its tail and let go. Feeling the string slip past my fingertips was like exhaling for the first time.

The only other picture I've put up is one Katie emailed me. It's our whole group on the ropes course, at the very highest point, backed by sky and treetops. Katie's arm is across my shoulder. Jenna's next to us, smiling primly but not touching. Dominic has Omar in a fake headlock. They're both mugging for the camera. Zoe is in the background, arms crossed, wearing her perma-smirk.

At the bottom of the picture is a shadow. The head and shoulders of the person holding the camera.

Andrew.

I know Katie sent me this picture because he isn't in it, but I'm glad that trace of him is there. When I look at the photo, I see everything that mattered about that place. And Andrew mattered. He matters. Even if we never meet again.

I study my own image in the photo. I'm sweaty and frizzy. The ropes-course harness is squeezing my body in strange ways. There are lumps and rolls that shouldn't be there. I'm squinting into the light. And I'm smiling.

"Sam, we're leaving!" Suzanne, from the hallway.

I unplug my phone. Slip on my sandals and grab my messenger bag. Bounce up and down a few times to shake away a burst of nerves. And then I swing the door open and step out into what's next.

acknowledgments

IT MAY BE A CLICHÉ TO SAY IT TAKES A VILLAGE TO publish a book, but for this particular book, it's absolutely true. I could not be more grateful to my own little village of publishing pros, fellow writers, friends, and family members for helping me get this book out of my brain and onto the shelves.

Thanks to my agent, Alyssa Eisner Henkin, for brainstorming with me and encouraging me to find the best possible version of my "dancer with body-image issues" idea. This book would not be what it is without your initial guidance and your support throughout its journey.

Thanks to my editor, Alexandra Cooper, whose insightful notes helped me push myself and my characters and dig deeper into the book's soul. Your comments gave me what I needed to turn an uncooperative, meandering manuscript into a finished product I'm proud to have written. Thanks also to Alyssa Miele and the rest of the team at HarperTeen: art director Erin Fitzsimmons and designer Katie Fitch, production editor Renée Cafiero, production managers Allison Brown and Lillian Sun, marketing manager Kim VandeWater and marketing assistant Lauren Kostenberger, and publicist Olivia Russo. It's a privilege to have all of you working on and with my book.

I would be lost without my writer community. Huge thanks to Michael Ann Dobbs, Heather Demetrios, Ghenet Myrthil, Lauren Morrill, and Jodi Kendall, who read and critiqued drafts of this book at various points during the process. You provided both the positive reinforcement and the kick in the pants I needed to get through revision after revision. On the support and cheerleading front, thanks go out to the Fearless Fifteeners, the YA Buccaneers, and all the other writers in my life. It's so great to feel like we're on this crazy ride together.

One of the earliest seeds of inspiration for this book came from a freelance article I wrote for *Dance Spirit* magazine a few years ago. For that article, I interviewed sport psychologist and mental-skills coach Justin Su'a—and he was kind enough to act as a resource when I was first mapping out this book as well. Psychologist Dr. Nadine Kaslow, who has worked with dancers at Atlanta Ballet, and nutrition therapist Anastasia Nevin, who has worked in eating-disorder-treatment settings, also answered questions as I researched this project. When the manuscript was complete, Stephanie Kuehn read the whole thing and offered notes on the clinical-treatment elements. Thank you all for sharing your expertise with me. The finished product is so much better for it.

Also in the research realm, thanks to Gail Nall, who helped me fill in figure-skating details, and Diana Gallagher, who did the same for gymnastics. I really appreciate your willingness to answer every question I emailed your way. In the category of life-as-research, thanks to my "dance family"—the people I've studied under, trained alongside, and performed with over the years. May we never stop moving.

Thanks, again and again, to my wonderful family: Mom and Dad; Ben, Kate, Turner, Benton, and Miles; Mary-Owen (who read so many early drafts of this book!); Sheila and Jack; and Niki, Ed, Max, and Henry. I cherish your love and support.

To my husband, Justin: I'm so lucky to have you by my side. Thank you for everything.